COULD IT BE MAGIC?

FAY KEENAN

Boldwood

First published in Great Britain in 2025 by Boldwood Books Ltd.

Copyright © Fay Keenan, 2025

Cover Design by Alice Moore Design

Cover Images: Shutterstock

A CIP catalogue record for this book is available from the British Library.

Paperback ISBN 978-1-83617-645-9

Large Print ISBN 978-1-83617-646-6

Hardback ISBN 978-1-83617-644-2

Trade Paperback ISBN 978-1-80635-273-9

Ebook ISBN 978-1-83617-647-3

Kindle ISBN 978-1-83617-648-0

Audio CD ISBN 978-1-83617-639-8

MP3 CD ISBN 978-1-83617-640-4

Digital audio download ISBN 978-1-83617-642-8

This book is printed on certified sustainable paper. Boldwood Books is dedicated to putting sustainability at the heart of our business. For more information please visit https://www.boldwoodbooks.com/about-us/sustainability/

Boldwood Books Ltd, 23 Bowerdean Street, London, SW6 3TN

www.boldwoodbooks.com

For my own 'Saint Nick'.

1

Your tracker mortgage rate will be rising, in line with the Bank of England's increase of the base rate from 31 December. If you require advice or assistance about making repayments under the new rate, please feel free to contact us...

Thea Ashcombe threw the letter down on her small kitchen table in frustration. Lupin, the small tortoiseshell rescue cat she'd caved and allowed her children to adopt from the Purrfect Paws Rescue Centre regarded her warily. A feral kitten, who'd been born with her sisters under some decking and then had to fend for herself, Lupin was still nervous of sudden movements and loud noises, and although living with two affectionate children had cured her of much of that, she still jumped when caught off guard.

'Sorry, puss,' Thea murmured, putting out a hand and giving the top of the cat's head a rub. Lupin nosed her affectionately, and, despite the letter from the bank, Thea relaxed slightly. Glad the kids were still at school, so she could worry about things in peace, she picked up the letter again.

31 December. What a wonderful present just in time for the new year. And it would certainly put the brakes on her Christmas plans. Her eleven-year-old son, Dylan, desperately wanted the latest game for the Nintendo Switch his great-grandmother, Lorelai, had bought for him for his birthday, and while her twelve, very-soon-to-be-thirteen-year-old daughter, Cora, was at the age where cold, hard cash was preferred for a January sales shopping spree in lieu of an actual 'big' present, Thea felt guilty that she'd have to amend her budget for that, too.

Thea pushed a hand through her hair, which was long overdue a trim, and glanced back at the shopping list. Queen of budgeting, she'd recently discovered the Too Good To Throw app, and, on the days she wasn't in the classroom of the primary school in the next village, she kept an eagle eye out for bargains to make her part-time teaching salary go a little further. While she was thankful for the job, she really could have done with more hours, especially now the kids were getting older. Three days a week had been great when they were younger, and she'd saved on nursery fees at the time, but now Cora and Dylan could get the school bus home from the secondary school four miles away, a full-time teaching post would have been ideal. In a school where teachers moving on was rare, though, it was unlikely.

That left her with a rising mortgage rate and a stagnant bank balance. There was no point asking her ex-partner for money: even if she knew where he was, he probably wouldn't have any to give her. Ed wasn't what anyone would call reliable. It was a shame she hadn't worked that out before she'd had two children with him. She shushed that bitter thought: she wouldn't be without Cora and Dylan for the world. But it had been difficult raising them by herself, and she lived in constant fear of the rug being pulled out from under her. Financially and emotionally, things had always been a bit of a strain. Ed had walked out soon after Dylan's first birthday, and Thea had moved from where they'd been living for some years on the outskirts of Chippenham. First, and with nowhere else to go, she'd moved into her grandmother's one-bedroomed annexe and then, when it hadn't been practical to stay there any longer, to a series of rented properties on the outskirts of Taunton, one of the three bigger towns that formed a loose triangle around Lower Brambleton. She'd managed to stay put for several years, ensuring some continuity for her children, but when the opportunity had arisen nearly two years ago to purchase a small house on the newly built Observatory Field estate through a shared ownership scheme, Thea has applied for it. Now, she was the proud owner of her own home, and after so much uncertainty, she definitely wanted to keep it that way.

With this unwelcome news from the bank, it seemed the seams of her finances were going to be put under more stress. She sighed and crossed a couple of things off the shopping list. She was an accomplished economiser, and had, for years, shopped at the local supermarkets when it was yellow label and discount time, but with the cost of living rising at a rate of knots, even that wasn't enough. She hated to admit it, but she was going to have to find another way to boost her income if she wasn't going to fall into debt. Perhaps it was time to start looking at other schools.

The very thought of owing money filled Thea with a clammy, panicky dread. She'd experienced it at the sharp end when she'd been living with Ed. He'd been a man who was completely held hostage by his own impulses and addictions, and by the time she'd found out what had been happening to their hard-earned cash, it had almost been too late. She sent up a silent prayer of thanks that she'd never married him, much as she'd longed for that after the children had been born. Because of that, she'd been able to make a cleaner break. The horror of losing the house and being in such a financially precarious position once again made the bile rise in her throat. She'd been through all that before, when Ed had left them on the verge of bankruptcy, and she was terrified at the idea of it happening again.

'Hi Mum!' Cora came barrelling through the front door, shedding possessions and outside layers as she went, and breaking into Thea's gloomy thoughts.

'Bag and coat on the hook, please,' Thea replied, hearing the familiar thud of the Vans backpack hitting the laminate of the hallway.

'What's for tea? I'm *starving*!' Cora, with that beanpole-stretch of adolescence, was always grazing on whatever she could find in the cupboards. Thea was grateful she wasn't obsessing over her weight, as so many of her friends seemed to be, but was also mindful of the sheer amount of refined sugar the girl could put away in one sitting.

'Spag bol,' Thea replied.

'Again? We had that last night. Can't we get a kebab?'

Thea swallowed down a bite back of irritation that had been on the edge of her tongue. 'Not tonight, love.'

'But Milly says *Just Eat* have started delivering out here,' Cora whined, obviously still intent on her choice of evening meal. 'And we haven't had one for *ages*. Pleeeeeease, Mum?'

Thea shook her head. She wished it was that simple, but the thoughts of the financial strain the family was soon going to be under were a little too close to the surface, after the correspondence from the bank.

'Maybe at the weekend,' she said, hoping that, by the time Saturday came, Cora's attention would have shifted elsewhere.

'OK,' Cora muttered. She was already engrossed in her phone, and Thea once again marvelled at the ease at which her daughter could text with two thumbs, make a cup of coffee and grab for the biscuit tin all while watching something on the small screen.

'Got any homework?' Thea asked as she busied herself with locating the last of the pasta spirals in the cupboard.

'Dunno.' Cora didn't look up until she went to the fridge, threw open the door and put the last of the bottle of milk into her coffee mug. 'Milk's gone, Mum.'

Thea sighed. She could do without many things, but a milk-free cup of tea first thing tomorrow morning was a sacrifice too far. Glancing at her watch, she realised that it was almost time to pick Dylan up from his best mate's house, where he'd gone after school. 'I'll pop out and grab some from the farm shop when I pick up your brother.' She reached for her phone and her purse.

Just as she was about to start the engine of her aged Volvo, she remembered she'd been perusing the Too Good To Throw app before Cora had come home. On impulse, she re-opened the app and noticed that Saints' Farm Shop on the outskirts of Lower Brambleton had recently joined the scheme. Perhaps, given the bad news from the bank, it would be good to get one of their 'Throw' bags while she was there? The place was usually a little too expensive for her, but a bargain bag from there was bound to contain some tasty treats, and she was nothing if not inventive. Even if she ended up with three swedes and a parsnip, with a bit of imagination she'd be able to make some soup out of them for the next few school lunches.

Clicking on the 'request Throw Bag' button, she paid the fee, which guaranteed to be at least 50 per cent less than the face value of the products contained in the bag and then got into the car. She noted, with irritation more than worry, that her fuel gauge was on empty. Given the age of her car, she wasn't that concerned – she wasn't a gambling woman, God knew she'd had enough experience of terrible odds not to be so stupid, but she did like to play the empty tank challenge every so often. So far, she'd never lost. As she started the engine, which coughed to life, she hoped the contents of the Throw Bag might provide some inspiration for cooking. However, if it was going to be swede and parsnip soup, she thought, at least it would be nice to have some fresh milk to put into it.

2

Nick Saint ran a hand through his hair and tried not to give away just how stressed he felt by the bombshell his sister, Annabelle, had just dropped. Busying himself with rearranging, for the fifth time, the locally cooked Christmas puddings and mince pies that had just arrived from Evie Brown's artisan bakery in the nearby village of Everscombe, he plastered what he hoped was a reassuring smile on his face and turned around to give Annabelle its benefit.

'Wow,' he said, summoning as much enthusiasm as he could. 'A second honeymoon? That sounds amazing, Annie. And a dream destination, too.'

'It's been a bit of a surprise,' Annabelle replied. Nick noticed that she was playing nervously with the tie on the front of her apron. His sister had lost a lot of weight recently and could now wrap the apron cords around herself twice. He wondered if their father's comment about her being a 'Somerset apple dumpling' had hit home a little too hard. Annabelle had always been touchy about her weight.

'But a lovely one,' Nick prompted. 'I mean, it'll be good for the two of you to get away. After... everything.' Nick kicked himself as he saw Annabelle blinking away sudden tears. He should have known better than to allude to the miscarriage back in the summer that she and her husband, Jamie, were still mourning. It had been late, at twenty weeks, and only discovered at the scan.

'I know.' Annabelle's face was brightly determined not to give in to another round of tears, he could tell. 'Jamie reckons we need a change of scene, and a chance to relax. And it was a proper deal, too, as it was so last minute. I've barely had the chance to think about what to pack.'

'When do you fly?'

'At some ungodly hour on Monday morning,' Annabelle replied. 'Thank goodness the passports haven't expired!' She gave her brother a brief smile, before moving around from where she was standing behind the counter of the farm shop they jointly ran, under the managerial eye of their father, Robert. Nick met her gaze as she looked up at him, and a silent understanding passed between them. Stepping forward, he wrapped his arms around her in a quick hug.

'You'll have a great time,' Nick murmured as he released her. 'And don't worry about this place – we'll muddle through.'

'Are you sure?' Annabelle replied. 'I mean, it's not like it's not busy enough in the normal run up to Christmas, and now, with this extra thing...'

'Don't worry about that,' Nick said quickly, although his own thought processes had been sprinting that way ever since Annabelle had told him the news. 'Dad and I have got it covered, and if the worst comes to the worst, we'll get someone from the agency in.'

'Don't you remember what happened last time we did that?'

Annabelle grimaced. 'You spent most of your time re-balancing the till because the guy they sent couldn't add up, even when the till did it for him! And don't get me started on what he did with the sausages!'

Nick laughed. 'I'll make sure whoever we get will be somewhat more experienced than him, I promise.'

'Thanks, Nick.' Annabelle smiled again. 'I appreciate it, and you, you know.'

'What are little brothers for?' Nick smiled back. Annabelle was only eighteen months older than him, but sometimes it felt like eighteen years. She'd always been the responsible one, and he wasn't about to begrudge her a Caribbean holiday when she'd been working so hard for so long to make Saints' Farm Shop the success it was becoming.

As a younger man, Nick had thought his future had been mapped out. He'd felt unstoppable, invincible, as though he could handle anything. He'd been set for a degree at the same agricultural college he'd done his post-sixteen qualifications at and spent most of his time either on a tractor in the fields or haring around the country lanes, and although he planned, eventually, to take over the farm, the next three years would be more of the same, academically and socially.

Then Robert Saint had had a heart attack at forty-seven years old and Nick's life had changed. Although his dad had made a full recovery, his sudden illness made a difference to the family. Nick had chosen to help take over the family business with his sister, early, which, back then had been a larger farm and a smaller shop, gradually streamlining things until Saints' Farm was a more commercial enterprise. It was still a hard slog, and even though the majority of what they now sold came from other suppliers, Robert still kept his hand in on the agricultural side. As a result of Robert Saint's illness, the family farm had become more of a large market garden over the years, but they had made more money out of it.

Nick had taken the reins at eighteen, with Annabelle, and they'd spent over a decade and a half working together, realising the full potential of what had been a gently dying family farm. Robert, who still missed the vast swathes of land that the family once owned, was still involved in the business, on the managerial side but, much to the relief of his wife, didn't have the day-to-day stress of keeping things going. What the family had lost in acres, they'd gained in quality of life, and Nick was grateful for that.

All the same, he wondered what might have been if his father hadn't been forced to downscale the farm. Would he, himself have taken it on by now, and would Annabelle have made different life choices? The farm was in their blood, but she'd always harboured dreams of city life, at least for a few years. Now they were both firmly tethered to Lower Brambleton, and it looked as though that wasn't going to change.

Not that he minded. Much. At thirty-seven, however, he knew time was marching on, and he'd been rooted here for decades. He'd had a few relationships over the years, but nothing that had persuaded him to take the final plunge and settle down, as Annabelle and her husband, Jamie, had. He often joked that he was married to the business, but as time went on, that was beginning to feel like less of a joke.

The trill of the shop's doorbell, signalling the arrival of a customer, snapped them both back to the more pressing issues of the day's trade. The shop was quiet for a Wednesday afternoon, and Nick was just about to head out the back to do an inventory on the non-perishable goods that he'd been putting off for about a week. However, when he saw the figure coming through the door, he decided the back-room stuff could wait a little longer.

'All right, but only a small one.' The boy dashed off to the sweet treats section at the back of the shop, and Thea Ashcombe glanced after him, before approaching the counter. Nick smiled at her, as he always did. Seeing Thea always made him feel brighter. They'd been friends for years and had known each other since they were kids. Although time had interceded and they didn't spend as much time together as they had when they had been part of the same friendship group at school, Nick was fond of Thea and his day always felt as though it improved when he saw her.

'Hi Thea,' he remembered to say as she approached. 'How are you?'

'Not bad, thanks,' Thea replied, but, to Nick, who'd known her for almost the whole of his life, the brief grin that she gave him in return seemed a little forced.

'Lovely afternoon,' Nick continued. 'Not much sunshine around this time of year, and it's always nice when it does break through.'

'Hmm,' Thea replied. She seemed a bit distracted.

'So, what can I do for you?' Nick asked. 'Can I tempt you to a pack of mince pies? Fresh in today from our local supplier.'

Thea shook her head vigorously. 'Er, no, thanks,' she replied. 'I don't think I'm quite ready to feel the Christmas spirit just yet.'

'Fair enough.' Nick smiled. 'How about a free sample, then? I was just about to open up the packet to tempt a few impulse buys!'

Thea did, at least, smile then. There was something about her expression that concerned Nick, and he found himself wanting to keep her smiling. If a freebie mince pie was what it took, then it seemed a small price to pay. He and Thea had been gradually renewing their friendship since she'd moved back to Lower Brambleton a couple of years ago, but their paths didn't tend to cross much. She was busy with school and her own children, and he was kept equally frantic with the demands of the farm shop. Whenever he saw her, though, he felt a warm glow of pleasure. It was always good to reconnect with people you'd grown up with.

'Oh, go on then,' she replied. 'Lunch was a bit of a rush, so it'll be a nice treat.'

'Too busy at school?' Nick asked. He knew how hard Thea worked at the primary school where she taught, and he always marvelled at how she had the patience. Some of the children who came into the shop didn't seem to have very many boundaries, and he'd often had to clean up the mess when little hands grabbed things from shelves. He held a healthy respect for anyone who could spend their working life with children, as well as having their own.

'It's a hectic time of year.' She reached for a mince pie from the packet Nick was holding, and he felt a little jolt as their fingers touched. 'That's amazing. Your supplier's got a wonderful way with shortcrust pastry.' Nick watched the colour infuse her cheeks as she realised she was talking with her mouth full, and he felt his own cheeks flushing slightly when he realised he was looking directly at her.

Just then, Dylan approached the counter with a cellophane wrapped packet of marshmallows. 'Can I have these, Mum?'

'Not today, darling. How about a packet of crisps instead?'

'I want something sweet,' Dylan insisted. 'Pleeeease...?'

Nick watched Thea suppress a sigh. 'Oh, all right then. But you'll have to share them with your sister.'

'Thanks, Mum!' Dylan gave a gap-toothed grin.

Thea finished the mince pie and turned back to the counter. She looked a little unsure of herself again, and Nick wondered why.

'Is there something else I can help you with?' he asked.

'Well, yes, actually,' Thea replied. 'I, er, I haven't done this before, but there's this app... Too Good To Throw? You guys have just registered on it, and I've reserved a Throw Bag?'

Nick tried to hide his surprise. Thea hadn't ever struck him as the penny-pinching type. Then, he checked himself – just because someone took advantage of a good offer on an app, didn't give him the right to judge.

'Sure,' he said. 'Bear with me – we put the bags together about an hour ago and they're just out the back. I'll pop and get you one.' He hurried out to the area beyond the shop floor where there were six Saints' Farm carrier bags already assembled and being kept cool in one of the fridges. He'd put them together himself, and all had a selection of chilled and baked goods that were expiring today. Glancing inside the bags, he looked for the one that had an extra Chelsea Bun in it – there'd been one spare, and rather than pinch it himself for after dinner, he'd shoved it into a bag. There were three in the bag in total, as well as a bottle of milk, a loaf of bread and a couple of swedes, again from a local organic farm. On impulse, he grabbed a box of the mince pies and popped them in, too. His dad wouldn't approve of the free-bie, but he wanted to give Thea another reason to smile. She looked as though she needed one. As he brought the bag back through to the counter, he wondered what was on her mind.

'Here you go,' Nick said, putting the bag with the marshmallows. As he rung up the discounted price, he noticed the pint of milk Thea had nipped off and got while she'd been waiting. 'No need for that, unless you're going to be using a lot over the next couple of days,' he added. 'There's a four-pint bottle in the bag.'

'Oh, that's lucky.' Thea smiled more convincingly this time. 'I, er, I only popped in for milk, really, but the Throw Bag seemed like a great idea.'

'Well, I hope you can make use of what's in there,' Nick replied. 'I hope you like swede!'

Thea grinned. 'Funnily enough, I suspected there might be one in the bag. I'll have to look up some recipes.'

'Well, let me know how it turns out.' Nick smiled back at her. 'See you soon.'

As Thea turned to leave, Dylan was already reaching for the marshmallows, and Nick couldn't resist another grin. He remembered how his mother used to tell him he ate the family out of house and home when he was that age, and it seemed as though Dylan was going through the same stage.

'I'm going to start bringing in the baskets from the front,' he called to Annabelle as he caught sight of her out the back. 'It's already getting dark.'

'OK,' Annabelle called back.

Nick sauntered to the front door and towards the baskets of fruit and veg on the far left of the shop's generous frontage. It was a job that kept him fit, bringing them out and then back in again every evening, so he couldn't really complain about it. And if anyone needed an emergency sack of spuds before closing, they were just inside the front door.

The car park was empty apart from Thea's Volvo, and Nick found his eyes drawn to her as she put the shopping in the boot and then slid into the driver's seat. Hefting a basket of carrots off the wooden units that sat outside the shop, he brought it inside and then walked briskly back to collect the next one. He noticed that Thea was still sitting in the car but assumed that she was talking to Dylan. He grabbed the next basket of veg and stacked it carefully on top of the first one.

On his third trip outside, he looked briefly towards Thea's car again. She still hadn't moved. Perhaps she was checking her phone before she left? By the fourth trip to the front of the shop, he wasn't so sure. When he chanced another glance towards her, he noticed a look of upset and frustration on her face and watched as she hit the steering wheel with her right hand. Shaking her head at Dylan, she appeared to be trying to turn the ignition key, but the Volvo's engine just spluttered and died, rather than firing into life. As she got back out of the car, he could clearly see how worried she looked.

3

Great. That's just great. Swallowing back the urge to let rip with all the swear words she knew, and kick the car in frustration, Thea made do with leaning against it instead. Fuel tank roulette had finally failed her. The irony of this situation, after what had happened between her and her ex so many years ago, was too irritating to be entertaining. Ed had risked a lot more than an empty fuel tank when he'd gambled away their savings and they'd had to sell the house they'd bought. Somehow, by playing the fuel tank game, it felt as though someone up there was laughing at her. But, whichever way she gave herself a bollocking, it wouldn't solve the immediate problem. The car really was empty, and didn't even have enough fumes to catch from the ignition. And she'd not renewed her RAC membership to cut costs.

'Mum? Are we going home?' Dylan's voice cut through her annoyance, and she turned and gave him a quick smile.

'In a sec, darling. Just got to sort something out.'

It was five miles to the nearest petrol station. In resignation, she pulled her phone out of her pocket and dialled her grandmother's number. Lorelai lived in a charming cottage on the other side of Lower Brambleton and hopefully would be able to give her a lift to the pumps. She hoped a few litres of diesel, plus, irritatingly, a can to put them into, wouldn't set her back too much. So much for saving money with the Throw Bag – that saving would now be cancelled out immediately.

Lorelai wasn't answering her phone. As she ended the call, Thea realised that her grandmother had mentioned she was heading into Taunton to do some Christmas shopping that afternoon, and she huffed in frustration. Perhaps her twin brother, Tristan, could help? Another flare of frustration hit her when she remembered that he was working on a project on the other side of the county and so wouldn't just be able to drop everything and help her.

Who else was there? Charlotte, Tristan's partner, might be working from home today. Charlotte was a historical astronomical archivist who was based at the University of North West Wessex in Bristol, but she often chose to work from the house she shared with Tristan on the outskirts of Taunton. Hurriedly, she rang her.

'Oh God, I'm so sorry, Thea,' Charlotte said once Thea had filled her in. 'I'm at the archive today so I won't be back until after six o'clock. Have you tried Tristan or Lorelai?'

'Gran's shopping and Tristan's on that job two hours away, isn't he?'

'Oh yeah.' There was a pause. 'Will the RAC come out for no fuel?'

Thea didn't want to admit that she'd cancelled her membership, and that she wasn't sure they'd come out for that, even if she hadn't.

'Look, keep me posted,' Charlotte said. 'I'll see if I can get off work a bit early and get over to you.'

'Thanks, but I'm sure I'll work something out.' Thea injected

as much brightness as she could into her tone. 'See you soon.'
She raised the phone to her temple, tempted to knock herself out
with it. What an idiot she was. 'Shit...'

'Everything all right?'

Nick Saint's voice cut into her gloomy thoughts, and she
snapped her head back up quickly to see him standing a few feet
away from her.

Thea shook her head. 'Not really.'

'Anything I can help with?' His tone was light, and gentle, and
his eyes were full of concern.

'I've just made a stupid mistake,' Thea said, surprised that her
voice trembled a bit. 'I should have filled the car up at the start of
the week, but I, er, didn't. Now it's completely out.' She didn't
want to admit to Nick that she'd hit ten quid from the top of her
overdraft on Monday and still had two more days until payday,
which was why she hadn't put fuel in the car. The Throw Bag and
marshmallows had cost another six pounds, so there was no way
she could fill the car until Friday without incurring bank charges.

Nick looked relieved. 'Well, I can help with that. We've got
some jerry cans of diesel in the tractor shed. Should be enough to
get you started and home, at least.'

'Won't that be red diesel?' Thea asked. 'I'm not sure I fancy a
fine on top of everything else!' Red diesel was strictly controlled
and for agricultural use only, and should you be found to be
using it in other vehicles, fines and even vehicle confiscations
were possible.

'Most of them are cans of red, but we keep a couple of smaller
ones for emergencies, too. Hang on, I'll pop down and see what I
can find.'

Thea's sense of relief that Nick had so casually come to her
rescue must have shown on her face as Nick added, 'It's no trouble, really. I'll be back in a sec.'

'Thank you so much,' Thea replied before Nick turned in the direction of the outbuildings behind the farm shop. She felt weak with relief. The easy way that Nick had apprised her situation, and immediately found a solution, felt as if a massive weight had lifted from her shoulders. She was so used to solving problems on her own, it felt nice to have someone else stepping in and sorting this one for her. No fuss, no drama, just a guy with a fuel can and a nice smile. She had to admit, Nick *did* have a nice smile. Especially when he was coming to her rescue.

'Are we going home now, Mum?' Dylan's voice interrupted her thoughts.

'In a sec, darling,' Thea replied. 'Nick's just gone to get us some fuel for the car.'

In a jiffy, Nick was back with a diesel can. 'Happens to the best of us,' he said as he waited for Thea to unlock her fuel cap. 'I once ran out of juice two miles from a college party and fifteen miles from home. Dad was not best pleased when I called him at two in the morning begging for a lift!'

Thea grinned. She could well imagine the gruff Robert Saint giving his son short shrift at being pulled out of bed. The reassuring glug of the diesel helped to still her racing heart, and as Nick put the fuel cap back on and turned back to her, she thanked him again.

'It's no bother,' he replied. 'I wouldn't leave you stranded, Thea.'

Thea's face grew warmer at the gentle friendliness of his tone. She'd always thought Nick was a sweetheart, but over the years, with one hazy, it-may-not-have-even-happened moment as the exception, she'd placed him firmly in the friend zone. It would have been too weird, when they were teenagers, to think of him as anything else. Now though, he'd definitely been her saviour.

'Well, it's still very kind of you.' She fiddled with the bracelet on her right wrist for a moment. 'How much do I owe you?'

'Oh, don't worry about that,' Nick replied with a smile. 'Call it a favour for a friend.'

'Are you sure?'

'I'm sure.' Nick paused. 'Next time you're in the pub, you can, er, buy me a drink if you want.'

'It's a deal.' Thea smiled at him. 'Well, I'd better get off. Dylan's already eaten his share of the marshmallows and if I don't confiscate them, he'll have had Cora's half as well.'

'See you soon,' Nick said as he picked up the diesel can. 'Take care, Thea.'

'You too.'

Thea turned the ignition key and, thankfully, the Volvo started. She glanced in Nick's direction before she pulled out of the parking spot and couldn't help lingering. His long-legged lope across the car park with the jerry can seemed so assured, and yet she knew how shy he could be, as well. She'd often heard Tristan teasing Nick about his terrible conversation skills with the opposite sex. And yet the Nick who'd quickly and efficiently solved her mini fuel crisis had been confident and sure of himself. On his home turf, he seemed so much more at ease. As a teenager he might have been shy, but he definitely wasn't now.

Shaking her head, she began the short drive home. Dylan, as was his habit, was keeping up a constant flow of chat as they travelled. The marshmallows had added fuel to this natural tendency and Thea half listened, saying yes and no in the appropriate places and also trying to put her mind to the rest of the evening.

'So, do you think Father Christmas will bring me *Sword Fighter 3* for Christmas, Mum? *Mum!*'

'Sorry, darling, what was that?' Realising she needed to give a better response, Thea glanced into the hopeful eyes of her young son.

'*Sword Fighter 3* for my Switch? Do you think Father Christmas might bring it?'

Thea's heart sank again. She had been pleased, initially, when her grandmother had bought Dylan the Nintendo Switch for his birthday earlier in the year, but now he expected to increase his collection of games for it fairly regularly, and Christmas seemed, to him, the perfect chance to add to it.

'Wait and see,' she said, after a beat. She didn't want to rule it out, but she'd definitely have to shop around to find the best prices for Christmas presents, this year more than ever.

Dylan grinned at her through a mouthful of marshmallows. 'Thanks, Mum.'

As she drove towards home, Thea tried to put Christmas out of her mind. Usually, she looked forward to the time off and the chance to eat, drink and be merry with the family, but the financial worries were beginning to infringe on that sense of relaxation. She knew, come the new year, she'd have to work something else out to get more money coming into the house, or things were going to get a whole lot more stressful.

4

The following Monday, Thea found herself back at Saints' Farm. The mobile library stopped in the car park once a fortnight and this was the last chance before Christmas to stock up on some books. It was a lovely, mutually beneficial arrangement because people returning books often popped into the shop for impulse buys, and those already coming to the shop were prompted to start, or continue, their book borrowing habits. Thea had been taking both children to the large, cheerful bus since they were toddlers, and although Cora's reading habits had declined since she got a smart phone and started secondary school, she still tagged along with Dylan and Thea to see what new titles had been added to the collection.

The bus was staffed by volunteers, and the Saint family had taken to providing them with a coffee when they made their stop at the farm shop. As Thea pulled up and parked, she could see Nick retrieving the coffee cups from the bus, and he waved a hand in greeting as he headed back into the shop. Thea resolved to pop in after the kids had chosen their books – she owed him another thank you after he came to her rescue last Wednesday.

She'd also reserved another Throw Bag, after the varied contents of the first one, and wanted to pick it up. With the much-needed cash injection of her part-time teacher's salary hitting her bank account on Friday, the first thing she'd done was fill the tank of her car, so she wouldn't end up in the same predicament again.

'I thought you'd read that one?' she said to Dylan as he pulled one of the Percy Jackson novels off the shelf of the fantasy section.

'Nope,' Dylan said confidently. 'I skipped ahead in the series 'cos someone got it before me, so I want to catch up with what I missed.'

'Fair enough.' Thea smiled at her son. 'Have a look and see what else you want.' She glanced over at Cora, who was engrossed in something on her phone, as per usual.

'Anything catch your eye?' she asked her daughter pointedly.

Cora shook her head, not bothering to look up from the screen. Thea suppressed the urge to stride over and snatch the damned device from her daughter's hands. She hoped Cora would come back to reading in her own time, which was why she still insisted that the girl visited the mobile library regularly. The novelty of having the world on a screen in your pocket had yet to wear off, though, and Thea had to accept it as a necessary evil, for now.

'I'm just going to pop into the shop,' she called again to Cora. 'Can you keep an eye on your brother for me?'

Dylan rolled his eyes. 'I don't need keeping an eye on, Mum.'

'I know.' Thea ruffled the top of his hair affectionately. 'But indulge me.'

Grumbling, Dylan ducked away from her and continued to look at the shelves. Cora looked up and gave Thea a brief grin of acknowledgement and then returned to her phone. Thea smiled at Bess, the volunteer who staffed the Monday afternoon session, and stepped back down into the car park.

As she entered the farm shop, Thea was surprised by how festive the place looked. In the few days since her last visit, Saints' had gone all out to make it feel like Christmas. Hanging from the wooden beams that ran in parallel lines across the shop were strings of warm white fairy lights, twinkling away and catching the colours of the decorations on four pine trees, one in each corner of the shop, themselves glinting with coloured lights. Each tree had a colour co-ordinated theme, and Thea was amused to see that the one nearest the counter was decked out in the navy blue and gold colours of the shop's branding. An unobtrusive compilation of seasonal songs played softly over the shop's PA system, and Thea had to suppress a laugh when she saw Nick behind the shop counter, sporting a very fluffy and festive Christmas bobble hat.

'It suits you,' she said as she approached him. 'Maybe you should think about wearing it all year.'

Nick grimaced. 'It was Annabelle's idea, although I'm half tempted to chuck it up onto the roof now that she's left the country!' He pushed the white band of the hat up a little, where it had sagged over his forehead.

'Have they gone for some winter sun?' Thea asked, then sighed. 'I could certainly do with some!'

As Nick filled her in on Jamie's last-minute deal and the holiday destination, Thea felt envious. How lovely to be married to someone who'd plan something like that and then make it a sun-drenched surprise. No chance of anything happening like that for her and the kids, she thought. Getting through Christmas without blowing a fortune on the central heating was about as glamorous as it was going to get for her.

'So, it's left me in a bit of a pickle,' Nick was saying as she caught the thread of the conversation again. 'Dad and I are working flat out, but we really could do with some extra staff in the run up to Christmas. Mum's cracked a hip, so can't really help too much, either.'

'Sounds stressful,' Thea commiserated. 'How did she do that?'

'She slipped on the back steps of the cottage while she was going out to put some bread on the bird table,' Nick replied. 'Thankfully it's only a hairline fracture so it'll mend with rest and time, but it's giving her a fair bit of gyp.' He paused before adding, 'She didn't let on to Annabelle how bad it was before Annabelle and Jamie left because she didn't want Annie to worry, but it does leave me rather short-handed with just Dad to call on during the week.'

'Poor Maggie,' Thea said. 'If I know your mum, she's going to be really frustrated about not being able to help out here.'

Nick grinned briefly. 'She is. And the bloody film crew are coming back at the end of this week, too.'

'Film crew?'

'Yup.' Nick paused, seemingly embarrassed. 'A couple of years ago, we were featured on a TV show for Channel 5 – *Britain's Loveliest Farm Shops*. It was Annabelle's idea, and because it was so soon after we'd had a refit, we all thought it would be great publicity to apply to be featured. Anyway, it all went so well that they asked us back in the summer if we'd mind doing another segment for a festive catch-up show. They're going to be using a lot of the footage from the first time around, but they want to do a kind of "Farm Shop at Christmas" thing. Annabelle said yes to it, but didn't realise she was going to be whisked off on holiday during the filming, so it's down to Dad and I to handle that, on top of everything else.'

'Can't you pull out?' Thea asked. 'I'm sure they'd understand.'

'Nope. It's all been arranged, and they're coming in on

Thursday to do some filming. They hope to have it all done by the middle of next week so they can air it over Christmas. Their schedule's quite tight, and the publicity's too good to pass up.' He smiled ruefully. 'I managed to stay off camera when they were here before, although they did catch me a few times, but now they want me front and centre.'

'Makes sense, really,' Thea teased. 'I mean, filming Nick Saint at Christmas – what a coup!'

Nick looked briefly thunderous, but then, much to Thea's relief, he laughed. 'OK, so I suppose it is kind of inevitable, but that doesn't mean I'm looking forward to it. But never mind – I'm sure we'll work something out.'

'I used to work in the local shop in the village, years ago, if you're desperate,' Thea joked. 'The tills are probably a bit different now, but I'm a quick learner.'

Nick's pause made Thea a little nervous.

'Is that a serious offer? I mean, don't take this the wrong way, but I'm pretty desperate and out of ideas...'

'Thanks,' Thea said dryly. Then, her mind began to fill in some gaps. A bit of extra work, even if it was only for a couple of weeks before Christmas, would certainly come in handy. And while the money wouldn't match her teaching salary, it would be less demanding, she hoped. 'Seriously, I could help out, if you wanted me to.'

'Aren't you working at school?'

'Only Monday to Wednesday,' Thea replied. 'I've been trying to get more hours, but it's not that easy in a nice school where no one ever leaves. From Thursday onwards, I could be here, if it helps.'

Nick's relieved face gave Thea's heart a little, joyful lift. He had looked so stressed when she'd come in, and it felt good to be able to do something to help him out, especially since he'd saved her bacon with the diesel. Working in the farm shop for a couple of weeks would be a nice change from school, and it would mean a little extra cash for Christmas, which would come in very handy indeed.

'Any time you can give us would be great,' Nick said. 'And since the film crew start on Thursday, the tail end of the week is where we might need the most help. If you're sure?'

Thea nodded. 'To be honest, you'd be doing me a favour, too. Christmas is an expensive time of year, especially now the kids are old enough to tell me exactly what they want. And what they want tends to cost more money, the older they get!'

'Well, that sounds like a plan, then.' Nick reached over the counter. 'Shake on it?'

Laughing, Thea took his hand, which felt warm and firm against hers. 'It's a deal.'

As Nick let go of her hand again, he added, 'Would you be OK to come in on Wednesday afternoon after school for a couple of hours' training? I can take you through the till, show you the ropes a bit, that sort of thing.'

'I'll have to check with my gran that she can pop over and keep an eye on Dylan, but I'm sure that'll be fine,' Thea replied. Lorelai was always happy to see her great-grandchildren, and she was sure a couple of hours wouldn't be a problem.

'Great! I'll see you then.' Nick gave her a smile, and Thea's heart gave that little, joyful lift again. 'Was there, er, anything else you needed?' he added as she lingered at the counter.

'Oh, right, yeah.' Thea grabbed her phone from her bag and clicked to find the reference for her next Throw Bag. 'I liked the bag I got last week, so I thought I'd take a chance with another one.'

As Nick headed to the stock room to retrieve her Throw Bag, Thea realised she hadn't done what she'd come in for and thanked him for the diesel. She was lucky she had a friend like him, she thought as she waited for him to return to the counter. Nick was the kind of person who'd do anything for anyone, and she yet again found herself wondering why he hadn't been snapped up by some lucky girl years ago. Maybe he had some terrible habits she wasn't aware of, she thought in amusement. After all, she hadn't a clue, when she'd fallen in love with Ed, just how destructive some of his 'habits' were going to be. Somehow, with Nick, who seemed much more straightforward, she doubted it, though. Perhaps he just hadn't found the right person yet?

5

Wednesday afternoon arrived, and Thea felt a flutter of apprehension. She then felt daft for being nervous. She'd had plenty of retail experience, even if it had been a fair few years ago, and although the technology might have changed, she was sure she could adapt. It wasn't as if Saints' Farm Shop was a hypermarket, either – she hoped she'd have plenty of time to learn the ropes, and if things didn't work out, it was only until Christmas anyway.

She'd told herself these facts a few times between agreeing to help out and actually arriving to be trained by Nick. Confident in her own abilities as a primary school teacher, a job she'd been doing for fifteen years, she wouldn't have thought twice about learning a new skill or trying a new technique in her classroom. This really wasn't so different. As she locked the car and headed in through the farm shop's doors, she could already see Nick behind the counter, bidding someone goodbye, and as the customer turned to leave, she saw it was Mollie Wakefield, owner of the Purrfect Paws Feline Rescue Centre and part-time manager of the charity shop in the village that had been opened to support the work of the centre. Mollie gave her a friendly smile as she passed by and a conspiratorial whisper.

'I've just had some Pokémon cards in, if Dylan's still interested in them. I'll put them out the back for Saturday if you get the chance to pop in with him.'

'Thanks, Mollie.' Thea smiled. 'I'll bring him by and see what he thinks.'

Mollie had the knack of being able to source a great deal of things that the Lower Brambleton locals had on their wish lists, especially the children, and the 'magic' of the Purrfect Paws Charity Shop seemed to work whatever time of year it was. Thea's keen eye for a bargain approved.

'Hi,' Nick said as she approached the counter. 'How was your day?'

'Long,' Thea sighed, but brightened when she saw Nick's look of sympathy. 'It's always a bit of a slog getting the children ready for the nativity play, but at least it'll all be done and dusted by the end of next week. If I have to adjust one more wonky tinsel halo or discourage the donkey from growing his role to more than just a few well-timed "hee-haws" one more time, I think I might bury my head in the manger!'

Nick laughed. 'I don't know how you do it. I certainly wouldn't have the patience for that kind of gig.'

Thea couldn't help a rush of pleasure when he laughed. She also noticed how well the dark blue Saints' Farm polo shirt suited him. It offset his beech-leaves-in-autumn coloured hair to a tee. He'd filled out over the years, too, because of the intensely physical nature of running the farm shop, and she had to concede he'd grown very attractive.

'It's kind of sweet, really,' Thea replied, fearing she'd come across as a bit too cynical. 'They all try very hard, and the parents are so proud of their little darlings on the stage. I just wish it wasn't quite so repetitive, getting them all word perfect.'

'Well, speaking as someone who had a strictly non-speaking role as one half of the stable door in the Christmas nativity play thirty years ago, I'm sure they'll all look back and feel proud.'

'Which half of the door were you? I can't remember.'

Nick pretended to look hurt. 'I'm offended that you've forgotten. Don't you remember the lengths Mrs Rossiter went to drill the script into us? The poor woman's hair turned white by the end of it, I seem to recall.'

'I don't think we were that bad,' Thea replied. 'I think she was just too busy to dye it before the end of term!' She paused, and then teasingly added, 'And I bet you can't remember what part I played, anyway.'

'Of course I can! I'll always remember you with one of Lorelai's tea towels strapped to your head with a dressing gown cord, cuddling that fluffy lamb. You and Tristan made quite the pair of shepherds, although I can't remember which of you had the line.'

'He did,' Thea replied. 'He always was the bigger drama queen out of the two of us.'

'And Tris, not here to defend himself!' Nick was smirking now, before his expression fell. 'Oh God, Thea, wasn't that the first Christmas after your parents...' he trailed off, clearly feeling as though he'd made a misstep in the conversation.

When Thea and Tristan were five years old, their parents had been killed in a car accident near what had been the Lower Brambleton Observatory. They had been raised by Lorelai at Nightshade Cottage, just down the hill from the observatory. The tragedy had rocked the family and the wider village of Lower Brambleton, and still, over thirty years on, it lived in the memories of the residents.

Thea gave him a reassuring smile. 'It's all right,' she said. 'Tris and I enjoyed the distraction of things like the school plays after we lost Mum and Dad. It wasn't as if the pain stopped, but it gave us other things to think about for short bursts of time. And Gran was in the audience that year, cheering us both on in the way that only she could.' She looked at him. 'And you didn't answer my question. Which half of the stable door were you?'

'The better half,' Nick said dryly. 'The other boy fell over and nearly took me with him.'

'That's right, I'd completely forgotten about that! Talk about a scene – or scenery – stealer! I wonder what happened to him?'

'Became a carpenter, from what I've heard.' Nick's tone was so deadpan that Thea couldn't be sure if he was joking or not.

'Well,' Thea said, glancing at the clock behind the counter. 'Are you ready to get started? I'm all yours for the next couple of hours, if you think that'll be enough time.'

'Should be more than enough to show you the basics,' Nick replied. 'And anything else you need to know, you can just ask me or Dad as we go along.'

'Thanks. I really do appreciate the chance to earn a bit more money before Christmas, and I'll try to do my best for you.'

'You're welcome. In fact, you're doing me a favour, too, so it's all worked out quite well.' Nick turned and reached for an apron that was hanging up on a brass hook behind the counter. 'I've got you one of your own, and although I haven't had time to get your name put on it, Mum made you a badge to pin on.'

'Thanks.' Thea took the apron and swiftly tied it around her waist. 'Well, where do we start?'

And as Nick started to take her through the operation of the till, and where the price lists were for the loose produce, as well as how to operate the scales, Thea quickly caught on. It felt good to be out of her cosy comfort zone of the classroom and learning a new set of skills, or, at least, refreshing some she'd not used in a long while. Retail might not be where she thought she'd end up at this point in her life, but it certainly beat some of the alternatives, not least worrying even more about paying the bills.

'So, the film crew are coming in tomorrow morning to set up and do some exterior shots and decide where the interior cameras are going to go. Are you all right with them being around while you're working?'

Thea hesitated. It would be her first 'real' day on the job, and she wasn't sure how she felt about being caught on TV learning the ropes. But then, Nick had warned her about the film crew when he'd suggested the job to her, so she didn't feel as though she could really say no. 'I'm sure it'll be fine,' she said cautiously. 'But if there's any way I can be out the back, or doing things just out of the eye of the cameras, I think I'd feel more comfortable.'

'Fair enough,' Nick replied. 'I suspect they'll just want lots of shots of pretty looking stuff in the shop anyway, and since Annabelle "volunteered" me to be the main talking head, and Dad's rather fond of showing off to the camera, you probably won't need to be in front of shot. Are you all right with being shown in the background?'

'Sure,' Thea said. 'I'm more than happy to be a non-speaking extra.'

'Much like you were in the Christmas play?' Nick teased. 'Maybe I should have asked Tristan to do a few hours here, instead!'

Thea laughed. 'He'd be constantly asking the director for his motivation in every scene, he's such a perfectionist!' Thea adored her twin brother, but Tristan was a stickler for things to be just right, and she wasn't above teasing him about it, and laughing about him with their friends.

'Best stick with you, then,' Nick said softly. When he smiled at her, Thea felt something start to fizz in her stomach. He really did have a lovely smile. She'd begun to notice things about him recently, but had put it down to feeling a bit lonely. Who lusted after their friends after all this time, anyway? She'd never really wanted to examine how she felt about him – past experiences with Ed had made her very risk averse, and Nick had been in and out of relationships himself, but she knew, from what Annabelle had mentioned the last time they'd spoken, that Nick hadn't been with anyone seriously for quite a while. And she hadn't had anyone, serious or otherwise, for even longer than that.

'Yeah,' she said, slightly nervously, trying to push those thoughts to one side and concentrate on the job at hand. 'Best stick with me.'

6

Thea, to her frustration, didn't sleep well on Wednesday night. It felt daft to be quite so nervous about starting a temporary, part-time job, but she couldn't help it. She might have joked about Tristan being a perfectionist, but she had a bit of a streak of it herself, and she didn't want to let Nick down. What if she really couldn't hack being behind the shop counter again? She was a bit worried that she really was an old dog, about to learn, well, if not exactly new, then long-forgotten tricks. And would working full time for the next few weeks just knacker her out before Christmas, so that she wouldn't have the energy to make the festive period as lovely as she wanted to for Cora and Dylan?

In the cold light of day, these worries felt ridiculous: plenty of parents worked full-time jobs, or more than one job, and they managed somehow. She was always at her best when she was busy, and it wasn't as though the children were babies any more. It was a short-term situation, and she'd deal with it, as she had dealt with everything life had thrown her way over the years. Resilience was in her DNA, after the loss she'd suffered as a young child, and she'd been coping with things ever since.

That didn't mean it wasn't hard, though. She often wondered what it would have been like if her parents had been alive to meet their grandchildren. She hoped they'd have been close. Lorelai was a wonderful great-grandmother to Cora and Dylan, but there was no escaping the fact that she was getting older and wouldn't be around forever. Thea was grateful for every day they had together, and all the time she'd spent with Lorelai as she'd grown up. The thought that she and Tristan might have ended up away from Lower Brambleton, or worse, split up to go to different families and different lives, still filled her with a retrospective horror. All things considered, they'd both been very lucky that Lorelai had been there to take care of them, but that didn't mean she didn't wonder what things might have been like had her parents not been taken so suddenly and dreadfully.

Restless and lacking the ability to get back to sleep, at 5 a.m. she shrugged on a pair of jogging bottoms, a sweatshirt, thick socks and her fleece-lined parka jacket. Pushing her feet into her wellies, since the ground underfoot had been soggy for weeks, she slipped out of the front door and onto Orion Close. Cora and Dylan, still fast asleep upstairs, wouldn't miss her for a few minutes.

The Observatory Field housing development had been built on the site of its namesake, the Lower Brambleton Observatory, after the site of special astronomical interest had closed and fallen into disrepair some years ago. The site had been in Thea's family, jointly inherited by Lorelai and her brother, Phillip, after their father had died but had only recently been demolished and redeveloped. Tristan had overseen the development for Flowerdew Homes, a company that had promised a sustainable and sympathetic development of houses to help to bring new life to the ever-sleepier hamlet of Lower Brambleton.

Thea had never been wealthy. When her parents had died,

the proceeds from their estate had been held in trust for both herself and Tristan until they were eighteen. The inheritance was substantial, and both she and Tristan had used some of the money to put themselves through university. Then, wisely, Tristan had put his share into property and now owned his house outright, having bought a decrepit townhouse on the outskirts of Taunton's city centre and renovated it.

Sadly, Thea's fortunes hadn't been so lucky. Even now, the sting of what she'd had, and what she'd lost, stayed with her and tainted every decision she made. She'd fallen in love with a charming man, who'd swept her off her feet and had promised to give her the security that she'd craved in the wake of her parents' death. She'd fallen hard for Ed and had been blind to his gambling problem that eventually became an addiction which inevitably caused tensions, a rift, and, eventually, a separation. Unfortunately for Thea and her two children, by the time she'd realised what was happening, Ed had left her and what was left of her inheritance was sunk into a house that was more mortgage than mortar. That the Observatory Field site held painful memories for her, there was no doubt, but the development was a stone's throw from her grandmother's cottage, and she couldn't bear to pass up the opportunity to own her own home.

It was funny, she thought, how she and Tristan had felt so differently about Observatory Field. Tristan had headed up the development as a kind of catharsis: it allowed him to control the destiny and future of the site and finally see the building that had been so much a part of the family's life, and their tragedy, razed to the ground. In Tristan's eyes, it was just what the place deserved: the final piece in the long, painful puzzle of the Lower Brambleton Observatory's history. Taking charge of that last step was Tristan's way of gaining closure after a lifetime of living with the traumatic memories the place evoked.

Thea glanced up at the sky, which was still dotted with bright stars, even though dawn would start greying the velvety blackness over the next couple of hours. Her parents had loved being here, in this space, and had spent many hours observing the night sky through the great telescope inside the dome of the observatory. They'd even discovered something hitherto unseen; an eclipsing binary, a pair of orbiting stars that moved in perfect harmony on the tip of the Volucris constellation. Although that discovery had been lost to time for thirty years, due to the bitterness and frustration of Lorelai's brother, here had been a posthumous accolade for her parents, and while this would always be bittersweet, she was delighted that it had happened.

But Thea would never stop missing them. Even though they were blurred memories in her mind, she was still brought up short by the scent of Yardley's *Lily of the Valley* if she happened to smell it or had to blink away sudden tears if she saw a copy of *Better Than Life*, her father's favourite science fiction novel, on a charity shop bookshelf. Something that always made her smile, though, was whenever Chesney Hawkes' 'I Am the One and Only' came on the radio. She had a faded memory of her mother bopping along in the kitchen to the catchy pop song, and she could never be sure if she actually did remember her rather more serious father rolling his eyes whenever she did, or if it was just her own childish mind filling in the gaps.

Her gentle, pre-dawn meandering had taken her to a familiar spot. When the housing development had been conceived, a late addition had been made that had necessitated the adjustment of the plans for one part of the land. Inset into a small, paved area where the observatory itself had once stood was a burnished bronze plaque with a by now very familiar inscription:

This plaque is dedicated to the tireless efforts and passion for discovery of the members of the Lower Brambleton Astronomical Society.

In 1994, Laura and Martin Ashcombe, esteemed members of LBAS, made the remarkable discovery of an eclipsing binary star, expanding our understanding of the cosmos. Their dedication and contribution to the field of astronomy continue to inspire future generations of stargazers and scholars.

'Per Aspera ad Astra'

Through hardships to the stars.

'I miss you,' Thea murmured as her eyes traced over the memorial plaque. She ran a tired hand over her face. 'I wish you were here.'

Thea didn't often feel lonely, although the loss she'd suffered was always with her. Children, both her own and those for whom she was responsible in her classroom, stopped her from feeling that emotion, and she knew that Tristan would always be there for her, come what may. And Lorelai, too, for as long as she was still around. But in the darkness of what felt like yet another morning of an unending winter, loneliness hit her like a smack to the stomach. The gap that her parents had left in her life had translated itself to a longing for love that, in turn, had led her to her relationship with Ed. He'd sensed that longing, but in the end, it hadn't been enough for him. His own, addictive desires had been too great. Ed had burned her and made her more cautious than she should have been about entering into new relationships, so, for a long time she'd steered herself away from anyone who might be interested in getting involved with her.

But there was no getting away from it. She missed the feeling of arms around her. She missed being able to laugh with someone over the antics of the children, and she missed being able to call someone up and make plans for a shared evening, day or weekend together. As she glanced at her watch, and wearily contemplated the beginning of another long day, she touched her fingers to her lips and then placed them in the centre of the memorial plaque. It felt cold under her touch. Then, straightening herself back up, she headed back to the house, where, in about an hour's time, she'd be back into the familiar routines of getting the kids up and out of the door for school. She wouldn't be thinking about how lonely she was, then. It was only when things were quiet, in these early hours, that it seemed to creep up on her. She'd be busy at Saints' Farm, too – the learning curve was going to be steep for a few days, and she hoped she wouldn't have time for gloomy thoughts. Letting herself back into the house, she closed the front door quietly and went through to the kitchen to make a cup of tea before the day really got going.

7

The sight of Nick's smile of welcome as she pushed open the doors of the farm shop did a lot to calm Thea's nerves. Nick, who'd always been the shy and reserved one of their friendship group at school, had, in adulthood, developed a quiet confidence that Thea found calmed her down. They'd drifted apart over the years, but whenever their paths had crossed, Thea always felt the better for it afterwards, no matter how stressed she was. When she'd been living away from Lower Brambleton, during those years spent with Ed, she'd not seen much of him, or any of her school friends. Even when she and Ed had split, she'd been working so hard to provide for the children she hadn't really had the emotional bandwidth to reconnect with her friends. However, whenever she'd returned to the village to visit her grandmother and bumped into Nick, her day had always seemed to improve. She'd always put it down to the strength of a friend-ship formed in early childhood, but as she walked towards him now, she wondered if something else had been behind that emotion.

'Morning,' he called from where he was picking up the last

sack of spuds to go out on the display by the front door. 'All set for today?'

Thea couldn't help noticing the ease with which he handled the twenty-five-kilo sack, and the slight bulge of his biceps as he did so. This kind of work obviously kept him fit. He was in great shape, with broad shoulders and lean hips, hugged snugly by well-fitting light blue jeans, and as he brushed his hair back from his eyes as he straightened up again, she found she was looking at him rather too intensely.

'I think so,' she said hurriedly. 'Where do you want me to start?'

Nick, who'd swiftly returned from outside the front door, grinned. 'Well, why don't you stick the kettle on? It's usually pretty quiet between nine and ten – you've missed the people who tend to pop in to get lunch on their way to work.'

'Sounds good,' Thea replied. She donned her apron from where she'd hung it back up behind the counter after her training had finished the previous evening. Nick had shown her the small back office and the kitchen next to the storeroom, so, ascertaining if he wanted tea or coffee, she set to making it while he put the rest of the produce outside.

On her return, Nick was taking a phone call. She tried not to listen in and busied herself with looking through the price list for the loose produce, as well as some of the other documentation she might need. She couldn't help noticing Nick's tone of voice, though; he sounded a little stressed.

'OK. No, look, you take things easy. Yeah, it's not ideal, but I'm sure we'll manage here. I'll pop over after work and give you a hand. OK, bye.'

'Everything all right?' Thea asked as Nick ended the call.

Nick slipped his phone into the back pocket of his jeans and gave her a slightly less than convincing smile. 'Er, not exactly, no.

Dad's put his back out. Silly sod was shifting the Christmas tree into the house last night and he felt it ping.'

'Oh no,' Thea sympathised. 'How is he feeling?'

'Irritated, mainly, but it means he can't really come into work for a day or two until it settles back down. He's doped up to the eyeballs on painkillers, so it's not a great idea for him to muck around with the forklift and the tractor, and with Mum's hip still mending, that leaves us even more short-handed.' Nick gave a grimace of frustration.

Thea, who was at her best when she had to think on her feet, put a reassuring hand on his arm. 'We'll manage. I'm a quick learner and the film crew will only be around for a few days, won't they? I'm sure we can muddle through, between the two of us.'

Nick gave her a smile. 'Shouldn't it be me trying to make you feel better? I'm in charge now, after all!'

'I'll try to remember that,' Thea laughed. 'Although I'm sure you'll have to talk me through quite a bit if we're going to keep this place running, between the two of us.'

'I'm here to help in any way I can,' Nick replied, and Thea felt a shift in the atmosphere between them as he held her gaze with his piercing blue eyes a fraction longer than necessary. 'You're really helping me out, Thea, and I'm grateful.'

Thea's hand was still on Nick's arm, she realised, with a self-conscious jolt, and she hastily removed it. Clearing her throat, she took a step towards the counter again, and slid behind it, creating a bit more of a barrier between them. 'Shall I look after here while you do what you need to do?'

Nick nodded. 'Sure.' He also looked a bit flustered. 'There's a delivery from the bakery coming in any time now, and another from the wholesalers, so I'll do a quick stock check of the fruit and veg, and the baked goods sections, and then I'll have to put the surplus from the wholesalers in the barn. If you can keep an eye on the till, and, if you get the chance, check the stock in the dairy fridge, that would be a great start.'

'Will do, Boss!' Thea quipped, trying not to overthink the pleasant frisson of tension that had developed between them. She needed to stay focussed on the job, even more so now that it looked as though it was just going to be herself and Nick running the place for the next few days.

'It'll be fine,' Nick said as he headed off to check the stock. Thea wasn't sure if he was talking to her, or to himself, but she promised herself she'd do her best to help him out as much as she could. That was what friends did for each other. And that's what she and Nick were. Friends. She tried to forget the way she'd felt when she'd seen him shifting the spuds just now, and the way her hand had just settled so naturally on his arm when she was trying to reassure him. And the way they'd gazed at each other when he'd been doing the same for her. They'd been friends for so long, now, it would be daft to think of him as anything else. Wouldn't it?

8

Thea was feeling pleased with herself by the time the hands of the large clock behind the counter edged towards lunch. She'd got the hang of the till quickly, and in the lull between customers had managed to sort out the dairy fridge as well as rearrange some of the biscuits and other sweet treats so that they looked their best on the shelves. Thea rather got the impression that, with Annabelle away, Nick and Rob had been doing the heavy work but not had the chance to keep the interior of the shop looking at its best, and so she was pleased she could help.

In the run up to Christmas, and especially with the film crew arriving, Thea wanted to make the inside of the shop as camera-worthy as possible. Annabelle had put up some fabulous wreaths at strategic points, but behind the counter Thea had found a box of artificial pine fronds that would look festive and enticing hanging from the oak beams that crisscrossed the shop's roof, and also a smaller box of decorations that must have been meant for the real Christmas tree that Nick had placed to one side of the counter. She was gradually sorting through these in the quiet spells.

Nick was making frequent trips back to the shop from the barns, where he'd been shifting the bulkier items from the wholesaler since they'd arrived about an hour earlier. He'd left her with a walkie-talkie so that she could contact him if she ran into a problem, or a question she couldn't answer, and he could make a sharp return to the store. So far, though, everything had been pleasingly straightforward.

Just as she was wondering if she dared nip out to the loo, which was, rather conveniently, situated near the back office, a large van drew up in the car park and shortly after a couple of guys in polo shirts got out. Assuming they were contractors stopping in for a quick bite to eat before their next job, Thea welcomed them with a cheery smile and a hello.

'All right?' the first guy said. 'Is the gaffer about? We've come to set up the equipment for the film crew.'

'I'll just see if I can get hold of him,' Thea said, and then radioed through to Nick. Thankfully, he wasn't far away, and within a minute or two he'd arrived back in the shop.

As Nick and the two men talked through where they could set up, Thea took the opportunity to slip out to the loo. Being as quick as she could, she was relieved to see that there hadn't been any customers when she'd left the counter and Nick was still chatting. Thea took some time to observe Nick, who seemed perfectly at ease as he spoke to the men from the TV company. She figured that he, like a lot of people, probably felt more relaxed when he was hiding behind his 'official' role as co-proprietor of a very desirable farm shop, than when he didn't have that context. She liked seeing him in action and observing how knowledgeable he was.

'The rest of the crew and the talent'll be here after lunch,' the other of the two men was saying. 'So I daresay there'll be some changes, depending on what Jez and Tally want to do, but we'll try not to get in your way too much.'

'That's great,' Nick said. 'Just let me know what you need from us – we're happy to help.'

'Cheers, mate,' the first guy said. 'And sorry to hear about your old man's back. Bet he's gutted not to be on camera this time!'

'I think he probably is, secretly!' Nick laughed. 'He grumbled about the intrusion last time, but I actually think he enjoyed his fifteen minutes of fame!'

Thea lost the thread of the conversation then, as she served a customer who'd come in and had quite a bundle of shopping. She did feel a bit nervous, though. With Rob and Maggie Saint out of action, and Annabelle and Jamie on holiday, it seemed it was down to her and Nick to be the faces of Saints' Farm Shop for the television, and she wasn't sure that was what she'd signed up for. Suddenly, her vision of just being in the back of shot was feeling far less realistic. She hoped that the focus would be on Nick for most of it, and that she could still manage to fade into the background.

The rest of the morning went smoothly, and by the time she was due to have her lunch break of half an hour, Thea felt as though she'd settled in well to the job. Nick had checked in frequently and had spent the past hour or so on the shop floor, ready to step in if she needed him. Thankfully, though, she was able to handle most things by herself, although she was ready to sit down for a bit out the back and have a well-deserved cuppa, and the sandwich she'd brought from home.

Just as she was about to head to the office at the back of the building, she was distracted by the sight of a tall, willowy and undeniably attractive blonde woman hurrying through the front door of the shop.

'Nicky, *darling!*' The cry sounded straight out of central casting, and Thea watched, fascinated, as the woman, who appeared to be in her late twenties, hurried across the shop floor and threw her arms around Nick before he could respond to her call.

'It's *so* good to see you! You look just as gorgeous as I remember, and it's been too long.' The blonde's ringing voice commanded everyone's attention, and Thea saw the two customers who were picking up items from the bakery counter craning their necks, intrigued.

'Hi Tally.' Nick's voice was slightly muffled because he was still caught in the blonde's very enthusiastic embrace. 'It's good to see you again, too.'

'Don't try to schmooze me,' Tally teased. 'I was hoping you might give me a ring, you naughty thing, after we wrapped here last time, but no, it wasn't to be.'

Finally released from her hug, Nick took a step back from the woman, obviously keen to put a little distance between them. Thea's curiosity was piqued; it seemed as though Nick and Tally had been a little more than acquaintances on a TV shoot, from the broad grin on her face when she looked at him.

'Oh, you know,' he said quickly. 'Things have been busy. Really busy. I'm sure you've been really busy, too.'

'Yes, that much is true! But now I'm back, perhaps we could squeeze in a little drink before I have to bugger off again. What do you say?'

'Yeah, sure,' Nick agreed, although Thea sensed he wasn't completely committed to the idea. She wondered what the story was there. Tally was all over him, but it could just be showbiz blarney. Perhaps she was just as effusive with all of the people she worked with.

'So, I'm staying at the Star and Telescope again tonight,' Tally continued. 'They've given me the same room as last time.' She raised an eyebrow at Nick. 'You know the one...'

Thea tried to look as though she was counting the number of Wookey Hole leaflets on the counter as Tally continued to talk. As Nick responded to Tally's endless chatter, she felt intrigued by what she was seeing. Nick hadn't mentioned an involvement with any members of the crew, but then he might not have wanted to divulge it to her, she supposed. She was surprised to feel a little bit put out, though, that he hadn't.

Eventually, irritated by Tally's prattling, she called out to Nick. 'Is it all right if I take my lunch break?'

'Sure,' he replied. 'I'll cover the till while you do.'

'OK then.' Thea headed to the back office before he could say anything else. She was oscillating between amusement and irritation about what she'd just witnessed between Nick and Tally. The amusement she could make sense of, but the irritation felt odd. She didn't have any right to feel it... Oh well, she thought as she unwrapped her somewhat soggy cheese and pickle sandwich from its reusable beeswax wrapper.

9

'So, we'll do some cover shots of the exterior today when Jez and the boys get here, and then some interior shots when things get a little busier.' Tally glanced around at the quiet store and shook her head. 'And if we could get things looking even more Christmassy in here, that would be great.'

Short of hanging huge Santas from every corner, Nick wasn't sure what else they could do to improve the décor, but he didn't say anything. He knew from the last time Tally had descended that she threw out ideas like birdseed. Once the rest of the crew arrived, she'd be kept in check.

'Well, let me know when you need me,' Nick said, as Tally paused for breath.

'Oh, I will.' Tally's eyes twinkled mischievously. 'It's so sad your mum and dad won't be available this time around, but it means you get to take centre stage.'

'Hmmm.' Nick remained to be convinced about the merits of this particular plan, but he figured he could put up with the intrusion for a couple of days. Realising that Tally was waiting for a better response, he hurriedly filled her in on the amendments to the staffing. 'Thea, who's just gone on a break, is an old friend of mine who's agreed to step in and help out, but she'd rather not be on camera if she can help it, so it would be great if you could bear that in mind.'

'Sure, sure,' Tally replied. 'Believe me, darling, my focus will be entirely on you.' She looked soulfully into his eyes and Nick knew that she was thinking back to the last time she and the crew had been here. They'd shared a couple of very exciting nights together, but both of them had known it probably wouldn't go any further. He wasn't the kind to just hook up with someone, but the weather had been hot, and the cider had been cool, and things had just happened. Fun as it had definitely been, though, in the rather cooler light of a winter's day, he wasn't sure he wanted it to happen again.

'Look, Tally,' he began, 'last time you were here was great, but, er, I'm not sure I'm in the market for anything like that, this time around.'

Tally grinned. 'Darling, never rule anything out. These filming days can be long, but they can also be euphoric, as I'm sure you remember. Let's just see how it goes, shall we?' She paused. 'Unless, of course, you're spoken for? In which case, I shall definitely keep my hands off!'

Nick dithered. This might well be his 'out' from Tally, who, while she was incredibly attractive, he didn't want a repeat of last year's one-night stand. It was fun for sure, but he just wasn't looking for a repeat performance. But then, he wasn't very good at lying, and he felt that Tally deserved better than that.

'Not spoken for,' he said carefully, 'but very, very busy. Mum and Dad are both poorly at the moment, and I'm rushed off my feet here. But thank you, Tally.' He paused before adding. 'It really is great to see you.'

Tally's smile back suggested she wasn't entirely convinced by his excuses, but Nick put it to the back of his mind. He really didn't feel like rekindling anything with her, and as he began to think about why, he was caught off-guard when his mind seemed to drift towards Thea.

10

Thea polished off her sandwich and then wondered what else she could do for the remaining break time she had. As a teacher, she was so used to working through her lunchtime that she felt somewhat at a loss. Tomorrow, she'd bring in a book to pass the time. Just as she was putting her lunchbox back into her bag, she saw Nick sidling into the back office.

'Everything OK?' she asked. 'Do you need me to come back out the front?'

Nick shook his head. 'It's all right, I can cover the till until you've had a proper break.' Nick was leaning up against the doorframe and seemed in no hurry to get back to the shop. She was intrigued by the connection she'd observed between Nick and Tally when the glamorous TV producer had arrived, and thought about asking Nick what the story was there. While she'd been living away from Lower Brambleton, she'd lost track of many aspects of her friends' lives, Nick included.

'Tally seems nice,' she said, when Nick showed no sign of pushing back off to the shop. 'Did you two, er, get on well the last time she came down?'

Nick nodded. 'Yeah. She's great. She really knows her stuff, and made this place look amazing last time.'

Thea smiled. 'I know. I saw the programme. The shop looked fantastic. And you did really well, too.'

'Thanks.' Nick smiled at her. 'I get the feeling she wants me to get more involved this time, what with Dad being laid up, but I'm not sure how I feel about that.'

'Involved?' She wondered who was looking after the shop while Nick was back here chatting to her. 'In what way?'

'I'm not quite sure yet.' He straightened up and Thea noticed that he kept glancing back towards the shop counter, just checking to see if anyone had come in.

'Perhaps I should get back out there?' Thea suggested. She moved towards the door, but as she did, Nick moved towards her, and for a moment they were in each other's space. Thea noticed, with a jolt, the aroma of a spicy-scented cologne emanating from Nick, a scent she hadn't smelt before, and wondered, with a little stab of envy, whether he'd splashed on something new because Tally had arrived today. Tally was certainly a good-looking woman; maybe Nick fancied his chances with her while she was down here on the shoot?

'If you're ready,' Nick replied. He smiled down at her and she felt her mouth going a little dry. What was going on? She'd known Nick for years; why, after being around him for a couple of days, was she suddenly physically reacting differently to him?

'I think so.' She laughed a little nervously. 'I've got through the morning... how hard can it be with a camera crew watching my every move?'

Thea's heart sped up as Nick put a warm hand on her forearm. 'I promised I'd keep them away from you if you didn't want to be on camera, and I will. I don't want you to feel uncomfortable, Thea.' His blue eyes were sincere, and Thea found herself holding his gaze for a few pulses longer as she saw his pupils widen. She was counting her own breaths as they both stood there, something warm and unspoken hanging in the air between them.

'Nicky? Are you back there? Can we sit down and have a natter about the shooting order, if you've got a sec?'

Tally's voice was more effective at shattering the moment than a sledgehammer against concrete. Nick hastily removed his hand from Thea's arm and, with an apologetic smile, turned in the direction of the voice. 'Yup, no problem, Tally. Just checking on a couple of things. Be there in a minute.'

'You'd better get out there before she tracks you down!' Thea gave a slightly nervous laugh. 'I'll get back on the counter so you can have a proper chat.'

'Thanks.' Nick smiled again, before his face became more serious. 'I meant it. I'll keep the cameras away. You just focus on being brilliant behind the shop counter, like you have been all morning, and leave the rest to me.'

Something about the protective tone in Nick's voice and the way he had taken charge of the disruption of the film shoot, made Thea feel suddenly less nervous. She liked seeing him like this: decisive, in control and, dare she admit it to herself, sexy?

11

Thankfully, Tally was far too preoccupied with setting up the logistics of the TV shoot to spend much time talking to Thea or Nick over the first afternoon. In addition, by the time Friday was nearly over, Thea was also relieved that she'd only been caught on camera in background shots for the documentary, as Nick had promised, so she hadn't had to take direction from Tally or anyone else. She couldn't help noticing the way Tally still flirted outrageously with Nick at every chance she got, though. It irritated her, the way Tally kept putting her hand on his back, giggling at his tritest utterance and charming him. Thea wondered what the story was. She tried to put Tally's OTT behaviour down to natural exuberance and a very PR-focussed way of doing things – after all, Tally needed to get the best out of the people who were appearing on camera, and Nick's role was going to be larger this time around. All the same, there seemed to be a few too many casual touches, whispers in ears and flirtatious giggles for Thea to completely ignore. And every time she noticed, she wondered why she cared so much. It wasn't as if she was Nick's girlfriend: he could flirt with whom he wanted, and Tally was certainly flirting with *him*.

'Right, Nicky darling, we're going to do a few more cover shots today, so if we can follow you about to the barns and back again, that would be great, and then I'll give you the weekend to rehearse your big piece to camera, which we'll shoot on Monday, early. Then, if we can do some footage of the Festive Market on Tuesday evening, we'll be wrapped.'

It was the *Nicky darlings* that did her head in. But Nick himself didn't seem to mind. Thea kept her head down and did her job, and when the time came for her to knock off for the day, she hung up her apron gratefully. Working here wasn't taxing, but being on her feet was hard, and she was looking forward to getting home.

'Well done,' Nick said as he closed the front door and flipped the sign to closed. 'You've really helped me out over the past couple of days, and I know it's been even more tricky with the film crew being here.'

'It's been fine,' Thea replied. 'I'm trying not to be offended that the camera clearly doesn't love me, as, unlike you, I haven't been singled out!'

Nick laughed. 'Well, I did ask them to leave you alone! I can always tell them you've changed your mind?'

'Definitely not,' Thea said firmly. 'I'm more than happy just to bimble about in the background and make you look good.'

'Well, I'm grateful you've been here,' Nick said, his tone a little more gentle. 'Um... would you like to go out for a drink? As a thank you for all the help today?'

Thea's heart gave a little flutter. After their moment at lunchtime the day before, she actually really did want to spend a little more time with him, but she had a lot to do before Saturday arrived. She had family coming over to celebrate Cora's thirteenth birthday, as well as a couple of Cora's friends sleeping over, and she really wanted to make it special for her daughter. With a little twinge of regret, she declined.

'Another time, maybe?' Nick said. 'I've really enjoyed working with you over the past couple of days, and it would be nice to have a chat away from this place.'

'I'd like that.' Thea smiled up at him. They lingered together a while, before Thea looked at her watch. 'I'd best be off. I've got a house full for Cora's birthday tomorrow, and a lot of balloons to blow up tonight!'

'You never stop, do you?' Nick grinned at her. 'I don't know where you get the energy. I'm knackered just working here, and there's only myself to look after when I get home.'

'I thrive on hard work,' Thea replied, 'but yeah, it does get pretty exhausting.' She stifled a yawn. 'I've really enjoyed working here, though – are you sure you don't need any more help when Annabelle's back?'

Nick looked thoughtful. 'Well, she does keep saying we should take someone else on to ease the pressure a bit. Would you be up for something a bit more long term?'

'I'd definitely think about it!' Thea purposely injected a light tone into her voice, but Nick looked concerned.

'Are things a bit tight?'

'Well, the wolf isn't quite at the door, but he's getting peckish!' Thea's quip didn't sound convincing, even to her own ears.

Nick ran a hand through his hair. 'If a few more hours after Christmas would help, then I'll definitely see what I can do.'

'Thank you.' Thea was touched and suddenly felt the urge to cry. 'But only if there's a need – I don't want to be taken on as a charity case!'

'As I said, you've done a great job, and with the film crew here it's been a bit trickier.' Nick glanced at the clock behind the counter. 'I'd better let you go. See you next Thursday, if not before?'

Thea nodded, and then they said goodbye. As she was driving home, she couldn't help wondering, not for the first time, why Nick still only had himself to look after. He was gorgeous, and he didn't even have to try very hard. No wonder Tally had set her sights on him while she was here.

12

Saturday came, and Thea rolled over in bed and thanked the gods she wasn't going to be on her feet today. Two full shifts at the shop had been fun, but they'd taken their toll on her back and her feet. She was used to moving around a lot in the classroom, but shop work had put a different kind of pressure on her body, and she was feeling it. This weekend was going to have its own energy, though: it was Cora's thirteenth birthday, and her daughter was having a couple of friends to sleep over. Thankfully, Thea had bought some pizzas in last month when she'd done a big supermarket shop, and the mobile phone Cora had received at the start of the school year had been a joint birthday and Christmas present, so there wasn't any additional spending to worry about. Thea felt she could relax and enjoy her daughter's birthday without the fear of losing control of her finances.

Lorelai was coming over that morning with a home baked birthday cake, and Tristan and Charlotte were also popping round with a present and to celebrate before Cora's friends arrived later that afternoon. Thea was glad that they would all make it: she never stopped feeling relieved that her family was all nearby. Over the years, especially when the children had been younger, it had been a blessing to have her grandmother and her brother on hand for support, and as Cora and Dylan had grown, they'd felt all of the wonderful emotions that came with having a close-knit family. It wasn't quite the same as having her parents, still, but it was a near substitute for which she was grateful.

Swinging her feet out of the bed and wincing as they made contact with the bedroom floor, she realised she'd have to toughen up if she was going to cope with even a couple of weeks' worth of shop work. *You're not seventeen any more,* she thought ruefully as she made her way to the shower. Back in the day, when she'd had a weekend job working in the local convenience store, she'd do a shift and then go out on the town straight afterwards. Those days were long behind her, or at least that's what her aching feet were telling her.

* * *

A little while later, Cora was sitting impatiently in the living room, waiting for the rest of the family to arrive. Thea, whose newly washed hair hung blow-dried straight down her back, almost to her waist, hugged her daughter warmly.

'I'm so proud of you, Cora-Dora,' she said. 'Happy birthday, my darling.'

Cora shoved her mother away playfully. 'Eww! Get off, and stop being so lame, Mum.' But there was returned affection in her eyes.

The sound of the doorbell distracted them both, and there were footsteps overhead as Dylan rushed from his bedroom.

'Must be Uncle Tristan and Charlotte,' Cora commented. 'I think Uncle Tristan promised Dylan he'd kick a few balls around while he was here.'

'Bit cold for that, today,' Thea replied. 'And I'm not sure the lawn'll take it.'

'Your fault for having me in the winter,' Cora observed. 'Should have thought about that.'

Thea grinned at her ever-cheekier and more grown-up daughter. 'I'll remind you of that when you're pregnant one day!'

'Gross!' Cora wrinkled her nose. 'That's never gonna happen.'

Secretly, Thea quite liked the fact that any mention of boys, or babies, was enough to provoke that kind of reaction in her daughter. She wasn't looking forward to the days, which would inevitably be approaching, of boyfriends and conversations about keeping safe.

Both mother and daughter turned as Dylan's footsteps thundered down the stairs and the front door was rapidly flung open. It only took a few seconds for Tristan and Charlotte to appear, bearing a posh looking gift bag and a birthday card for Cora and followed by Charlotte's bouncy spaniel, Comet.

'Happy birthday, squirt!' Tristan grinned at his niece and handed over the bag. 'Hope you like your present.'

'Thanks, Uncle Tris,' Cora replied, flumping down on the sofa to open it.

'Don't thank me, thank Charlotte. She chose it.'

'I'll take the win!' Charlotte replied, before adding to Thea in an undertone, 'My mate, Gemma, helped me to choose something. I was a bit of a nerd as a teenager, I'm afraid, so I wasn't quite sure what to get her.'

Thea smiled back at Charlotte. 'I'm sure whatever you've chosen is great.'

She didn't have to reassure Charlotte further, as Cora's squeals of excitement did the job for her. 'New Generation Air Pods? Thanks, Uncle Tristan, thanks, Charlotte!'

Thea felt uneasy about the extravagance of the gift, before

Tristan, obviously clocking her mood, murmured, 'I know it's a bit OTT, but let Charlotte have this – it's not every day your niece becomes a teenager.'

Thea smiled at her brother, who always had the knack of knowing what to say to make her feel better. The gift was a lot of money, but Cora was obviously thrilled, so she decided to let it go.

'It's very generous of you,' she replied. 'Thank you.'

Cora had already opened the box and was busily trying to sync the earbuds with her phone. 'Ella's going to be well jell when she sees these,' she said. 'I can't wait to wear them on the bus.'

'I don't think you should take them to school, Cora,' Thea cautioned. 'You don't want them nicked or confiscated.'

Cora rolled her eyes. 'I'll look after them, Mum, I promise.'

Thea opened her mouth to respond, but a gentle nudge from Tristan stopped her. There'd be plenty of time to hash that one out later. For now, she'd just let Cora enjoy her present. Comet, who was sniffing around the room, gave a high-pitched bark as he caught sight of Lupin, the tortoiseshell cat, but the cat was speedier and she gave a hiss before retreating back upstairs.

'Still ruling the roost, I see?' Tristan grinned. 'At least this time poor Comet hasn't felt the sharp edge of her claws!'

'She always needs him to know who's in charge.' Thea grinned.

'Yoo-hoo! Anyone home?' Lorelai's voice drifted through from the front door, which Dylan, who left all doors ajar in his chaotic wake, hadn't closed.

'Hi Gran,' Thea called. 'We're in the living room.'

Lorelai appeared seconds later and handed over Cora's present to her excited great-granddaughter. This time, it was an envelope, and as Cora opened it up, she squealed in excitement.

'Ooh! Thanks, Gran! Mum, we're *so* going on a shopping trip in the Christmas holidays. Can we go to Cribbs Causeway? Or Cabot? Pleeeeeeeease?'

Thea smiled. 'I should think so.' She didn't stop to allow herself to worry about what else a trip to one of Bristol's premier shopping centres might cost her. For today, Cora and her birthday were all that mattered.

'Tristan, dear, could you just get the birthday girl's cake out of my car for me?' Lorelai smiled at her grandson. 'It's on the front passenger seat.'

'Sure.' Tristan strode out of the living room.

'I hope she likes the cake,' Lorelai whispered to Thea. 'I was up icing it until gone midnight!'

'Gran, you shouldn't have gone to so much trouble.'

'It was no trouble, darling. Honestly. Keeps my mind active, and goodness knows it needs to be.' Lorelai gave Thea a warm smile. 'You know I'd do anything for you and the children, don't you.'

'I know.' Thea gave her grandmother a hug. 'But don't go overdoing it – we want you around for a few more years yet!'

'I'm not going anywhere!' Thea watched as her grandmother's gaze shifted to Cora and Dylan, who were, for once, sitting side by side in relative harmony on the sofa.

'Has their so-called father been in contact?'

Thea shook her head. 'Nope. But that's for the best. He'd only upset them if he did.'

'Still, not even a card? I don't know how he can just forget about them like that.'

'I prefer it that way,' Thea said, surprised at Lorelai's line of thought. 'Don't you, after all he put us through?'

'Well, yes, but after all this time, he might at least have sent his daughter a birthday card.'

'And where would he send it? It's not as if I gave him our address when we moved into this house. Some things are better left in the past, Gran.'

'You're right,' Lorelai conceded. 'I suppose I just can't help feeling maudlin on days like this. We suffered so much loss as a family, and Ed just threw the life he had with you and the children away. I don't understand it.'

Thea, who'd been through the reasons for the split with Ed a thousand times with Lorelai, didn't immediately reply. She knew that Lorelai struggled to comprehend how someone could walk out on their children for the reasons that Ed did, but now wasn't the time or the place to try, yet again, to help her to get her head around it. 'Well, sometimes things just don't work out, Gran, no matter how much you might want them to.'

Before Lorelai could reply, Tristan had returned from Lorelai's car with a cake box. And behind him, looking extremely nervous to be intruding on such a family occasion, was Nick.

13

'Sorry to just drop in,' Nick said. 'I was passing with a delivery and I suddenly remembered I needed to ask you something, if you've got a sec?'

'No worries,' Thea said, slightly too warmly for it to sound casual. She'd been caught off guard at the sight of Nick's handsome face, and she tried to regain her equilibrium. 'How can I help?' Blushing at the ridiculousness of the question, remembering she was, in fact, in her own home and not behind the counter at the farm shop, she added hastily, 'I mean, it's good to see you. What brings you by on a Saturday afternoon?'

Nick had moved into the living room now, and closer to Thea's side, as Tristan had, with an inquisitive glance at Thea, settled onto the sofa to help Cora with her continued attempts to get the Air Pods working with her phone.

Thea glanced at Tristan, and then at Lorelai and Charlotte. She hadn't yet told any of them that she was working at Saints' Farm Shop. She didn't want to alert them to her worries about money and was hoping to keep it a secret while the second job lasted, at least until after Christmas. Her family would only try to 'help', and while their intentions were good, Thea had been used to solving her own problems for too long to accept their good intentions, or their loans. Her pride had a lot to do with it, too. After the humiliation she'd felt when Ed had left, she wanted to be able to stand on her own two feet.

'Come into the kitchen,' she said hurriedly, moving in that direction before he had the chance to say more. 'And we'll have a chat.'

'I honestly didn't mean to intrude,' Nick said as she led him into the kitchen and closed the door behind them. 'I can come back when you're less busy.'

'It's fine.' Thea gave him a quick smile. 'It's just that, er, my family don't know I've picked up some extra work. If it's all the same to you, I'd rather they didn't find out just now.'

'Of course.' Nick's expression registered confusion, but he didn't ask why she might be keeping things quiet. 'Your secret's safe with me.'

'Thanks.' Thea relaxed fractionally. She looked at him directly for the first time since he'd arrived. The dark blue Saints Farm polo shirt really did suit him, setting off the beech-leaves-in-autumn coloured hair to perfection. And the way he'd shoved his hands in his pockets, possibly out of nerves, was endearing. 'So, er, what was it you wanted to ask me?'

'Well, this is a bit last minute,' he said, 'and I suppose I could have just sent you a WhatsApp, but I was wondering if you'd be free next Tuesday evening?'

Thea's heart, only just calming down from Nick's unexpected arrival, started to hammer again. She remembered how she'd kicked herself for turning him down when he'd asked her out for a drink last night.

'Um, yes, I think so. What did you have in mind?'

Nick pulled a hand out of his pocket and ran it through his

hair. 'I meant to ask you this a lot earlier,' he continued, 'but we've been so busy that I just didn't get the chance. If you can't make it, that's fine, but I thought, while I was passing I'd just pop in and ask—'

Thea couldn't help smiling. 'Nick,' she said gently. 'Why don't you just spit it out?'

'Oh, yeah, sure,' he replied. 'I, um, guess, you've got a party to get back to, as well.' His face coloured slightly. 'I really am sorry to just barge in.' He looked her in the eye, and Thea held her breath.

'The thing is, the Christmas late night shopping evening is coming up next Tuesday,' he said in a rush. 'And there are stall-holders coming for the night, who set up in the car park. I was wondering if you'd be able to do an extra shift in the shop, since we're bound to be busy with more trade.'

Thea breathed out again, and she'd be lying if she said she didn't feel a deflating sense of disappointment. Then, frustrated with herself for jumping to conclusions, she gave Nick a brighter-than-bright smile. 'How long does the evening go on for? I remember popping in early doors with the kids a couple of years back, but we didn't stay too long.'

'Should be all done and dusted by nine o'clock,' Nick replied, thankfully seemingly oblivious to Thea's disappointment. 'I mean, even if you could cover the till for an hour or two, you'd really be doing us a favour. The film crew are going to be mainly focussed on the stalls outside, so there shouldn't be any extra pressure.'

'Of course,' Thea said. 'Look, let me work a couple of things out – I'm at school all day, so I won't be able to get to you until early evening, but I'll let you know.'

'Thanks, Thea.' Nick's smile of relief and gratitude made Thea's heart speed up again. *Stop it,* she told herself firmly. He'd always had a lovely smile, and what was lovelier was that he seemed completely oblivious to the effect it had on her. 'I'm sorry, as I said, to just drop this on you, but I forgot to check the staffing for the extended hours. Annabelle's the one who handles most of the admin, and I'm not used to being in charge of that, too!'

'It's fine.' Thea smiled. They stood together in a slightly loaded silence until she added, 'Would you, er, like to stay for a cuppa and a piece of birthday cake? Gran's baked one big enough for all of Lower Brambleton to have a slice!'

Nick kept smiling but shook his head. 'Thanks, but I've left Roseanna, who works Saturdays, in charge while I get the deliveries done. Mum's sitting in the back office in case of an emergency, but she'll need to get back to Dad, who's still laid up with his back, as soon as she can, so I really ought to head back to the shop.'

'No worries.' Thea opened the kitchen door again and walked him past the living room to the front of the house. 'I'll hopefully see you on Tuesday evening, if not before.'

'See you then.' Nick looked back at her as she stood in the doorway. 'And thank you, Thea. It means a lot to know I can depend on you.'

'You're welcome.' This time, Thea could feel her own face growing pink. She tried to put it down to the contrast between the warmth of the house and the sudden chill from outside, but something inside her was suggesting otherwise. It might have been the fact that they'd been working together, but she felt a definite stirring of attraction for Nick, as she watched him head briskly towards the Saint Farm van. *Careful*, she thought. *He's been a good friend, over the years; do you really want to jeopardise that?* She shook her head. Loneliness had a lot to answer for, and she didn't want to push something with Nick just because it felt convenient. All the same, something did feel different. He'd known about Cora's party, and he could have just WhatsApped her to ask her about the Christmas market. He didn't need to come and ask her face to face. Pondering that as she closed the front door and headed back into the party, she allowed herself a moment or two to think about him. It couldn't do any harm to imagine, could it?

14

As soon as Thea walked back into the living room, all eyes were upon her. Tristan, who never could resist needling his twin sister, raised an eyebrow.

'Secret meetings in the kitchen, sis? Have you finally let Nick Saint out of the friend zone?'

'Eww!' Cora squealed, glancing up from the Spotify playlist she was compiling to try out her birthday present. 'That's gross, Uncle Tristan!'

'No,' Thea shot back, feeling more defensive than she should have. She thought fast, realising that her family were intrigued by the way she'd hustled Nick out of the room, and she needed to give them at least a brief explanation, or they'd be on her case for the rest of the afternoon. 'He's, er, asked me if I'd help out at the shop for the late-night shopping event next Tuesday. He was moaning about being short-handed when I, er, popped in there last week and he's obviously hit the panic button and is pulling in all hands to help.'

'Why you, though?' Tristan asked. 'I mean, isn't it a bit odd just to grab random customers to help out at a moment's notice?'

Thea's mind went into overdrive. She didn't want to 'fess up to the extra job right now, not in front of the children, and the inevitable conversations this would raise. 'I, er, happened to mention I'd done some shop work years ago, and I guess he remembered. He's desperate for an extra pair of hands, with Annabelle and Jamie being out of the country and his folks being off their feet, so I said I'd help out for the evening.'

'He's desperate for *something*, all right!' Tristan grinned. 'Any excuse to spend a bit of time with you, I reckon.'

Thea rolled her eyes. On the whole, she'd been delighted when Tristan had fallen in love with Charlotte. He'd always been a little too serious for his own good, keeping his thoughts and emotions strictly in check, even with her, for most of their lives. Charlotte had brought a little levity and fun into his life and altered his outlook on things. The inevitable result of this was that he tended to joke around a whole lot more than he used to, and while this was mostly lovely to see, it did mean she was often the target of his good-natured teasing. It was as if, now he'd finally found someone, he wanted Thea to hurry up and do the same.

'Shall we light the candles?' Thea asked, making a very obvious subject change. She hurried back to the kitchen and grabbed the matches and focussed her attention on the cake. After the obligatory round of 'Happy birthday' singing, and the wish making, and then handing round the carefully cut slices of Lorelai's exceptionally moist and rich chocolate sponge, Thea felt that the attention was away from herself and back onto Cora, where it should be.

'So, what are you going to put on your shopping list to spend your birthday money on?' she asked as she tucked into a generous slice of cake.

'Dunno yet,' Cora replied through a mouthful of her own

cake. 'Genevieve's got this lush Carolina Herrera perfume – the bottle's in the shape of a shoe – I might get some of that, if we're gonna go up to Cribbs Causeway.'

Thea suppressed a sigh. This current generation of teens was so much more brand aware than she'd ever been. The advent of social media and the internet meant that they were bombarded with products every hour of the day, on every platform they visited, and it made the job of a parent both daunting and potentially very expensive. But at least Lorelai's gift of cash would help to soak up some of that expense.

'And maybe Genevieve could come with us? And we could go for lunch?' Cora's hopeful expression made Thea's heart lurch.

'Let's think about it during the holidays,' she said. It was her standard response when she wanted more time to work things out. Thankfully, term ended on 20 December this year, so she'd have finished her fill-in shifts at the farm shop before the school holidays started. She hoped she could bluff her way through the next couple of weeks without Cora or Dylan discovering her extra job. She'd managed to persuade them she'd been at appointments and running errands for the first couple of days this week, to explain her absence from home when they'd finished school, but she wasn't sure she'd be able to keep it up for the next couple of weeks. It wasn't that she was ashamed, as such, but she hated the thought of them being worried about money, especially so close to Christmas. If Nick offered her a more permanent gig for the new year, then she'd own up to it.

Lorelai might be a different matter, however. She imagined herself diving behind the counter if her grandmother popped into the shop and realised that just wasn't going to work. She resolved to let Lorelai know about it when the time was right. Tristan and Charlotte could be kept in the dark, though – she didn't want to provide more ammunition for her brother, who'd only tease her about working with Nick.

The party went on for another hour or so, before Tristan and Charlotte said their goodbyes. They were Bristol bound tonight and meeting with some of Charlotte's work colleagues for a Christmas meal. Term had ended the day before, so it was a good chance to get together before the Christmas season got into full swing. As they left, Charlotte grabbed Thea for a quiet word in the hall. 'Don't let Tristan rile you up about Nick,' she said. 'He's always suspected that Nick carries a torch for you, and you know what he's like when he thinks something, it takes an army to persuade him otherwise!'

'I know.' Thea smiled ruefully. 'But he's wrong. Nick and I are just friends, and that's all we've ever been. I'm not ready for anything else, and even if I was, I don't think Nick wants the kind of baggage I'm carrying.'

Charlotte crooked an eyebrow. 'Baggage?'

'I come with a couple of non-optional extras!' Thea smiled in the direction of Cora and Dylan, who were both now immersed in a game of *Mario Kart* on the Nintendo Switch.

'But he's great with the kids,' Charlotte said. 'I mean, whenever he's been part of the group, he seems to get on really well with them.'

'Saving a few penalties is one thing,' Thea replied. 'But taking them on full time is a lot more responsibility. I don't think he'd have a clue!'

'You never know until you try,' Charlotte said, then held up a hand in apology. 'I'm sorry, I'm getting as bad as your brother. Ignore me. It must be the time of year. I've been watching a lot of Hallmark and FilmFlix Christmas movies since December started, and they've obviously gone to my head.'

'I never had you down as the cheesy Christmas romcom type,'

Thea said in surprise. 'I thought you were far too clever for all of that rubbish!'

'Oh, I'm rather partial to a seasonal love story,' Charlotte laughed. 'And don't knock it until you've tried it. There was one that came out a few years ago with Finn Sanderson and Montana de Santo that I can't help watching on repeat – God, what was it called? Oh, that's right, *A Countess For Christmas*. Cheers me up every time. Makes me believe that, with a bit of mistletoe, anything's possible.'

'Well, that's as may be, but I'll stick to watching Christmas romcoms rather than trying to star in them!' Thea laughed. She said goodbye to Charlotte and Tristan and then set to tidying up the plates and the remainder of the cake. Perhaps she'd take a slice in for Nick when she had her next shift at the shop.

'Well, that went well,' Lorelai remarked as she brought through the rest of the crockery and helped Thea to put it in the dishwasher. 'I can't believe Cora's officially a teenager! Doesn't seem like yesterday that you brought her home from the hospital.'

'I know.' Thea smiled. 'I remember you saying that the toddler days, and then the primary school ones, would pass in the blink of an eye, and you were right.' She flipped the switch on the kettle to make her and her grandmother a last cuppa. Now was the time to let Lorelai know about the job, she figured, while the kids were still racing each other on the Switch and they were alone.

'Nick's a nice boy, isn't he?' Lorelai said, just as Thea was drawing breath. 'I wonder why some girl hasn't snapped him up by now.'

'He's hardly a boy any more!' Thea laughed. 'He's as old as I am.'

'He seems to like you,' Lorelai continued.

'As a friend,' Thea said firmly. 'We've always been friends, Gran. As a matter of fact, I'm doing him a favour in the shop. That's why he popped round.'

'Oh, yes?' Lorelai said. Thea rather got the impression that she was working hard to keep that neutral tone in her voice. 'What's that, then?'

'I'm, er, filling in on my days off while Annabelle and Jamie are away,' she said. 'Just until Christmas.'

'That's good of you,' Lorelai replied. 'Well, if you need me to keep an eye on the children while you're helping out, let me know. I don't have anything major planned in the run up to the holiday, so feel free to ask.'

'Thanks, Gran.' Thea leaned forward and kissed her grandmother on the cheek. 'I appreciate all that you do for us.' She was relieved that Lorelai didn't give her the third degree about her finances.

'I know you do,' Lorelai replied. 'But if you find yourself under a sprig of mistletoe with our Mr Saint this year...'

'Gran...' Thea warned, but she was smiling. She couldn't help but be amused by what she imagined Nick's reaction might be if he was ever caught under the mistletoe with her. He'd been nervous enough, asking her to work the late-night shopping evening!

15

Monday morning arrived with two pieces of unwelcome news for Nick. His father's back was still bad, so Robert was reluctantly confined to barracks, and the agency worker Nick had been expecting to cover the first three days of the week had cried off, ostensibly with the flu, but Nick suspected a better offer had come their way. Working in a farm shop in the sticks didn't have the same appeal as working closer to home, and the trek from Taunton may have proved too much for them, he thought in resigned irritation.

That left him with a gap in the staffing and a bigger problem: the film crew would be spending most of today trying to shoot cover shots and also a short interview with him, but if he had to look after the counter as well as take in the deliveries and do his media-personality bit, he was going to be spread as thin as his Aunt Gladys's servings of roast beef. The easiest thing to do would be to pull out of the filming, but the publicity was too good to refuse, and they needed all the help they could get.

'Shit...' he muttered as the net of carrots he was carrying from the trailer of goods he'd just brought from the barn split.

Hurriedly picking them up, he jumped a mile when a voice behind him rang out.

Nick straightened up and mustered his best friendly smile before he turned around. 'Hi Tally. You're early.'

Tally gave him a grin. 'I'm always prompt when I'm on a job. And I wanted to get a recce before the rest of the crew arrived. We've got a lot to cover today if we're going to catch the light.'

'Well, just let me know what you need from me and I'll do my best,' Nick replied. He considered letting her know about the staffing issue, but didn't want to risk her pulling out of the shoot. No matter how tricky it was going to be, it really would aid their visibility as a business.

'Oh, Nicky, darling, I'd be delighted to tell you what I need,' Tally murmured suggestively. She gave him a mischievous grin. 'Do you fancy a proper drink and a catch up once we've wrapped for the day?' Her denim-blue eyes met his, and he got the definite impression that a drink might just be for starters. 'We had such a great time last time I was here...'

'It was nice, Tally, but—'

'How do you feel about a repeat performance?' Tally interrupted softly. 'I meant to call you when I got back to London, but, well...' She shrugged. 'You know how it is.'

Actually, he didn't, but that didn't matter. Tally was fun, and gorgeous, and perhaps a bit of fun was what he needed right now. He'd been at a loose end in his personal life since his last relationship had ended, about a year ago. Tally had been his 'get over your ex by getting under someone new' moment, and she'd certainly managed that. If she was free, and so was he, then where was the harm? He hadn't been keen, initially, when she'd hinted at it earlier in the week, but what was stopping him, really? Yes, work was busy and his folks weren't at their best, but it wasn't as though he didn't have *any* spare time...

All of a sudden, and to Nick's surprise, Thea's face flashed into his mind. They'd definitely shared something in the doorway on Thursday, and he'd enjoyed his brief time with her when he'd popped into her place on Saturday to ask her about the festive night. It was daft, but he felt as though they'd got closer in the time they'd been working together than they'd been in years. He shook his head. He'd always liked Thea, a lot, but perhaps he was overthinking things. Just because they'd been spending time together at Saints' Farm didn't mean they were attracted to each other, although, he had to admit, he had always had more than a soft spot for her.

'For now, I'll show you some coffee,' he teased gently back, trying to shake off the indecision that he felt.

'Fair enough. I could do with the caffeine hit.'

They walked through the shop, and Nick found himself automatically checking the shelves for untidy stock. The place needed to look its best today. Over coffee, they discussed the running order, and, given the staff shortages, Tally agreed to shift Nick's piece to camera to the top of the list, before the shop officially opened at 9 a.m. There was a beautiful, rolling mist still drifting over the fields behind the farm shop, which was just starting to burn off from the winter sun, and Tally said it would make a great backdrop, if her camera and sound technicians could get here in time to catch it. After she'd made a couple of calls, Nick found himself standing behind the shop, in front of the fields of fast dissipating fog, trying desperately to wax lyrical about why this time of year was so special for Saints' Farm.

'This is my home,' he said softly, as he turned to look out across the wide expanse of field behind him. 'And over the years, things have changed. We're not the farmers we were, four generations ago, we've had to adapt with the times and innovate to stay at the top of our game.' A slight breeze rolled the mist behind him and lifted his hair, and he swept the front of it out of his eyes before he continued. 'But Saints' Farm is, and always will be, home for me, and I wouldn't ever be anywhere else. I love it here, and it's in my blood. At Christmas, it's even more special.'

There was a pause as Tally gestured for him to hold the last pose, before she briskly called, 'Cut!'

Nick breathed out. He'd managed to get through it without stammering, and he felt a swell of pride.

'That's great,' Tally said. 'You can relax now, darling.' Nick watched her as she had a quick look through at the playback and then double checked that the sound and camera operators knew what the rest of the running order was going to be. Then, she turned her attention back to Nick. Her eyes twinkled at him. 'You really should consider a career in front of the camera – you've got presence, Nick.'

'Yeah, right,' Nick laughed, relieved that the cameras had stopped rolling. 'You'll say anything to flatter the talent!'

'I'm serious!' Tally punched him playfully on the arm. 'Look, the production company's got something in the pipeline that I think you'd be perfect for. Would you at least think about it?'

Nick shook his head. 'This is fun for a few hours, but I don't think I've got it in me to be a TV star.' He gazed out over the ruddy red brown ploughed fields, fields he knew as well as the back of his hand, and then back at Tally. 'I've got responsibilities to this place.'

'I get that,' Tally replied, 'but you could be the next Matt Baker if you wanted to – all it takes is a little coaching.' She looked into his eyes. 'I'd be happy to advise you.'

'I appreciate that, Tally, but the answer's still no.'

'Oh well.' She gave a theatrical sigh. 'Can't say I didn't try. And you know where I am if you ever change your mind.'

'I'm sure my dad would be up for a role in a TV show, if you've got space for a grumpy old Somerset farmer!' Nick said, to break the tension. 'Shall I give him a call?'

Tally laughed then. 'Sorry, darling, but Clarkson's cornered the market on grumpy old farmers for now. I'm not sure there's room on television for two of them.'

'Dad'll be chuffed to be compared to Jeremy Clarkson.' Nick grinned. 'He reckons he's done more for the countryside than anyone else over the years, with that show.'

'Farming is a very hot topic right now, Nick, and with a charismatic lead at the helm... the possibilities are endless.'

Nick knew that Tally still had a mind to convince him to think about the TV show, but he knew himself well enough to know it wouldn't be his style. Saints Farm was his home, and he wanted to preserve its legacy. Gallivanting around in front of the camera was not on his list of life goals, despite the fun he'd had being a part of the farm shop show.

'Well,' he said, making a move back towards the shop, 'I'd better get everything open. I'm on my own today, so it's going to be busy.'

'Can't get the staff?' Tally teased. 'I did some shop work when I was at university to pay the bills – shout if you need a hand.'

'Thanks, but I'm sure I'll manage,' Nick replied. He liked Tally, but he didn't want to give her any more encouragement.

'Thank goodness we did most of the heavy lifting last week!' Tally said as she strode off to rejoin the crew. 'Oh, but if you do change your mind, I could always pitch you to the production company.'

Nick shook his head, although for a split second he did allow himself the brief fantasy of what it would be like to host a TV show. *Hello, and welcome to Countryside Today, your one stop shop for all things rural!*

Nope. He wasn't the next Matt Baker, no matter how much Tally tried to persuade him otherwise.

'Well, I'd better get back to it,' Nick said.

'We'll touch base with you later, once we've done some cover shots of the exterior,' Tally said. 'And then you can guide us in the direction of anything in particular you'd like us to focus on inside the shop.'

'All right then,' Nick said as he headed off in the direction of the farm shop. Tally didn't press him about meeting up with her later, so he wondered if she'd gone off the idea. To his relief, he wasn't that bothered.

16

As Thea packed away the debris of another educational but exhausting afternoon with her class of eager Year Four students, she braced herself for an equally long evening. When Nick had asked her to help out at the festive evening, it had seemed like a perfectly reasonable idea. Now, having masterminded her class's participation in the upcoming nativity play, she felt more than a little worn out and even less prepared for an evening on her feet.

'I think they're coming along really well,' her friend and colleague, Jan, who ran the breakfast and after-school clubs as well as providing in-class support at busy times of year, commented as she stuck her head around the classroom door.

'They're definitely better than they were last week! I have to admit though, it will be a relief when the performances are over, and we can just relax until the end of term!'

'You've done a great job,' Jan said. 'And that Christmas break will be very well earned, when we get to it.'

Thea smiled. This time of year was always hectic but there was great satisfaction and fun to be had in seeing the children performing on stage and the armies of proud parents who all came to support them. Teaching was never going to be an easy profession, but the rewards kept her in the job.

'Are you going to late-night shopping tonight?' Jan asked as she helped Thea to hang up some of the costumes that had been shoved on coat hangers willy-nilly by the children as they'd hurried out of the door that afternoon.

'Wouldn't miss it.' She still hadn't told anyone at school about her job and figured that if anyone spotted her later, she could just fudge it and say that Nick had asked her to help out since the shop was short-handed with both Annabelle and Jamie being away. If she headed home now, she'd be able to grab a bite to eat before shooting back out to Saints' Farm for the six o'clock start.

'See you later, then.' Jan gave her a last smile and walked towards the school hall, where she wrangled and shepherded the members of after-school club until their parents came to collect them at 6 p.m. Jan was a firm favourite of both children and parents alike, and Thea had got to know her well over the years. She'd used the club regularly when she'd been working in another school, but less in recent years when she'd got the job here. It was rare to find someone with the patience and the staying power to entertain a wide range of ages, but Jan did it with aplomb, and the kids loved her.

A short time later, as she pulled her car onto the driveway, she tried to fight off the inevitable exhaustion that a day in the classroom always created. She couldn't remember the last time she didn't feel tired, whether that was from the demands of being a teacher or a parent, she could never really tell. *You need some fun,* she told herself wearily. But fun, even at Christmas, seemed in short supply when money was tight.

Shrugging off the increasingly gloomy thoughts, she called a quick hello to both children, before falling back on her trusty and economical Bolognese sauce that she'd had the foresight to pull out of the freezer before she'd left that morning. She wondered, as she bolted down her own portion, if the amount of garlic she'd put in it would be off putting if she got too close to the customers tonight. As soon as she'd finished, she nipped upstairs and made free with the Colgate and the mouthwash.

'Right, you two, I'm off to help Nick out at the late-night shopping,' she said. 'Gran's on standby, but I should be back by nine o'clock.'

'All right,' Cora replied. 'Have fun.'

Dylan, immersed in the antics of Mr Beast on YouTube, waved a hand in dismissal.

'Love you, Dyl!' Thea grabbed hold of her young son and managed to plant a kiss on his forehead before he squirmed away from her, grumbling that she'd made him miss the best bit of the live stream.

One thing she could be thankful for was her children, Thea thought as she reversed briskly off the driveway. They were growing up so well, despite the early upheavals they'd faced, and she felt relieved as well as thankful. As a parent, one day at a time had often been her mantra, and she'd learned to cherish the calm moments.

As she approached Saints' Farm, she could see that a lot of stallholders were already getting ready to showcase their wares. Tables were springing up like flat-topped mushrooms all over the car park, and strings of fairy lights were adorning them, casting the space in a festive light. She parked her car at the side of the shop, well out of the way of the event itself, and then hurried in to find Nick and discover what he needed her to do.

'Oh, come on, Nicky.' A sweet, playful voice drifted from the direction of the shop's counter as Thea walked through the front door. 'The viewers'll love it, and you'll look adorable in it.'

'Not on your life!' Thea heard Nick replying. The tone of his voice oscillated between flirtatious and a cry for help. 'It's bad enough that my actual name is Nick Saint, I'm not going to dress like my namesake!'

'Do it for me?' the voice purred, and Thea felt a surprising stab of jealousy. As she moved through the store, she caught sight of Tally standing at the side of the counter. She was carrying an expensive looking Santa suit and wearing an expression that was halfway between flirtation and frustration.

'No, Tally.' Nick's voice, firmer this time, sounded resolute. 'I've danced to the tune of the production company for this shoot long enough. I draw the line at dressing up like Father bloody Christmas! I'm sorry Dad's not well enough to do it like he did last year, but it's one job I'm not prepared to take on.'

Well said, Thea thought. She gave Nick an imaginary fist bump of satisfaction for not letting Tally have her own way. Nick had set his boundaries, and that of the shop, very firmly throughout the shoot so far, and Thea was glad to see him sticking to them. There was something very compelling to her about seeing him in action on his home turf, and Thea was beginning to realise, the more she worked with him, just what a depth of knowledge and expertise he had. Including, it now appeared, telling attractive TV producers where to get off.

Tally tossed her head in frustration. 'Oh well,' Thea heard her say, 'I suppose I can't win them all.' She dropped her voice seductively. 'But I'll be waiting under the mistletoe for you later...' Smiling mischievously, she sauntered away from the counter.

'Hi,' Thea said, a little too brightly, as she approached the shop counter. 'Everything all right?'

The sweet smile that crossed Nick's face when he saw her made Thea's heart do a little flip. *Stop it,* she told herself. *Get a grip.*

'Fine, fine,' Nick said, smiling at her in that genuine, open way that made her feel as though she was the sole focus of his attention. 'And better now you're here.'

Thea's heart definitely sped up at the compliment. Something about the way his gaze lingered on her face, and the smile tugging at his lips made her want to lean over and kiss him. *Stop it. You're no match for five feet eleven of blonde television-producing goddess.*

Still though, it was nice to get that kind of greeting from anyone. The fact it was Nick who said it made it even nicer.

Some time later, the Christmas market was in full swing outside, and Thea was going great guns at the counter inside the farm shop. She'd seen Nick striding about, bringing in a few more boxes of mince pies from the stock room and chatting amiably with the locals who'd come from all parts of Lower Brambleton to sample and buy the wares of the sellers in the car park. She was tickled to see him accept a pint of cider from the Carters Cider concession, who'd come over from the factory about thirty miles away in the village of Little Somerby. Local knowledge had it that Rob Saint had been good friends with the Carters Cider patriarch, Jack Carter, back in the day, and the business relationship, as well as the friendship, was remembered with great fondness on both sides, even years after Jack's death. As a result, Carters always sent a few barrels and a bartender to the Christmas market to warm the Somerset locals.

The cider truck was over in the corner of the car park next to the hog roast. A pint and a pig roll sounded like a great proposition to Thea, whose stomach was growling. She'd eaten early so she could get to the farm shop on time, and the Bolognese seemed a long time ago, now.

'I hope that old rogue, Rob Saint's paying you overtime for the night shift!' Lorelai's amused voice cut into Thea's musings, and Thea smiled back at her.

'Don't worry, Gran, Nick's sorting out the pay check!'

Lorelai paid for her box of mince pies and Thea breathed a sigh of relief as her gran made to leave.

'Don't you work my granddaughter too hard tonight!' Lorelai chided Nick lightly as they exchanged a quick hello when he arrived at the counter to check in. 'She's got a lot of work on at school, good of her as it is to help you out.'

'I'm very grateful to her.' Nick smiled down at Lorelai. 'She's been a star.'

'That's Thea all over.' Lorelai smiled back at Nick and glanced at them both, a look of amusement in her eyes. 'Make sure you give her a proper Christmas bonus for all of her hard work!'

'Gran!' Thea admonished Lorelai lightly. She caught Nick's eye, and she couldn't help noticing a slight, almost unnoticeably raised eyebrow in her direction. Feeling a sudden urge to giggle, as if she'd regressed to being a teenager again and had been caught doing something she shouldn't, she stammered, 'If you're headed to the stock room, we could really do with a few more organic Christmas puddings, if there are any out there.'

'Er, OK,' Nick said, looking as though he was about to laugh himself. 'I was going to offer to relieve you on the till so you could have a look around the fair, but I'll check for some of those puds before I do, if you say we're short out here.'

'They're selling like hot, er, puddings!' Thea quipped weakly, but she felt a sense of relief as Nick moved past her to the stock room.

'Well, I'll see you later in the week, dear,' Lorelai said, shouldering her canvas tote bag and making a move towards the shop door. 'Don't work too hard.'

'I won't!'

A couple of minutes later, Nick was back with a tray of Christmas puddings and an inquisitive expression.

'Your gran's incorrigible!' he said as he popped the puddings down on the counter.

Thea laughed. 'You could say that.' She paused. 'Look, er, I just wanted to thank you again for taking me on here. I've really enjoyed it, and the money's going to make Christmas a bit easier.'

'You're welcome,' Nick replied. 'I mean, you've got me out of a tight spot. If you hadn't stepped in, I'd have had to have propped Dad up behind the counter, and he's so zoned out on codeine at the moment he'd be giving away the profits!'

Thea laughed. 'Well, I'm glad I've spared you that.'

'Are things really that tight for Christmas?' Nick asked, suddenly serious.

Thea paused, unsure whether she wanted to go too much into detail about her money worries. 'Oh, you know,' she said quickly. 'It's an expensive time of year. Especially with the children. I'm trying to manage their expectations, but it's not easy.'

'Fair enough,' Nick said, a soft tone to his voice. 'But it's nothing to be ashamed of. Things are tough right now, for a lot of people. I think it's very strong of you to face it head on and try to work things out by yourself.'

Thea's eyes felt prickly all of a sudden, and she blinked furiously. 'It doesn't feel that way,' she said quietly. 'Sometimes it feels as though all I'm doing is keeping the wolf from the door by offering him a rapidly diminishing pile of meat, and as soon as it's gone, he'll be in to eat me, the kids and the bloody cat, too!'

'Nah,' Nick replied. 'That cat's a feisty little torty: she'd take down a wolf without shedding a claw!'

Thea gave a slightly shaky laugh. 'You always know how to cheer me up.'

'I'm always around to try, when you need me.' He put a tentative hand on her forearm. 'You're my friend, Thea, and I care about you.'

Thea looked up and saw his clear blue eyes were full of warmth and compassion. Something held between them, until Nick cleared his throat and broke the gaze.

'Well,' he said, taking his hand off her arm, 'did you want to take a break and have a look around? I'm happy to man the till for a bit.'

'Thanks.' Thea smiled, trying to disguise the fact that her own face felt hot and her heart was hammering nineteen to the dozen. 'I won't be long. I'm on the lookout for some reasonably priced things to fill the kids' stockings with, so I'll zip around and see what I can see.'

'Take your time,' Nick replied. 'The more I'm behind the counter, the less chance there is that bloody Tally will try to strong-arm me into that stupid Santa costume!'

'She seemed rather, er, *persistent*,' Thea said carefully. She didn't want to let on that she'd overheard too much of the banter between Tally and Nick earlier, but she was still intrigued by their dynamic.

'That she is.' Nick rolled his eyes.

'She's a very attractive woman,' Thea observed. Some part of her knew she was testing the waters here, seeing if Nick was going to agree with her.

'Yes, she is, but I don't like it when things get complicated. And Tally's always struck me as the type who loves complications.'

'Oh, bless you, Nick,' Thea teased. 'Ever since I've known you you've tended to shy away when things got a little, um, busy for you.'

'What can I say?' Nick grinned. 'I'm a simple country boy at heart.'

Thea grinned back. 'You always were a sentimental fool, Nick Saint.'

'Oy!' Nick protested. 'Don't cheek your boss or I'll cancel your tea break.'

'No, you won't,' Thea shot back playfully. 'You'd never hear the end of it from your mum if you treated the staff badly.'

'Fair point.' There it was again, his heartbreakingly lovely smile, complemented by the twinkle of his gorgeous blue eyes. Thea gave herself a mental shake. What was wrong with her tonight? Putting it down to tiredness and the near hysteria of a day coaxing her Year 4 class into word-perfect harmony for the nativity play, she moved away from the counter and took the break Nick had offered her. Perhaps a little wander around the market would help her to order her thoughts. Goodness knew, there'd been little enough time for that lately.

As she walked out into the car park where the stallholders were in full swing, she caught sight of Tally, clipboard in hand, directing the camera crew to catch a few cover shots of the market. She really was quite stunning. If Nick decided to have a fling with Tally while she was here, she'd feel more than a little jealous, whether she had any right to be or not.

17

The festive evening had been a success. The weather, while cold, had remained dry and ready refills of both coffee and mulled cider from the Carters concession had ensured Christmas spirit was in good supply all round. It was the first time that Nick had been left in sole charge of the evening; Annabelle usually master-minded the whole thing, but from the tone of the WhatsApp she'd sent the family group, just before kick-off tonight, she wasn't missing the responsibility and, to his surprise, Nick had found managing the evening more of a pleasure than he'd anticipated.

Even the antics of the camera crew with an enthusiastic Tally at the helm couldn't disrupt his mood for long. They managed to get some gorgeous shots of both of the market and the shop itself, and Nick knew how valuable this publicity would be in the coming months for a business such as Saints' Farm. Tally was excellent at her job, and he knew the end product, Santa suit or no Santa suit, was going to be a success.

As the evening drew to a close, and weary stall holders packed up a great deal less of what they'd arrived with, Nick circulated the shopping area which was gradually returning to its original purpose as a car park. He smiled and shook hands with a few of the regulars, including Mollie Wakefield, who'd somehow managed to transport what looked like the entire contents of the Purrfect Paws Rescue charity shop and arrange it beautifully onto a couple of tables. Mollie was never one to resist a challenge and the micro concession of the charity shop had done well tonight with its selection of preloved books, toys and a small rack of clothing as well as beautifully designed merchandise with the charity's logo strategically placed to ensure maximum exposure for the good work that Purrfect Paws did in rescuing and rehoming the feline residents of the county.

Nick felt tired though: he was used to being on his feet all day but carrying out the requests of the film crew had added an extra layer of stress, and he very much felt in need of a drink and a debrief. He had breezily assured Annabelle and Jamie that they shouldn't worry about the business in their absence and for the most part that had been true, but this had been a long few days and, with a sinking heart, he reminded himself that it was only Tuesday!

For a second, his mind drifted back to Thea who'd also had a busy day at her proper job and yet had been helping him out like an absolute trooper all evening. Thea didn't often let things slip about the stresses in her life, at least not to him, despite the fact they'd been friends for such a long time, but tonight he got a glimpse. She was clearly very worried about her financial circumstances, and he was desperate to try to make things better for her. Any good friend would want to help, wouldn't they?

Nick wandered back towards the entrance of the shop, and began to move the produce inside the entrance once again. The routine nature of this job was such that most evenings he did it on auto pilot, but he couldn't help glancing towards the counter where Thea was still standing, serving the last of the customers before the shop closed. She had such a great way with people, he thought as he observed her ready smile and the way people really responded to her. He could imagine that gentle, approachable manner of hers being a real winner with both children and parents alike. It was her warmth and empathy that he'd always loved about her, he realised. Then, as that unguarded thought registered in his brain, he nearly dropped the tray of parsnips he'd been bringing in.

Loved?

Where the hell had *that* come from? Shaking his head, as if trying to rid himself of those treacherous thoughts, he focussed his attention on bringing in the rest of the baskets and trays. It didn't help that his eyes seemed constantly drawn back to the shop counter every time he walked back through the front door. He realised if he didn't stop staring soon, Thea was going to accuse him of being some kind of stalker.

'Well, that all went rather swimmingly.' Tally's unmistakeable voice broke into his thoughts as he paused just to the right of the front door. There was one more tray of carrots to bring in and he was reaching for it as she approached.

'I'm glad,' Nick replied.

'Would've been better if I'd managed to wrangle you into that Santa suit though!' Tally teased.

'Never in a millennium of Sundays!' Nick shot back.

'Oh well,' Tally replied, 'a girl can dream.' She looked coyly at him from under her lashes. In the soft light that emanated from the strings of tiny amber bulbs that hung from the low rafters of the front of the shop, Tally's eyes looked gentler, and more sincere.

'So is that a wrap?' Nick asked, unsure why Tally was still hanging about. The film crew had had even longer days than he had, and most of them didn't stick around when they'd stopped filming.

'I believe so.' Tally smiled at him. 'And as ever, it's been a real pleasure to be back here, Nick. Thank you for your hospitality.'

'You're welcome.' Nick smiled back. Despite Tally's continuous flirting, he had quite enjoyed having her and the rest of the crew here. It didn't hurt to step out of your comfort zone once in a while.

Tally didn't seem as though she was going to be the one to call it a night before he did, and she still hovered near the doorway, shuffling a little closer to Nick as the last customers departed with a cheery 'goodnight'.

'So how about that drink?' she said, still staring at him. 'It's my last night here... it would be lovely to spend the rest of the evening catching up with you.' The look in her eyes suggested that a drink would just be the start of it. Nick felt flattered by the attention, and he couldn't help thinking back to the last time they'd gone for a drink together, and where it had ended. But, it had been a long day, and he wasn't really sure he wanted a repeat performance.

'I've got a lot to finish up here,' he replied. 'Some other time, perhaps.'

'You really do play hard to get, don't you?' Tally tilted her face towards his. 'I'm going back to London in the morning. This is our last chance...'

Nick opened his mouth to reply, but before he could, Tally had planted a firm kiss on it. Her lips were warm, and as she kissed him, he could taste the somewhat strange combination of a synthetic, overly sweet raspberry lip balm and a very bitter coffee. It was a nice kiss, and took him back to the last time Tally had been in Somerset, but somehow it didn't feel quite right this time.

'Merry Christmas, Saint Nick,' Tally murmured as she moved away from him. 'I'll see you again next year.'

Nick took a breath to reply, but before he could think about what the hell to say, another voice, overly bright and trying hard to disguise its shock, emanated from just inside the shop.

'I'll be off now, Nick,' Thea said. 'See you on Thursday.'

As Tally gave him a long look, and Thea's departing back hurried across the car park, Nick cursed the mistletoe that was hanging innocently above his head.

18

Thea couldn't disguise the green, sick feeling of jealousy that shot through her, and continued to do so, as she hurried to her car and drove home. *This is stupid,* she thought. She had no claim on Nick, other than as his friend. If he wanted to kiss the glamorous and confident Tally under the mistletoe, then he was more than able to. The rational centre of her brain made all of these arguments calmly as she commuted the short distance between Saints' Farm and her house. The emotional core of her body just screamed louder and made her feel nauseated.

Nick Saint wasn't hers. He'd never been hers, and he never would be hers. They were friends, nothing more. *To say the truth, reason and love keep little company these days,* she thought wryly. The memories of *A Midsummer Night's Dream,* which Year 6 had performed a version of in the summer, provoked her face into a brief smile, despite her racing heart.

She pulled into her driveway and hurried through the front door, relieved, finally, to be able to sit down at last. Waves of exhaustion washed over her, and she was so tired that the sight of

Cora briskly filling the kettle and popping tea bags into two mugs, made her eyes fill with tears.

'Thanks, darling,' she murmured, placing a kiss on the girl's forehead as she ambled into the living room and collapsed on the sofa. It felt like the most comfortable seat in the world after a long, long day.

'Biccy?' Cora called from the kitchen.

'Two, please,' Thea replied.

'Must have been a tough night.'

You have no idea, Thea thought.

Five minutes later, she and Cora were sipping tea and deciding if there was enough time before bed to slip in a quick episode of *Friends* on Netflix. That might be another thing that would have to go in the new year, so Thea decided that there definitely *was* time. As Ross pined after Rachel for the umpteenth time, Thea wanted to scream at the television.

'Everything been all right here?' she asked.

'Fine,' Cora replied. 'Dylan crashed out about half an hour ago, but he asked me to remind you that you said you'd get the Christmas decorations down when you got back.'

Thea groaned. 'The last thing I feel like doing right now is going into the crawl space.'

'I don't mind doing it,' Cora said eagerly.

'Nope, sorry kiddo – there's no way I'm letting you loose up a ladder!'

'Well, you can break the news to him tomorrow, then,' Cora said.

Thea sighed. She knew she should really stand firm on it, but she had promised Dylan.

'Let me just finish this glorious cuppa and I'll get the stepladder out.'

The two of them drank their tea in companionable silence,

and as the credits rolled on the episode of *Friends,* Thea heaved herself back up from the sofa. 'Can you hold the steps for me?'

'Yeah.' Cora ambled through and put the mugs in the dishwasher.

A short time later, Thea was trying to locate the two boxes of decorations, along with the artificial Christmas tree that she'd stowed in the crawl space a year ago. She wasn't sure if it was tiredness or the darkness in the loft that was causing her to struggle.

'Can you grab my phone, darling?' she called down to Cora.

'Yup. Hang on...' Cora let go of the ladder and Thea waited. Then, just as Cora was returning, her phone started to ring.

'Bit late for an actual phone call,' Thea muttered, trying to stave off the inevitable sense of worry that the ringing phone evoked. She was of a generation that always felt instinctively concerned when the phone rang after eight o'clock at night, and she hoped it wasn't Lorelai on the other end, or Tristan.

Thankfully, caller ID on the mobile was a godsend in these situations.

'Nick's ringing you, Mum,' Cora called up. 'Do you want me to answer it?'

Thea nearly lost her footing on the stepladder. 'Nope. Let it ring.'

Cora looked up quizzically. 'Are you sure?'

The phone's noise was becoming irritating now, and in her current state, Thea didn't need any more provocation.

'Yes,' she said firmly. She really didn't want to speak to him right now. She still couldn't quite put her finger on why she was feeling so hurt: Nick could kiss whom he wanted under the mistletoe, but that didn't mean she wanted to speak to him.

Cora passed her the phone, and she pressed the ignore

button. Then, turning the torch on, she located the Christmas boxes, and the tree, and headed back down the ladder.

'There you go, squirt,' she said, passing the boxes to Cora. 'That should keep your brother quiet.'

'It'll be worth it, Mum, I promise.' Thea was surprised when her daughter leaned over and gave her a hug. 'You seem really stressed right now, and we just want to make everything look really special for you, and for Christmas.'

Thea blinked back tears. 'Thank you, darling.' Sometimes, in the throes of adolescence, Cora could still surprise her.

'Now, go and get in the bath and I'll bring you another cup of tea.'

Thea smiled. 'Sounds fab.' She hurried into the bathroom, phone still in hand, but, as she dumped it on the windowsill before she turned the taps on, it rang again.

'Not now, Nick,' she muttered. She knew it was childish, but she couldn't face talking to him after seeing him under the mistletoe with Tally. If he'd told her he was interested in Tally (and why wouldn't he be?), she'd have been fine with what she'd seen. It was the fact that he'd kept that from her that was really annoying. She felt as though they'd been rekindling their friendship while she'd been working at the shop, and that, by not being entirely straight with her, Nick hadn't respected that.

Trying hard to put him out of her mind as she sank, a few minutes later, into a warm, scented bubble bath that felt like the height of luxury, she found that she couldn't altogether shake her irritation. She knew her trust issues were embedded deeply after Ed had so monumentally abused her faith in him, and she also knew that she was probably projecting much of that onto Nick. Just because they were becoming friends again, it didn't mean he had to tell her everything. It was just that she did feel as though they'd had a couple of 'moments' of their own lately.

'Do I fancy Nick?' she asked herself. But then, was it really so ridiculous? He was her age, in good shape, handsome, and available. Well, maybe not after what she'd seen tonight. Sighing, she ducked her head below the waterline, feeling the warmth closing over her head and creating the temporary illusion of peace. If only she could stay underwater forever! Rising back to the surface, she steeled herself not to grab her phone to see if he'd called again. It could all wait until later. Tonight, all she wanted was to crash out into a warm bed and a dreamless sleep.

19

Thea felt relieved that she wasn't due back at the farm shop until Thursday: she had enough to occupy her in school with the nativity play rehearsals and the other Christmas activities that were taking place. Her mind kept sliding off sideways to think about Nick's kiss with Tally, and she firmly shut herself down every time it tried. Nick was a free agent, and he could kiss whomever he liked.

As such, by the time she got to the shop on Thursday, she was more at peace with herself. It wasn't worth risking a friendship over, and she had no intention of losing Nick as a friend. She'd finally 'fessed up to Cora and Dylan about working a few days here and there at Saints' Farm, but had said it was because Nick was short-handed in the run up to Christmas. They'd both seemed to accept this with little fuss, and Cora had even volunteered to make dinner tonight and tomorrow, to save Thea the trouble. Thea felt grateful that the two of them were so understanding.

'Hi,' Nick called from across the yard as she locked her car. 'I'm just heading out to the barn to pick up a few more bags of coal and nets of kindling. There's a delivery from the veg supplier due at 9.30, if you're all right to count it in?'

'Uh, yeah, of course,' Thea stammered. Nick's tone seemed a little off-hand, and she wondered why. Hurriedly, she walked into the shop, grabbed her apron and opened up the till ready for new customers.

It was an oddly quiet start to the day, and Thea found herself walking up and down the aisles of the shop, straightening wonky groceries and re-stacking bags of flour and dried fruit to pass the time. She hated to admit it, but she was as much of a stickler for order as Tristan was, especially when she felt under pressure, and this strange atmosphere that seemed to have fallen between herself and Nick since she'd witnessed him and Tally under the mistletoe seemed to be pervading.

Nick seemed to be absenting himself from the shop floor as much as possible during the morning, and once the veg order came in and Thea had ticked it all off and put it out, she was too busy to notice whether he'd checked in or not. It wasn't until midday that he came back in, and suggested she take her lunch break.

'I can man the till for an hour – I think I've got everything in from the barns, now.'

'OK,' Thea replied. She opened her mouth to say something else, but then realised she wasn't quite sure where to start. Feeling more than a little dispirited, she mooched into the back office and unwrapped her sandwich. Bloody Tally and her commandeering of Nick under the mistletoe! She knew she had no claim on Nick other than his friendship, but it still irritated her that he seemed to be avoiding her. In an attempt to take her mind off it, she pulled out her phone and was surprised to see a WhatsApp from Annabelle. She and Annabelle were good friends, but their lives often took them in different directions.

However, she smiled when she saw the message thanking her for stepping in to cover at such short notice. She messaged back replying that it was no problem, although she could have done without a bloody annoying TV director putting her stamp on the place quite so thoroughly. Annabelle's laughing emoji was swiftly followed by a wry:

> That'll be Tally, then. Did she try it on with Nick again, this time?

Thea paused before replying.

> Let's just say the mistletoe's had a good workout this year...

Annie's shocked face emoji made Thea smirk. The smile, however, disappeared when Annabelle replied with a:

> Well, he is STILL a free agent, poor lonely saddo that he is. He can kiss whomever he likes.

Thea paused before replying. Annabelle was right, but she still felt unsettled by Tally's behaviour towards Nick. She had the distinct feeling that Annabelle was leading her, trying to get her to admit to something, but she was wiser than that. She merely added, 'Yeah, but I thought he'd have better taste than that. She's so OBVIOUS!' before signing off. Perhaps she shouldn't be grumbling about Nick to his sister, especially since he was the one who'd given her this job, but she had to talk to *someone*. And Tristan was out of the question; he'd take the piss even more than Annabelle would. Sighing, she put her phone down and picked up her book. She'd tried to make more time to read, lately, and she had half an hour before she was back on the counter. As she tried to lose herself in the latest Mick Herron novel, she wondered if she ought to just have it out with Nick. It was going to be a bit tricky if he kept avoiding her, seeing as they were the only ones staffing the shop.

After about twenty minutes, she closed her book and headed towards the counter again. Just as she was about to walk through the doorway of the back office, she encountered Nick coming the other way.

'It's all right, I'll get back out there now,' she said. The doorway was tight, and as he stepped in, she stepped out. Their bodies brushed together, and Thea felt a jolt of electricity between them as they made contact. She laughed nervously and looked up at Nick, who was staring down at her, a look of surprise and consternation on his face.

'Look, Thea, can we talk?' he said.

Thea's gaze met his, and she was suddenly hit with such a sense of longing and desire that her knees wobbled. 'Um, sure,' she stammered. 'About what?'

'You know what,' Nick replied softly.

Just as Thea was about to reply, a 'Hellooooooo? Service?' came from the shop counter.

'Bugger.' Nick rolled his eyes and Thea, taking the opportunity to escape a conversation she wasn't quite ready to have, eased her way past him. 'I'll go. We can chat later, can't we?'

Nick nodded, and Thea hurried out to the front of the shop. Mollie Wakefield from Purrfect Paws was standing at the counter. Thea greeted her and rang up her purchases.

'It's such a gorgeous, sunny winter's day outside,' Mollie said, smiling at Thea. 'One could almost forget we're in the midst of winter. We see so little sunshine at this time of year, don't we? My cats all perk up when there's a bit more light and warmth in the air.'

'I know the feeling!' Thea joked, but she was half on autopilot. She heard Mollie mentioning something about a long-range forecast for snow in the West Country, but she didn't take much notice. Snow was a rarity in this part of the county, blessed as it was by south westerly winds from the Gulf Stream. Thea couldn't remember the last time they'd had more than a smattering of the white stuff in Lower Brambleton.

As Mollie left, there seemed to be a steady stream of afternoon customers, so much so that by the time there was a lull, Nick had disappeared again, ostensibly off to one of the other barns on site. Thea huffed in frustration, and not a little confusion. That interaction in the doorway had made her pause. She had a very strong sense that seeing Tally kissing Nick under the mistletoe had been a bit of 'moment' for her, too, but she also knew she couldn't trust her own instincts right now. There was too much going on for her to think straight.

20

Closing time came around, and Thea hung up her apron gratefully. She'd been nervous all afternoon about talking to Nick, and now she just wanted to speak to him and get home. The thought of another tense day tomorrow made her try to be more patient, though. The atmosphere between them had added another layer of stress that she just didn't need. As she closed out the till and put the drawer into the safe, she straightened up again and let out a long sigh. She was tired. Really, really tired. Thank goodness Cora was going to cook dinner tonight.

'Everything OK?' Nick asked as she went back through to the shop, having picked up her bag from the back office.

'All good,' Thea replied. 'Er, you said you wanted to talk to me?'

'Yeah, is now a good time?' As Thea watched, Nick rubbed the back of his neck, a classic nervous gesture she'd seen him do a thousand times before. Tonight, though, it irritated her.

'I do have to get home, Nick,' she said quickly. 'The kids have been on their own since they got back from school and I'd like to see them sometime tonight.'

'Sure, sure. Sorry.'

'Well?' she said, a little more sharply than she'd intended. 'What is it, Nick?'

Nick, obviously catching her tone, got to it. 'Look, there are a couple of things, actually. The first one is about what you saw the other night. It was nothing, honestly. Tally took things into her own hands—'

'And you, it would seem,' Thea interjected. 'You were very much *in her hands* from what I saw.'

Nick looked pained. 'She grabbed me before I had the chance to do anything!' he protested. 'And all right, she's a very attractive woman, but I keep telling you, she's not for me.'

'Not so much that you didn't hook up with her last time, though,' Thea observed. 'You must fancy her a bit.'

'Honestly?' Nick paused. 'I did then, but I don't any more. And that stupid kiss proved it to me. I think it might have proved it to her, too. She didn't exactly look thrilled afterwards.'

'I wouldn't know. I left pretty sharpish, but you probably didn't notice.'

'I did notice, and I wanted to explain.' Nick's tone was gentle, but firm, and Thea found her pulse beating a little bit faster.

'You don't have to explain anything to me. I'm your friend, not your—' She broke off, and started to blush. 'Look, I really do have to go.'

Nick shifted a little. 'Not my what?' he asked softly.

'Nothing,' Thea muttered. 'Forget I said anything.' She didn't want to admit to herself just how much seeing Nick kissing Tally under the mistletoe had affected her. She was frustrated she'd reacted so strongly, and it didn't make any sense, in her mind at least. Nick could kiss whomever he wanted; why, then, had a huge part of her wanted to be in Tally's place?

'Thea...' Nick murmured, and his tone made her look up

from the floor, where she'd been resolutely staring. 'Would it help if I said I was sorry?' His eyes showed concern, affection, and an obvious desire to make things right between them. She didn't doubt his sincerity, in that moment, but she was still unsettled by her own reaction to the kiss she'd seen.

'It's not that,' Thea muttered. She didn't want to admit how she felt to him: she was terrified about losing the connection they were beginning to strengthen. 'Honestly, Nick, it's fine.'

Nick's expression communicated all too clearly that he didn't believe her. Just as she was about to speak, again, he beat her to it.

'Come here.'

Nick moved towards her and Thea was enveloped in a hug. Nick, after a day hefting stuff in from the barns single handed, smelled warm, musky and delicious. The traces of sweat and deodorant assailed her senses, and she breathed in, relishing their closeness. 'Tally was a stupid mistake, and that's all there is to it. I'd hate for you to think otherwise. And I really do want to clear the air,' he said softly, his breath brushing her hair.

'Me too.' Thea rested in his arms, enjoying how good it felt to be held again, and by Nick. She glanced up at him, and as their eyes met, and their lips hovered a breath or two apart, her head started to spin. But just before she could close the gap between them, reality reasserted itself. 'You're a good friend,' she said, half-sadly, pulling back.

'You too.' He let her go. 'I'll, er, see you tomorrow?'

'Bright and early!' she replied. As she walked out of the door towards her car, Thea's heart was hammering faster and faster. It would have been so easy to tilt her face upwards and kiss him while they were hugging, but she wasn't sure how things might have ended, if she had. She was shocked by just how much she'd wanted to do that.

21

After a much easier Friday in the farm shop, with Nick thanking his lucky stars he and Thea had sorted things out the night before, Saturday morning arrived with a festive flurry of snow. He'd been constantly replaying the hug that he and Thea had shared, resulting in some highly erotic dreams that had left him feeling as frustrated as the teenager he'd once been.

As Nick pulled up in the car park of the shop, he was glad of the Land Rover that was his choice for getting around. It had almost two hundred thousand miles on the clock, and his father joked that it was held together by rust and hope these days, but Nick wasn't the vain, flashy type when it came to cars: the Landy suited him just fine.

He had a busy day ahead: he was still basically running the place on his own, but at least Roseanna would be in at 9 a.m. to manage the counter and keep the shop ticking over while he carried out the deliveries. Next weekend, the last one before they closed for Christmas, he'd be rushed off his feet with them. Today was somewhat less busy but he did have a rather special errand to run, and he wanted to allow enough time to do that.

He made sure the shop was ready for business, and then occupied himself with assembling the orders, ready to pack into the little dark blue van that bore the shop's logo. By that time, Roseanna had arrived and was calmly checking and rotating stock and writing down things to re-order in the little notebook that was placed by the till for that purpose. Annabelle used the notebook when she put in orders from their many local suppliers early on Monday morning each week.

Nick was grateful for Roseanna's calm, efficient presence. She was a reliable eighteen-year-old student at the nearby secondary school, and she'd been working at the farm shop on a Saturday since she turned sixteen. These days, Nick always felt more than happy to leave her in charge when he went out and did the deliveries on a Saturday morning. 'I'll be off now then,' he said. 'I might be a little bit longer than usual because of my final delivery, but you've got Mum and Dad's number and my mobile if you need anything. Call us if there's a problem.'

'It's all good,' Roseanna replied. 'You'd better get going or you'll be late.'

'See you in a bit,' he said, walking out towards the van.

A short time later, Nick had done the local rounds, including dropping off a large consignment of a locally produced luxury brand of raw cat food to the Purrfect Paws cattery and rescue centre. Although the unfortunate strays and rescues who hadn't found their forever homes would spend Christmas in the centre, Mollie and her dedicated staff were keen to give them a small festive treat ready for the big day.

After an hour or so, Nick had reached the last of his errands for the morning. The advantage of living in such a small hamlet as Lower Brambleton was that the deliveries weren't too much to handle and he enjoyed catching up with the locals who liked to source their provisions from the nearby area, and those who had come to depend on the Saints' Farm delivery service as a vital lifeline.

This last stop was no exception. Right at the top of one of the hills that bookended the hamlet was the Restful Oaks retirement home. With panoramic views across the beautiful county of Somerset, this was a very desirable place to spend your twilight years, and its residents were very well taken care of by its team of staff. They, too, liked a regular delivery of local produce and Nick always enjoyed a chat and, if time allowed, a cuppa and a biscuit with the residents in the lounge that overlooked the village.

Today though, his errand was slightly different. He pondered, as he got this very special delivery out of the van, why he was more than happy to don a Father Christmas outfit for this occasion, when he'd point-blank refused to put one on for Tally and her cameras. But tradition was one thing and making an idiot of himself in front of the nation was quite another, he conceded. As he made his way into the large, white, mock-Georgian style building, he observed that there were more cars than usual parked in the car park, even for a weekend. The festive season made people want to reach out and connect with their loved ones. He hoped that these meetings would cheer the residents of Restful Oaks and rally them for the season.

'Morning, Nick!' The cheerful voice of the receptionist, Amelia, rang out as he crossed the threshold with the first of a number of boxes. 'Let me call Geoff and get him to give you a hand with those.'

'Thanks.' Nick smiled at Amelia and made the familiar way through to the kitchen, which was at the back of the building. Placing the first of the boxes down, on his way back out he met with the home's weekend manager, Selina, and confirmed a couple of details.

'Yes, they're all present and correct in the dining room,' Selina confirmed. 'The local Guides and Brownies have come over this morning, too, to sing carols and provide a bit more Christmas cheer, so I hope you've remembered some extra mince pies and goodies!'

'Annabelle put a note on the order to throw in a few more boxes.' Nick smiled. 'Wouldn't want our carol singers to run out of steam, would we?' He paused before adding, 'Is there somewhere I can go to put this on?'

Selina smiled. 'Absolutely. Although, if you don't mind me saying, you're a little too young for the costume. Your father's back still giving him gyp?'

Nick nodded. 'Sadly, yes, or he'd be up here with me. Not that I mind doing it,' he added quickly, 'but Dad does enjoy coming here and being sociable.'

'Tell him he's welcome any time in the new year, when he's up to it,' Selina said. 'I know a lot of the residents really appreciate the conversation.'

'Will do,' Nick replied. He hurried into the staff room and quickly got changed. Then, once he was sure the daft beard and red costume were completely in place, he took a deep breath and made his way into the large dining area where the residents and their guests, as well as the Brownies and Guides were assembled.

'Ho, Ho, Ho, Merry Christmas, one and all!' he boomed in his best imitation of Santa Claus. While the residents looked indulgently delighted, the assembled girls of different ages looked excited and by turns too-cool-for-school indifference. There was a smattering of parents who'd stuck around to hear the carol singing, and as Nick looked around the room, his heart started to race. There, sitting alongside a couple of the residents and smiling broadly, not trying to disguise her amusement at all at the sight of Nick in the rather-too-large Santa suit, was Thea.

Well, if that wasn't the icing on the Christmas cake, Nick

thought in mortification as he felt his face growing as red as the suit he was wearing. He tried to put it down to the tropical temperature of the home's central heating, but he couldn't convince himself for long, especially when Thea gave him a highly amused wink.

Hurrying around the dining area, he handed out a beautifully baked mince pie to each resident, and then, under the watchful eye of the Brownie and Guide leaders, the younger guests helped themselves to the rest, which had been unboxed and brought in by Selina and her staff.

'Cup of tea, Santa?' Selina asked, with a twinkle in her eye.

'A glass of water would be even better!' Nick replied. The synthetic fluff of the beard was making his face itch, and he couldn't wait to strip it back off again. And Thea's amused glances weren't helping the situation. She hadn't mentioned she was going to be here, and he was beginning to feel increasingly uncomfortable, hot and embarrassed.

'Coming right up.' Selina bustled off to the kitchen.

'Nice job, Santa,' Thea murmured as she approached. 'I thought you'd sworn off that kind of get-up?'

'Not exactly my first choice,' Nick muttered back, 'but I had to step in for Dad, again.'

'Very noble of you,' Thea replied. Her tone was dry, but Nick chanced a direct glance at her and saw her eyes were smiling. 'I didn't realise this was part of your festive rounds today.'

'It's a Saints' Farm regular date in the calendar,' Nick replied. 'Seemed a shame to duck out just because Dad's not up to it this year.'

'Well, the mince pies are going down as well as the carol singing did,' Thea said. 'I think it's a job well done.'

There was a slight pause between them, before Thea added, 'It suits you, though. You always look your best in strong colours.'

Nick felt a flush of pleasure at the unexpected compliment. 'Thank you. If I'd known you thought that, I'd definitely have put the suit on for the TV cameras!'

'Hi Nick!' Cora's cheerful voice cut into their conversation. 'You look as though you're about to pass out from the heat in that costume.' She grinned at him. 'And apart from one or two of the younger Brownies, I think we're all over the existence of Santa Claus.' She glanced around the room, where, even accounting for the young age of some of the visitors, belief in Saint Nicholas was not going to feature high among this group's list of priorities.

'Ssh!' Thea said playfully. 'As far as you're concerned, you'd better start believing in Santa Claus if you want any presents this year.'

'Yeah, right, Mum.' Cora rolled her eyes. 'I think even Dylan has worked out where the presents come from by now.' She turned back to Nick. 'Nice effort though. And thanks for the mince pies.'

'Any time.' Nick smiled down at her.

'I don't suppose you could magic us up a Christmas tree as well, could you?' Cora asked cheekily. 'Ours is so old now, the branches won't stay on it!'

'What? You've got a fake tree?'

'Yup' – Cora's eyes glinted mischievously – 'and it's not even a good one. It's older than I am and so crap that the lights it came with don't even work any more.'

'Well,' he said, 'I'm sure it's nothing that can't be fixed. Your mum's great with stuff like that.'

'I don't think even Mum can fix it this time,' Cora said, glancing at Thea. 'But she's too tight to buy us a new one.'

'Cora!' Thea's face registered irritation and then worry before she forced a smile in her daughter's direction. 'You're exaggerating, as usual.'

'Whatever, Mum,' Cora replied. She'd ambled off again before either Thea or Nick could reply.

'Ignore her,' Thea said, and Nick knew she didn't want to talk about the tree. 'She does tend to over-dramatise.'

'She's such a great kid, though,' Nick said. 'It doesn't seem a minute since she was born. I remember when you and Ed came to stay with Lorelai, that first Christmas. She must only have been a couple of weeks old.' He shook his head. 'I don't know how you did it. And then Dylan came along too.'

Thea smiled. 'You just kind of do, at the time. And I was so pleased to be spending some time with Gran that Christmas. It was the first time we'd been back to visit in ages, and I really needed to be close to family.' She paused, before adding, 'I never should have let Ed talk me into moving away from the village. It's where we all belong, and I'm so glad to be back now.'

'I'm glad you're back, too.' Nick looked into Thea's eyes and he wished that, instead of being in a day room full of pensioners, Guides and Brownies, they were back where they'd been when they'd shared that delicious hug. 'I missed you.'

'I missed you, too,' Thea replied. Her eyes widened a little as she held his gaze, and something electric seemed to pass between them, a natural progression from their closeness the previous night.

Nick opened his mouth to respond, but as he did Cora arrived by Thea's side again and the moment was lost. As they both continued to rib him about his terrible costume, he wondered if there was ever going to be a right time to explore what seemed to keep happening between them.

22

On Sunday morning, Thea still hadn't got around to working out what she was going to do about the knackered fake Christmas tree. The poor thing was leaning like a drunkard up against the wall of the living room, looking sadder and more rubbish than ever. The price label on the box was a reminder of just how old the thing was, and she knew that, even a modest replacement would set her back more money that she didn't have. Perhaps, with the judicious application of some duct tape and a bit of creative positioning of the better branches to cover the more ragged ones, the tree could survive another year.

All the same, the box of tree ornaments that stood in a state of melancholy beside the tree, just waiting to be positioned and argued over by Cora and Dylan, also stared at her in quiet reproach. For a split second she entertained the notion of just nipping into the woodland behind the house and hacking down a dwarf pine from an unseen corner, but she didn't own a saw, and she couldn't, in all conscience, ruin a tree just for the sake of a couple of weeks in her house.

Glumly, she looked at a replacement tree on Amazon, but,

since it was so close to Christmas, any options that would arrive before the big day were wildly expensive and any within her meagre budget wouldn't arrive until January. What could she do?

The cheery ring of her doorbell made her jump, but at least it stalled the avalanche of self-pity that threatened to break over her head. The tree would have to wait. She hadn't planned to see anyone today: Tristan wasn't a dropper-in, and Lorelai hadn't mentioned that she was going to come over, but that didn't mean she wouldn't, if she'd fancied the short walk between her place and Thea's.

She didn't bother to check the Ring doorbell camera before reaching for the latch on the door. The cul-de-sac was quiet at the best of times, and on a Sunday morning there seemed little chance it would be an unwelcome visitor. However, when she pulled open the door, all she could see was the somewhat innocuous sight of a Norwegian spruce tree, propped up against the side of the bay window.

'What on earth?' she said in bemusement.

'If it's too much, I can find another home for it.' Nick, who'd been hiding around the corner of the house, emerged, looking both delighted and sheepish to be the bearer of glad tidings, as well as the Christmas tree.

'Nick...' Thea began. 'I... I can't accept this. And I certainly can't afford it.'

'Yes, you can,' Nick replied. 'It's the last of a job lot we got from a supplier. And it's the runt of the litter, look.' He pointed to a slightly brown looking branch that was poking out at an angle at the bottom of the tree. 'I'd have had to knock half off the price, anyway, and we're getting a few more in tomorrow, so it won't be missed. It needs a good home.'

'But I haven't got a pot to put it in,' Thea protested. 'Poor thing'll die of thirst.'

'I've thought of that, too.' Nick produced a Christmas tree stand from behind his back, which just happened to be a festive red colour. 'We have a couple of these in the store room at work – we won't miss one, this close to Christmas. Put a bit of tinsel around it and you're golden. Now you *have* to take it in.'

Thea smiled at him. 'You've convinced me.' She paused. 'But you're also a gullible fool. Cora really did a number on you about the state of our fake tree, didn't she?'

'Can't have a fake tree, anyhow,' Nick replied. 'It's not the same. And before you try to tell me that Christmas trees aren't sustainable, this one's got eco-credentials dropping as fast as its needles.'

Thea shook her head. 'You're ridiculous, Nick Saint.'

'So they tell me.'

There was that pause again. 'Well? Are you going to let me bring it into the house, or is it just going to live on your doorstep until the recycling comes in the new year?'

Thea shook her head. 'Well, I suppose since you put it like that...' She moved quickly out of the way as Nick grabbed the tree and briskly brought it into the house. She tried not to notice the dropping needles: the hall needed a good hoover, anyway.

'Where do you want it?' Nick asked.

'In the corner by the patio door would be brilliant,' Thea replied. She watched as Nick carefully positioned the tree in the stand and fixed it in place.

'Fill it up with some water and it's good until Twelfth Night at least,' Nick said as he straightened back up again. Thea watched him give a slightly disdainful glance in the direction of the remains of the artificial tree. 'And that old thing can go in the bin, now!'

'That's virtually a family heirloom!' Thea laughed. 'I think Ed and I bought it for our first house together.'

'All the more reason to dump the bloody thing, then,' Nick said. 'He always struck me as a bit of a fake.'

'Oh yeah?' Thea teased. 'And I suppose you're the real thing, are you?'

Realising what she'd said, she felt the colour creeping up her face. 'I mean, um, stop taking the mick, Nick!'

'Well saved,' Nick said, an amused tone in his voice. 'But yeah... I like the real thing. Feels more authentic, somehow. More... trustworthy.' He was tinkering with the tree, getting it straight in the stand, but as he spoke, he turned around to face her. 'Don't you think?'

The question hung between them, and Thea wondered if they were still talking about Christmas greenery. 'I suppose...' she began, before a squeal from the doorway cut her off.

'Oh wow! That's, like, *so* much nicer than our old tree. It looks awesome!'

Cora bounded into the room and immediately started rummaging in the box of baubles. 'Dylan!' she shouted towards the ceiling. 'We can decorate the tree now!'

Thea winced at the volume of her daughter's voice, but Nick seemed unbothered by it.

The thud of footsteps down the stairs, and an even heftier thump as Dylan did his usual and jumped down the last three into the hallway, announced her younger son's arrival.

'Cool,' he said as he hurried past Thea and Nick. 'Shotgun putting the angel on top!'

'Mum's going to do that, like always,' Cora chided her younger brother. She paused and stopped rummaging in the baubles box. 'Why don't you and Nick go for a walk or something while we do the tree? We want to make it look really nice.' Her eyes swivelled from Thea to Nick. 'You could even get a coffee at the pub if you wanted to.'

Thea tried to read the expression in her daughter's eyes, but she'd turned her attention back to the tree decorations.

'I'm sure you're really busy, aren't you?' She looked at Nick. 'I mean, you must have loads to do in the run up to Christmas...'

Nick smiled at her. 'Actually, I don't have any plans. Next week's going to be manic, so I deliberately didn't put anything in for today.' He shuffled on the spot a bit. 'We could go for a bit of a walk if you want, leave these two to bling up the tree in peace?'

Thea felt her heart do that little flipping thing she'd been trying to ignore whenever Nick did something adorable. 'I'd like that.' She had a bright idea. 'Give me a minute, and I'll whip us up a couple of lattes to take on the walk. I've got a couple of decent travel mugs.'

'Sounds great. Can you put an extra sugar in mine?'

'You're sweet enough already!' Thea quipped and then regretted it as her face grew hot and Cora threw her an enquiring glance. 'I, er, won't be a minute.'

As good as her word, within a few minutes they were heading out the front door towards the wooded area that divided the housing estate from the rest of Lower Brambleton. Sipping her coffee, Thea tried not to think about just how lovely it had been to open the door and find Nick on the other side of it. Shrugging deeper into her thick, quilted winter parka, she tried instead to concentrate on the gorgeous surroundings.

'Well, I think the tree is a hit, don't you?'

Thea nodded enthusiastically. Even though she was mid-sip from her travel mug. 'It really is,' she said after a moment. 'Thank you again, Nick.'

'What are friends for?'

There was something about Nick's tone that made Thea glance across at him. They were ambling down the winding path that led from the edge of the housing estate down towards the small centre of Lower Brambleton. It was a path that had been renovated since the houses had been erected, which made it easier to follow, but there were few other walkers using it on a quiet Sunday morning. The route they were following led to the village, but if they'd walked the other way, they'd have ended up on Buttermere Lane, where Lorelai's cottage was. Thea had been scanning the path as they'd walked, but Nick's voice brought her up short.

'I'm so glad you're my friend, Nick,' she said carefully. 'You and I... we've known each other a long time, haven't we? I mean, I know we've only been spending more time together recently, but old friendships count for a lot, don't you think?'

Nick grinned. 'Definitely! But you saying it like that makes me feel old.'

'Me too.'

They walked a little further. The sun was shining brightly overhead, casting a slight winter warmth through the bare branches of the beech trees and dappling the path when the beeches were interspersed by the conifers and pines that also grew in the wood. The heady scent of pine balsam gave the air a festive feel, and Thea breathed deeply. She'd never tire of that scent. It was tied to so many memories of her childhood: long, lazy afternoons with her friends, tucked out of the way of the enquiring eyes of well-meaning adults, walks with Lorelai, both with, and later without, Barney, Lorelai's rotund chocolate Labrador, and, casting her mind back even further to the hazy days of early childhood, spending time in the woods when her parents had been alive. Often, they'd take a break from their work at the observatory to stretch their legs, and that scent was a reminder of times lost and long past.

'Penny for them?' Nick teased, as Thea realised she'd gone silent.

'Sorry. I was just thinking that I don't get out here nearly enough any more. Sometimes I forget how much I need just to reconnect with nature, and how lucky I am to have all this on the doorstep.'

'I can't ever imagine living anywhere else,' Nick said. Thea noticed that he looked slightly embarrassed as he admitted that. 'That probably makes me sound like a boring old fart.'

'Not at all,' Thea protested. 'You're loyal to your roots. It's one of the things I've always loved about you...' It was her turn to look embarrassed, and, searching for something to comment on to move the conversation on, she instead took another gulp of her coffee.

If Nick read anything into her turn of phrase, he didn't show it. Thea was relieved. Things had been a bit odd between them since the incident with Tally and the mistletoe, and she couldn't get that hug they'd shared on Thursday night out of her mind. It was stupid, really; they had a friendly shorthand, but it seemed as though she'd been struggling to interpret it lately. She was probably just tired and stressed, but it really did feel as though one minute they were behaving like the friends they'd once been, and the next, she didn't know what to say or how to behave around him.

'Thea, Nick!' A voice called to them from up to their left, and as Thea turned at the familiar tones, she felt a maddening combination of relief and frustration. There, standing on the bank above the path were Tristan and Charlotte, and gambolling down the incline towards them was Comet, Charlotte's adorable cocker spaniel.

'Oh, hi you two,' Thea called up to them, before leaning down to ruffle Comet's ears. 'What brings you out this way?'

'Gran offered us Sunday lunch,' Tristan said as he made his way down the bank. 'And we said we'd come over early so I could get her Christmas decorations down from the attic. You know how much she hates asking us to do things, but I didn't want her getting up a ladder with no one else in the house.'

'I'd have been more than happy to do that,' Thea replied. She felt guilty that the only time she'd seen Lorelai that week was that brief chat at the late-night shopping evening. She usually popped in a couple of times a week, but she'd been so caught up at work, doing both jobs, that she hadn't had the chance.

'It's fine, sis.' Tristan, who was dressed in green wellies and scruffy jeans, as well as a thick woolly jumper, smiled. 'We were going to drop in on you later, anyway, just to see if there's anything you thought we should buy for Christmas dinner.'

'Not that I can think of, but I'll let you know,' Thea replied.

'So, what brings you two out here, all alone?' Tristan's enquiring gaze shifted from Nick to Thea. 'Don't tell me this is finally a first date? After all these years?'

'Don't be daft, mate!' Nick interjected. 'Your sister's got much better taste than that.'

Thea shook her head. 'I could do a lot worse, as we all well know!' As she explained that Cora and Dylan had thrown them out of the house so they could decorate the tree and surprise her with it, Tristan's expression softened.

'That's so cool. They're great together when they're not squabbling, aren't they?'

Thea nodded. 'They really are.'

There was a pause, and Charlotte, who'd slithered down the bank in Tristan's wake, cleared her throat. 'We should probably be getting back to Lorelai's, Tris, she'll be wondering where we are.'

'Yeah, you're right,' Tristan replied. He gave Thea a parting grin. 'I'll swing by later before we head back, just in case you can think of anything we'll need on Christmas Day.'

'Sure. See you later.'

As Tristan and Charlotte headed in the opposite direction, back to Nightshade Cottage, Nick looked thoughtfully after them. 'I still can't believe that your twin brother fell head over heels for someone after all these years. I could have sworn he'd have been a sad bachelor like me for the rest of his days!'

'Neither of you is sad,' Thea protested. 'You'll find someone, Nick, just like Tris has, and when you do, you'll be as happy as he is, I know it.'

Nick didn't reply. The silence stretched between them as the mellifluous carolling of a blackbird harmonised with a robin just above their heads in the branches of a sleeping beech tree. He took a step towards her, but just as he did, the rather less harmonious trill of Thea's phone broke the mood. Whipping it out of her jacket pocket, she read the screen and swiped immediately.

'Hello? Oh, great, yes, darling, we'll head back and see. In a bit. Bye.'

Putting her phone away, she looked at Nick again.

'Sorry,' she said. 'What were you saying?'

'Never mind.' He gave her a slightly crooked smile. 'Was that Cora?'

'Yup. Tree's all ready for the ceremonial placing of the retro plastic angel!'

'You'd better get back to it, then. Wouldn't want to keep the angel from her rightful place.'

As they walked back towards the house, Thea yet again wondered if she was reading things wrong. Nick, who'd always been so open with her, was giving her some very confusing signals lately. The problem was, if she didn't start working out what he meant soon, she was going to run the very real risk of making a complete idiot of herself and perhaps losing his friendship in the process.

Soon, they were at the front door again. Thea paused. 'Would you like another coffee?'

'No thanks, I'm good.' Nick passed her his cup. 'I promised I'd look in on Mum and Dad before lunch and see if there was anything they needed doing. Dad's still moaning like hell about his back, and although Mum's hip's on the mend, she'll break it again if she doesn't rest, so I'm going to go and mediate for a bit.'

'Sounds like fun!' Thea quipped weakly. *Damn. There's that pause again.*

'Well, I'll see you at work on Thursday, if not before,' she said, eventually.

'See you.' Nick leaned towards her, and Thea felt her knees going wobbly. The feeling of his hand on her forearm, warm even through the layers of her coat, sent a dizzying tingle up to her shoulder. As his lips gently brushed her cheek, she closed her eyes in reflexive pleasure.

'See you,' she replied, wishing she was brave enough to turn her head a little to the right. But it would appear that neither she, nor he, had the confidence to make that chaste kiss of friendship into something more. Not just yet, anyway. As she let herself into the house, her hands were still a little shaky.

23

The dazed look on her face must have registered with Cora as her daughter gave her a broad grin when Thea poked her head around the living room door.

'Nice walk?'

Thea nodded. 'Great, thanks.' The expectant looks on her children's faces needed a better response, though, and she turned her full attention to the Christmas tree.

'You've done a brilliant job!' she exclaimed, taking in the coloured riot of lights, baubles, decorations the children had made at primary school and even further back in nursery, and the tinsel that they'd wrapped around the Christmas tree stand. She turned back to them. 'I don't think we've ever had such a lovely looking tree.'

Cora grinned at her. 'Thanks to your good friend, Nick, of course.'

'Yeah,' Thea admitted, 'but you've both done such a great job making it look so festive.' She slid an arm around them both. 'I feel really Christmassy, now.'

Cora handed her the angel, which was waiting patiently on the table. 'You can do the honours, Mum.'

Thea, touched, nodded. 'Let's do it together, like we always do.' They all put their hands on the angel and guided it to the top of the tree. Dylan had recently had a growth spurt, and Thea felt a pang when she realised she didn't have to lift him up for this particular family ritual any more. As she hooked the angel's cord over the top spur of the tree, she wondered how much longer they'd keep doing this. Someday, when they'd grown up and left home, Christmases might not be spent this way.

Shaking off that maudlin thought, she smiled down at them both. 'How about a massive mug of hot chocolate each, and I might even have a stash of marshmallows I've been saving for Christmas to float on top?'

The children whooped, and Thea went to the kitchen to make the drinks while they bickered over which film to watch.

Upon her return to the living room, Cora and Dylan had flumped on the sofa and were arguing the toss between the latest Marvel offering and a young-adult romcom. Thea took a sip of her own drink. 'Do I get a say?'

'Nope!' Cora and Dylan chorused. Shaking her head, she was about to toss a coin between them to settle it once and for all when Cora, who'd wrestled control of the remote from her brother again, grinned at Thea.

'What about this one? I remember watching it all the time when I was younger.'

Dylan groaned and buried his head under a cushion. 'Do we have to?'

Thea looked at the screen as the beautiful, slightly gangling form of Jennifer Garner peered out of the place card for the movie *13 Going on 30*. Along with *Wild Child,* it had been one of Thea's go-to films of her teenage years, and Cora had loved watching and rewatching it when she'd been younger, too. Thea felt a frisson of nostalgia when she pressed play, and the opening scenes unfolded.

'We'll watch your film straight afterwards, I promise, munchkin.'

Still grumbling, but mollified slightly, Dylan relented and snuggled onto the sofa with them. The familiar plot line unfolded, and Thea found herself wondering what she'd do if she got the chance to go back to being her younger self, as the leading character does at the end of the film. Would she have done anything differently? As ever, she knew she wouldn't be without her children, who were the centre of her life, but there were some things she wished she could change.

A long-forgotten memory drifted into her mind when she began to drowse on the sofa. A house party at Saints' Farm, a few too many shots of flavoured vodka and a clumsy, cherry-infused kiss with Nick at the top of the stairs. It had been the only kiss they'd ever shared, and she wasn't even sure if, twenty-odd years on, it had actually happened, but buried deep within her memory, she seemed to think it had. Certainly, neither of them had mentioned it afterwards, which had always made her wonder if she'd imagined it. Maybe, if they'd both been less drunk, maybe if they'd both been braver, things might have worked out differently...

Thea jerked up as her head started to nod. She'd been dimly aware that Cora had shifted away from her and was surreptitiously scrolling on her phone.

'Film not holding your attention?' she said softly, giving her daughter a playful nudge. She didn't miss the guilty look that passed over Cora's face before she hurriedly locked her phone again.

'Says you,' Cora shot back. 'You were dribbling on the cushion just now!'

'Was not!'

'Was too!'

'Shut uuuuuuup!' Dylan grumbled as the two of them continued in this vein for a few more seconds. Surprisingly, he'd become invested in the outcome of the film, and he hated to be disturbed once he'd got into something.

Thea duly did, as did Cora, and as Mark Ruffalo and Jennifer Garner completed their cosy romantic journey, Thea felt a combination of warmth and envy. You couldn't turn back time, but maybe there was still a way to make the future better.

Later on, when the kids had got themselves organised for school the next day, and she'd made sure both of their phones were charging in the kitchen, she noticed that Cora had put a new passcode on her phone. She'd never changed it before, and Thea had made it clear that a condition of having a phone was that Cora had to allow Thea access to check the phone's contents from time to time. She hadn't mentioned changing it, but perhaps one of her friends had found out the original code. Making a note to mention it to her daughter in the morning, she was just about to switch the lights off and go to bed herself when a notification buzzed from the Snapchat app on Cora's phone.

She knew she should just go to bed, but curiosity got the better of her. Walking back to where both children's phones were lying on the kitchen counter, she looked down at the screen before it went black.

What she saw there made her blood run cold and her hands start to shake.

It couldn't be.

Could it?

Not after all this time?

She didn't dare touch the phone in case she accidentally opened the message, so Thea just stared at the screen until it went dark of its own accord.

24

Breakfast in the Ashcombe household was never a great time to hold a discussion, as Thea spent most of it chivvying Dylan out of bed and encouraging Cora to eat something before they both left the house to catch the bus that stopped at the entrance to the estate. So, swallowing her disquiet about the Snapchat notification as well as a few mouthfuls of porridge, Thea tried to put it out of her mind until she'd have more time at the end of the day.

'Don't forget to switch everything off and lock the door!' she called up the stairs as she prepared to get to school. She'd initially been concerned about leaving Cora and Dylan to secure the house, but they'd proven to be reliable and responsible, and now she didn't think anything of leaving them to it in the morning. There had been the odd mishap where the 'Grandparent Taxi' had been called upon, after one or other of them had missed the bus, but Lorelai never minded, and these were few and far between.

At school, everyone was gearing up for the nativity plays, which were happening the next day. Thea was swept up in last minute coaching of lines, encouragement of the less confident members of her class and at least one reminder to go for a wee before the play started, to avoid accidents onstage. All in all, though, it was a hectic but rewarding day, and just what she needed to take her mind off the potential issues with Cora.

Driving home after a long afternoon, eyes nearly crossing from an abundance of end-of-term marking, she at last had time to think about what she was going to say to her daughter. It wasn't as if she'd been snooping on her phone, after all – the notification had appeared just as she'd been going to bed, and she hadn't opened the message. But the name on the notification had sent a shock through her she kept reliving, and every time she did, the what ifs and why-on-earths kept stacking up like the world's most sinister house of cards.

She thought about popping into the farm shop on the way home to get some biscuits to soften the impact of the conversation, but she stopped herself. She still didn't quite know what to say to Nick after the nearly-kiss on the doorstep yesterday, and she didn't feel as though she had the bandwidth to think more deeply about that while the potential issue with Cora was still playing on her mind. Her daughter had to come first.

Pulling into the driveway, she was relieved to hear the familiar thump-thump-thump of her daughter's current favourite song emanating from the slightly open window. Hopefully, they could sit and chat before dinner.

'Cora,' she called up the stairs as she closed the front door. 'Can you come down here a minute?'

Cora didn't respond verbally, but the music stopped and a few seconds later there were socked feet on the stairs. Thea nervously filled the kettle and set it to boil.

'Good day?' she asked as Cora sat herself at the kitchen table.

'All right,' Cora replied. 'You?'

'Not bad.'

Once the teas were in front of them, Thea knew she couldn't delay things any longer.

'So,' she began. 'You know you were on your phone during the film yesterday?'

Cora looked instantly defensive. 'It's not like we haven't seen it, like, a million times, Mum.'

'I know, I know,' Thea said hurriedly. 'And it's not really about that.' She fiddled with the handle of her tea mug, trying to find the right words to proceed. Cora had long gotten over that instantly defensive streak she'd developed at around aged eleven, but Thea also knew she had to tread carefully.

'Was there, um, anything you wanted to talk to me about?' Thea said gently. 'I mean, we've not had much of a chance to just sit down and chat lately, what with one thing and another.'

Cora shook her head. 'Nope. It's all good.' She paused, a glint in her eye. 'Unless you want to write me a note to get me out of PE tomorrow. The 3G pitch is well bad to play hockey on in the cold.'

Thea smiled slightly. 'It's character building, or so they say.' She tried again. 'You know you can talk to me about anything, right?'

Cora's *pull the other one* expression was neither a shock nor particularly upsetting. Thea well remembered her grandmother broaching this kind of conversation several times during her own adolescence, and her response being distinctly similar to Cora's own.

'Nothing to talk about,' Cora replied. 'Unless you want to talk to me about your massive crush on Nick Saint!'

Thea choked on her mouthful of tea. 'What?'

The knowing look on her daughter's face knocked Thea for six. 'I don't, I mean I haven't, I mean, even if I had...'

'Relax, Mum.' Cora grinned. 'It's fine. He's nice. Dylan and I really like him and it's obvious Nick likes you. Go for it.'

Thea sat up straighter in her chair. Her daughter, much like Ed, had the gift of the gab, and an instinctive ability to divert attention away from the focus of a discussion onto an area she wanted to talk about. It would serve her well in the future, but right now it was an irritating tactic.

Assuming her best schoolteacher's voice, Thea replied, 'I'm not talking about Nick with you, young lady. That's between him and me for now.'

'Oh, so there's is a "him and you", is there?'

'Enough.' Thea's patience, worn thin by the repetitive nature of the dress rehearsal for the nativity play, was almost at its limit. 'I need to talk to you about the message you got from that boy last night.'

Cora's face registered shock and then anger. 'You've been sneaking on my phone?'

Thea shook her head. 'No. But even if I had, that's my right as your mother. That was the deal, remember? I saw the Snapchat message flashing up just before I went to bed last night.'

Cora seemed to shrink in on herself. She suddenly looked much more like the little girl she used to be than the self-confident teenager she'd become over the past year. She dropped her gaze to her mug and, in a voice barely louder than a whisper, replied, 'I didn't want to tell you. I thought you'd be upset, or tell me not to speak to him...'

'How long have you been in contact with him?' Thea asked.

'Only since my birthday.'

Thea let out a long sigh. 'He must be younger than your brother, isn't he? That's much too young to have a Snapchat account.'

Cora's look of disbelief made Thea give a brief smile. 'OK, so I know that's not the main issue here, but even so, it's a fair point. I told you that you couldn't get one until you were thirteen. It would seem he's not been given the same, er, boundaries.'

'He's called Ben and he's a year younger than Dylan,' Cora replied. 'And before you say it, he's definitely who he says he is.'

'How can you be sure, darling? You've only been in touch with him for a week.'

'He sent me some pictures of himself,' Cora replied.

'That doesn't prove anything.' Thea could feel her frustrations rising. 'He could have generated them from anywhere.'

Cora shook her head. 'No. He's legit.'

'Can I see them?'

Cora's face showed she was weighing up the options. 'All right.' She reached for her phone and scrolled through her photo gallery. 'Look. See.'

Thea took the phone from her daughter, and as she saw the image Cora had selected, she experienced such a flood of different emotions, she wasn't quite sure where to start. There was a picture of the boy, and standing next to him was someone else. Someone who Thea realised had moved on with his life, if this picture was anything to go by.

'All right,' she said softly. 'I believe you. The question is, what happens next?'

'I was hoping you could tell me, Mum,' Cora said, and then, much to Thea's shock and heartbreak, her daughter started to cry.

25

'Well, I won't say I haven't missed you, sis!' Nick said as Annabelle's smiling, tanned face appeared around the front door of the shop on Monday evening. It was closing time, and Nick was itching to get away, and had already stowed the produce from outside safely in the doorway.

'I've missed you, too,' Annabelle replied as she came around the counter and gave him a hug. 'I couldn't resist popping in before tomorrow to make sure the place is still standing.'

'As you can see, it most definitely is.' Nick tried not to feel put out. Annabelle was only ribbing him, but he felt as though he'd done more than enough over the past two weeks to keep the shop on an even keel, especially with the film crew.

'Perhaps I ought to go away more often,' Annabelle teased. She looked rested, relaxed and as if the holiday had done her a lot of good.

'Nah,' he replied. 'Place wasn't the same without you glaring at me.'

Annabelle grinned. 'Well, it'll be business as usual from tomorrow, anyway, so you can relax for a bit.' She paused. 'How did things work out, staffing wise, while I was away? Did Thea get the hang of things?'

'Yeah,' Nick replied enthusiastically. 'Thea was great. I'm so glad she agreed to cover a couple of days or I'd really have been pushed, especially since the agency couldn't get anyone out here at such short notice.'

Annabelle regarded him speculatively. 'Must have been nice... having Thea around all the time.'

Nick didn't rise to Annabelle's unspoken insinuation. 'It was nice to have her helping out, yes. She's a good friend.'

'I know.' Annabelle's eyes met his. 'It's nice to think of the two of you getting close again.' She paused, before adding, 'you've always had a bit of a thing for Thea, haven't you? I mean, out of all of the group, she's the one you'd do pretty much anything for.'

'Like I said, she's a good friend, and she means a lot to me,' Nick said firmly. 'History counts for a lot, you know.'

'I know,' Annabelle replied. 'But, oh, I don't know, don't you ever wonder if, now that she's finally moved back to the village, you should make a move once and for all? Just so you know for sure if she likes you, too?'

'Christ, you sound like Mum!' Nick snapped. 'And you make me sound like a right pathetic loser. It's not like I've been pining for Thea all these years.' He'd had his fair share of relationships; admittedly nothing serious since Thea had moved into Observatory Field, but that didn't mean he was holding out for her... just that he hadn't met the right person yet.

Nick could feel Annabelle's eyes on him, and winced when she added, 'Well, super stud, if you weren't going to make a move on Thea when she was right under your nose, did you decide to pick up where you left off with Tally, then, since she was down this way again?' She laughed. 'Come on, Nick, I've been in a gossip-free zone for two weeks... spill the tea!'

'Tally's not my type,' Nick muttered. 'Not any more.'

'What, a gorgeous, confident, independent, creative woman isn't for you? Jesus, Nick, what *are* you actually looking for?'

'Not that!' Nick could feel himself getting irritated, and his sister hadn't been back in the country for more than a few hours. 'She's great, but she's not...'

'She's not Thea?' Annabelle suggested gently. 'Seriously, Nick, you've got to get Thea out of your system. Either ask her out or give it up.'

'It's all right for you,' Nick countered, still irritated. 'You and Jamie have always been the perfect couple. Ever since school, he loved you and you loved him. You never had anything to lose.'

'That's not true,' Annabelle retorted. 'We've had our ups and downs, as you well know. But we've never been anything other than honest with each other. You need to be honest with yourself, and with Thea, if you're ever going to move forward.'

'How can I be honest? If I tell her how I really feel, it'll end our friendship for good, and I can't take that risk.'

'Not necessarily.' Annabelle's voice grew calmer again. 'I mean, you've been mates for thirty years – who's to say she doesn't want to try taking things to another level? You've always got on well together.'

'That's exactly why I can't say anything to her,' Nick said. 'What if she never wanted to speak to me again? I can't lose her friendship if what I'm feeling really is one-sided.'

Annabelle sighed. 'I don't think you need to worry too much about that.'

'What do you mean?'

Pulling out her phone, Annabelle tapped the WhatsApp icon and scrolled to Thea's name. 'I probably shouldn't be showing you this, but if it helps you to make up your mind...'

Nick's breath hitched in his throat as he read the exchange.

'Shit...' he murmured. 'I mean, we sort of talked things through after it happened, but I didn't know she was quite so pissed off about it.'

'Well, now you do.'

Annabelle looked him square in the face again. 'And, just because I think I really need to spell this out for you, don't you think, if she was that upset, you might not have much to lose if you just fronted up to her and told her how you *really* feel?'

Before he had the chance to reply, Annabelle had slipped her phone back in her pocket and was heading for the front door. 'Don't forget to put the till drawer in the safe before you go,' she called to him. 'I'll see you in the morning.'

Nick shook his head. When he and Thea had talked about the mistletoe incident, she'd seemed more upset about it than someone who wanted just to be friends would be. And, there *had* been a few times since then, especially after the walk in the woods on Sunday, that had made him think. Perhaps he had been missing the signs after all. There was only one thing to do; he'd have to level with Thea. He didn't know when, and he wasn't sure how, but Annabelle was right: he certainly couldn't go on like this.

It was time to lock up for the evening. He closed the front doors and headed into the back office to deposit the till drawer in the safe. As he was heading out of the back door, he glanced at the pile of post on the desk. There wasn't anything that demanded his immediate attention, but there was something he'd been happily ignoring for the past couple of weeks. The fancy, cream coloured envelope contained an invitation that usually he'd just pass onto Annabelle, but he knew for a fact that she'd had her own invite and so had their parents. He hadn't bothered to do anything about it, since Annabelle had 'fessed up she'd RSVP'd on behalf of the whole family a couple of weeks back, so he was obliged to put in an appearance. He'd have to dig out his dinner suit, since the event was black tie, but at least it should still fit him.

Switching off the lights in the back office, he headed home to his cottage. He tried not to think about when he might see Thea again; now Annabelle was back, she'd finished working at the shop, which he felt sad about. He hadn't spoken to Annabelle yet about potentially employing Thea after Christmas on a more permanent basis, and he made up his mind to discuss it with her and the rest of the family during the break. As he drew up outside his house, he realised he'd been on autopilot all the time he'd been driving home; he had absolutely no memory of getting there at all.

26

'Hey Gran!'

Thea let herself in through the utility room door of Night-shade Cottage and headed through to the kitchen. Lorelai called back from the living room, and after making them both a cuppa, Thea mooched on through.

'How did the nativity play go?' Lorelai asked as Thea kicked off her shoes and got comfy on the sofa.

'Really well.' Thea smiled. 'Only one member of Reception class forgot their lines and the angels' haloes all stayed on, so I count that as a win.'

'Oh, I remember seeing you and Tristan in your tea towels and tunics, back in the day,' Lorelai said, a faint trace of nostalgia in her voice. 'Tristan hated every minute of it, but you were a natural star. I could have sworn you were bound for the stage, from that moment on!'

Thea laughed. 'I've still got the picture the school took of the two of us. Tris looked like he was going to rip the head off the Baby Jesus doll, and I was blowing kisses to you and Uncle Phillip in the audience.' She was tickled that her gran remembered the event differently, having recently laughed, herself, with Nick about her brother's melodramatic tendencies.

They chatted amiably about the children and firmed up a few Christmas plans before Thea worked up the courage to broach the subject she'd come to talk about with Lorelai. She'd been flummoxed by Cora's admission last night, and while she'd assured Cora that they'd find a way through, she really needed to talk to her grandmother about what that way might be.

'So, you know I let Cora finally set up some social media accounts on her birthday?' she began.

Lorelai looked briefly concerned. 'Are you sure that was wise, dear? I hear such terrible things about social media these days. I know it's a part of life, but she seems awfully young at the moment to have an account of her own.'

'All of her friends have them, Gran, and I'm still policing her every move on that phone of hers, so hopefully it'll be all right.' Thea paused. 'The thing is, someone's got in touch with her, and I'm not quite sure what to do about it.'

'Who is it?'

It was crunch time. Thea took a deep breath. 'Her half-brother.'

Lorelai put the mug she was holding down on the coffee table with a thud. 'Come again?'

'Her ten-year-old half-brother. And you'd better believe that I was just as flabbergasted as you were when she told me that.'

'But... *how? When?*'

'Pretty bloody soon after Ed and I split, it would seem.'

'Oh, darling.' Lorelai went to hug Thea, but she shook her head.

'It's fine, Gran. I mean, it's not like we haven't been separated for years. It's just a bit of a shock that he's chosen to get in touch now. That he's aware that he has a half-sister. That bloody, frig-

ging Ed never saw fit to tell me he's started a whole new family!'
Thea felt a spark of anger. It wasn't that she wanted Ed back – he
was a destructive influence, and she knew she was far better off
without him in her life; it was more that he hadn't had the courtesy to let her know that there was now at least one more child to
consider in their complicated family dynamic.

'What do you intend to do about this... connection?' Lorelai
asked as Thea paused.

Thea shook her head. 'I really don't know, Gran. I mean, what
can I do? These kids have made a link over Snapchat, and it
would be so easy just to tell her to block him, but that doesn't
seem fair. The trouble is, I've no way of contacting Ed directly.
The last mobile number I had for him doesn't work, and he
deleted his Facebook account when we split up.' She gave a
mirthless laugh. 'I don't even know where he's living any more.'

'And you're sure this boy is who he says he is?'

'I've seen some of the photos he's sent Cora.' Thea sighed. 'He's
the spitting image of Ed, with a little bit of Dylan thrown in for good
measure. And in one of them, he's standing next to Ed.' Inexplicably,
her eyes filled with tears, and she rubbed them in irritation. 'It's not
that I'm hurt, exactly, but I'd have appreciated some indication from
Ed that he'd started a new family. I mean, when we separated, I still
expected he'd maintain contact with the kids, but when he didn't, I
hoped it would be for the best. He was in a bad place, and I was so
angry about all the money we'd lost that a clean break seemed like
the right thing to do. He had enough to sort out by himself, and
when he didn't keep in touch, even with the kids, I didn't push it.
Now, it feels as though he, through this boy, has come waltzing back
into our lives on his own terms, with no warning, and I'm expected
to pick up the pieces, like I always had to when we were together.'

Lorelai reached out a hand and squeezed one of Thea's. 'You

looked after your family after he nearly destroyed it,' she said gently. 'You've been so strong, Thea. But if this young boy is who he says he is and wants to get in touch with his half-sister and brother, you need to think about how that might work in practice. It means you and Ed will probably have to come face to face again and come to some agreement about how that's going to work.'

'It's early days, Gran,' Thea replied. 'And who knows how this is all going to turn out? You know what kids are like. One minute they're sending messages left, right and centre and the next they don't speak for weeks.' She paused, feeling ashamed of herself for the thought that this young boy might disappear as abruptly as he'd arrived in Cora's life.

'But that doesn't mean he won't try to get in touch another time,' Lorelai said reasonably. 'And that could be when Cora's more independent than she is already. It might be a good idea to make contact, proper contact, now, while you've at least got some say in the matter. In the blink of an eye, she'll be off to university, or leaving home, and you won't have any say.'

Thea hated it when her grandmother talked sense, but she knew it was also what she needed. 'You're right.' She sipped her tea. 'Much as it galls me, I suppose, if the kids are interested in meeting each other, then Ed and I need to start communicating too. I just wish it wasn't happening so quickly.'

'I'm sure you'll do the right thing, love,' Lorelai said. 'And if Ed's got any sense, he'll try to make this as painless as possible for you all.'

'Ed wasn't exactly great at painless.' Thea rolled her eyes. 'The man I knew, at the end, would have done anything to get another fix.'

'People do change, you know,' Lorelai observed. 'And no one's suggested that you have to be too cordial with Ed. But for the sake of the children involved...'

'I know, I know,' Thea interjected. 'We'll all have to behave like adults. I just hope Ed realises that, too.'

'So what are you going to say to Cora and Dylan, then?'

Thea sighed. 'I suppose I've got no other choice than to let them meet their half-brother, if they want to. And if that means getting back in touch with Ed, then that's a price I'll have to pay.'

Lorelai leaned forward and squeezed Thea's hand again. 'Good girl,' she said. 'But try to put that out of your mind until after Christmas. You've got enough on your plate, and this isn't going anywhere.'

Thea smiled at her grandmother. She'd learned a lot about compartmentalising things from Lorelai, who could juggle many things simultaneously without dropping any of them. Perhaps Lorelai was right: nothing would happen immediately, and she had plenty of time to work out the best way to proceed.

'Cora did pop in and see me on the way home tonight,' Lorelai said, after both of them had taken another sip of their tea. 'She didn't mention any of what you've just told me, but she did say a couple of other things.'

Thea's heart sped up a little. 'What did she tell you?'

Lorelai gave her a warm smile. 'This and that. Mostly how happy she is that you and Nick Saint seem to be getting on so well.'

'Nick and I are... well, to be honest, I'm not quite sure what we are.' She paused and looked away, slightly embarrassed, from her grandmother's gaze. 'But whatever it is... it's nice.'

'Glad to hear it.' Lorelai let the words hang in the air. It was an old trick of hers, from when Tristan and Thea were teenagers and she wanted to know more but was too clever to probe for details. 'It's good to see you happy, Thea. It's also nice to know you and Nick have been getting closer again.'

Thea smiled at her grandmother. 'Yeah. We have been spending a bit of time together lately.'

Lorelai smiled. 'That's nice to hear. You seemed to sidle around each other when you were teenagers, and I always wondered if there was ever going to be more to it. Whatever my differences of opinion with his father over Observatory Field, Nick was raised well, and he's always had a soft spot for you.' Lorelai had had a few run-ins with Robert Saint when the housing development had been approved, and although they were on more cordial terms again these days, the history ran deep.

'It's not as if he's been pining for me,' Thea said quickly. 'He's had a whole other life, and a whole set of girlfriends, and I've had two kids, for heaven's sake!'

Lorelai gave Thea a long look. 'Don't cut yourself off from potential happiness just because Ed might reappear like some deranged genie. You mustn't conflate these two things happening in your life. Nick's a good boy, and he's fond of you. If something happens and it makes you happy, then let it happen.'

'Nothing's happened, Gran!' Thea protested. She wasn't quite prepared to admit how pleasurably confusing the near misses with Nick had been. 'But I promise you, if it does, you'll be the first to know.' She finished her tea and kissed her grandmother goodbye. She always felt better after spending time with Lorelai, and she left Nightshade Cottage smiling.

27

Nick was in sore need of wise counsel after the revelation from Annabelle about the text from Thea, but he was fed up with going around in circles with Annabelle herself. She meant well, and she was probably right, but she couldn't help but be in big sister mode whenever they discussed things like this. What Nick needed, he decided with a rueful grin, was advice from a bloke. He toyed with the idea of ringing up his best mate, Andy, but then remembered he'd taken some time off to take his wife and children on a last-minute trip to London before Christmas properly hit, and he didn't want to disturb them. Nick's dad would just take the Mickey out of him for taking so long to get his act together about Thea, and his best mate, Tristan, was out of the question, being Thea's twin brother. That left only one option, and even that felt a bit incestuous. He really didn't know where else to turn, though. So, swallowing down his embarrassment, once Annabelle had arrived to do her morning shift at the farm shop, Nick made an excuse to get out of her way, and drove straight round to Mistletoe Barn, where Jamie, an agricultural land agent, was working in his office, a converted outbuilding in the corner of the garden.

Nick knew Jamie had a quiet morning and wasn't due to visit a client until after lunch, so, ringing him on the way, he was relieved when Jamie poked his head out of the office door.

'Back door's open,' he called across the garden. 'Let yourself in and stick the coffee machine on. I'm gagging for a caffeine hit. The jet lag's catching up with me and I need something to get through the afternoon, sorting out the conveyancing for Jim Philpott's smallholding over Everscombe way.'

After a couple of minutes, Jamie joined him in the kitchen and, while he sorted out a plate of biscuits and the mugs, Nick stuck to small talk. Jamie, though, with the perceptiveness that came from having known Nick almost as long as Thea had, cut to the chase once snacks and drinks were well on the way.

'So, what's really on your mind, mate?' Jamie poured them both a mug of coffee from the drip percolator and brought the mugs to the kitchen island, where Nick was sitting on one of the bar stools.

Nick added a generous slug of double cream from the jug on the island before he replied, 'How do you know there's something on my mind?'

Grinning, Jamie added cream and a heaped teaspoon of sugar to his own mug. 'Don't tell Annie – she thinks I'm cutting down.'

'Your secret's safe with me,' Nick replied. 'How's it, er, all going?'

Jamie raised an eyebrow. 'I won't bore you with the details, but we're taking it one day at a time.' Nick watched as his brother-in-law sipped his coffee. He noticed the uncharacteristic look of sadness on Jamie's face, and realised, for the first time, just how hard Annabelle's miscarriage had been on him, as well as his sister.

'But the holiday helped?'

'Yes, absolutely.' Jamie's face brightened. 'It was great just to get away from this place for a bit, you know. Annie's been working so hard, and she didn't really give herself enough time to recover after the...' Jamie paused and dropped his gaze. Nick watched him swallow hard before he looked up again. 'It hit us both pretty hard.'

'I can't imagine how painful it must have been,' Nick said softly. His heart ached for them. The loss of a much-wanted baby had been a terrible thing; he remembered feeling so nervous about talking to both Jamie and Annabelle in the immediate aftermath, but Annabelle, with her first instinct to always consider everyone else, had made it easier for him to give her support, even in the midst of her own, terrible sadness and grief. He wished he was half as good at putting people at ease as she was.

'But you didn't come here to talk to me about all that,' Jamie said, a brisker tone to his voice. 'You're good at deflecting attention away from yourself. What's on your mind? Is it that blonde from the film crew again?'

Nick shook his head. 'Nothing happened. She got the wrong end of the stick and thought there was more to it than there was, this time.'

Jamie gave a wry smile. 'Probably just as well,' he said. 'After all, she doesn't stand a chance against that massive flaming torch you're carrying for Thea, does she?'

'What?' Nick made the mistake of inhaling his coffee, and spluttered some of it back out on the pristine white marble topped counter of the kitchen island. Grabbing a paper towel from the reel that sat to one side of him, he hurriedly mopped it up, glad of the distraction. He'd wanted to talk to Jamie about just that, but he was blindsided by his brother-in-law's directness.

'Nick, mate, I've known you for as long as I've known Annie,' Jamie said, a gentler tone in his voice. 'And if there's one thing that's been bleeding obvious for all that time, it's that on-again-off-again thing you keep having about Thea.' He gave a laugh. 'It's not so much a torch you're carrying as a string of dodgy solar lights, flashing around your neck, right above your heart!'

'Thanks,' Nick muttered. 'Now I really do feel like some sad stalker.'

'Well, what are you going to do about it?' Jamie grabbed the coffee mugs and gave them both a rapid refill. 'Have you ever actually told her how you feel?'

Nick paused to take back his mug before answering. 'Nope. Don't want to risk it. Even with those texts Thea sent Annie, it doesn't mean Thea actually wants to make us more than friends. She could just have been really pissed off.'

'Pull the other one, mate' – Jamie passed Nick his new mug – 'no one sends WhatsApps like that unless they're a tiny bit jealous. I'd say you've as good a shot as anyone.'

Nick put his mug down and sighed. 'We've known each other for too long. It would be weird to actually ask her out now. People don't do that, do they? Not when there's as much history as we've got. And what if she said no? I'd never be able to look her in the eye again.'

'So, you do have a thing for her, then?' Jamie grinned. 'Annie'll go nuts when I tell her you've finally admitted to it!'

'Oh, fuck off,' Nick said good-naturedly. 'You tell her, and I'll make sure you're on chauffeur duty for that shindig up at Cherry Tree Court this weekend instead of me.'

'Speaking of... have you decided who your plus one's going to be for that? Would be a shame to fly solo. I mean, especially when the answer might be right in front of you.' Jamie raised an eyebrow.

Nick paused before answering. It wasn't as if the idea hadn't occurred to him already, but he didn't want to give Jamie the satisfaction of thinking he'd come up with it first. 'Maybe.'

'Mate.' Jamie's voice was suddenly a lot gentler. 'If there's one thing I've learned over the past year or so, it's that you have to take each day as it comes. I know you're worried about being rejected, but it might be time you put your big boy pants on and took the plunge. You've been on your own for a while now and hankering after someone just because you're too scared to know one way or the other if they feel the same way seems to be a bit of a wuss move, to me.'

'Says the man who's been with the same woman since he was sixteen,' Nick shot back. 'It's all right for you; you've got Annabelle and this life, and soon, with a bit of luck, you'll be starting a new family. You haven't had to take a risk for ages.'

Jamie shook his head. 'Perhaps,' he said, 'but that all comes with its own challenges. And unless you take a risk and see how Thea feels about you, you're going to end up always wondering what might have been. Are you all right with that, for the rest of your life?'

'Oh, don't be so melodramatic,' Nick snapped. 'My life is fine, thank you very much. I'm perfectly happy with things the way they are.' He put his coffee cup down. 'And speaking of, I'd better get back to work. I promised Annie I'd give her a hand with the Christmas shutdown stock take so we could all get away from the shop for a few days over the holiday.'

'For what it's worth, I think you should ask her. You can't go on being a martyr to your own love life forever, Saint Nick.'

'Don't call me that,' Nick shot back over his shoulder as he left. 'It was a stupid nickname in school and it's even dafter now.'

'Blame your mum and dad.' Jamie grinned at him. Despite

himself, Nick grinned back. 'They really didn't think when they put that on the paperwork, did they?'

As Nick drove back to Saints' Farm, he couldn't help wondering about the Midwinter's Eve Ball at Cherry Tree Court. Maybe it would fly with Thea if he framed the invitation as a simple thank you. And if it turned into more than that? His palms grew a little clammy on the steering wheel. Either way, perhaps it was worth the risk.

28

'So did you ask her?' Annabelle hissed on Friday afternoon as Thea disappeared behind the bakery shelf.

'Ask who what?' Nick, who knew all too well, played for time. He'd seen Thea coming in, and she looked stressed. He didn't want to add to her problems.

'You know damned well who and what,' Annabelle replied. 'Just get on with it or I'll—' She turned her attention away from him as Thea re-emerged and walked to the counter. 'Oh, hi, Thea. How are you doing?'

'Fine, thanks,' Thea replied, but to Nick's attentive eye it still looked as though she had something on her mind. 'How are you? How was the holiday?'

Annabelle beamed. 'It was fabulous and thank you so much for covering at such short notice. I really appreciate it, and I know Nick does, too.' Nick saw her glancing at him. 'I hope he told you that.'

Thea looked at him, and he felt his heart skipping around merrily in his chest as she did. When would that *ever* stop happening, he wondered. 'He did.' This time her smile seemed more heartfelt. 'And to be honest, he did me a favour. The extra cash'll come in handy over Christmas.'

'Well, I'm sure we could find you a more permanent job if you wanted one,' Annabelle replied. 'From what Nick's told me, you were brilliant behind the counter and in the rest of the shop.'

'He's being very kind,' Thea said, but Nick could see she was pleased to hear the compliment. 'He had to show me a fair few times how the till worked!'

'Oh, it takes a bit of getting used to,' Annabelle said airily as she started to ring up Thea's purchases. 'Do you, er, need a hand taking these out to the car?'

'Thanks, but I'm sure I'll be fine,' Thea replied, then slapped her forehead. 'Oh, bugger, I forgot, Gran's asked me to pick up a bag of the Somerset Ruby spuds as well. She's cooking Christmas dinner for us all and she forgot to get some when she came in last week. Can you put a bag through, and I'll grab one on the way out?'

'Sure.' Annabelle smiled at Nick, and he knew what she was going to say next. 'And don't worry about lugging them out. Nick'll take them to the car for you. Wouldn't want you putting your back out this close to Christmas, would we?'

'Oh, I can manage,' Thea said.

'Don't be daft.' Nick finally spoke, and to his relief, his voice wasn't shaking, even though his palms were sweating, and his stomach was flipping like a pancake. 'I'll go and grab a bag for you.'

Thea's smile made his nerves even worse. Why was he behaving like a lovestruck fifteen-year-old? He'd worked alongside Thea for three weeks and hadn't felt like this.

'Well, get a move on, little brother.' Annabelle gestured. 'That sack of spuds won't carry itself.'

'Yeah, right, OK.' Nick hurried out from behind the counter

towards the front of the store where the paper sacks of potatoes were. 'I'll, er, see you at the car.'

'Thanks.' Thea smiled at him again. Nick picked up the pace before he could put himself through the torture of eavesdropping on the rest of the two women's conversation. He didn't want to be mortified by his sister's attempts to matchmake. Hefting a twenty-kilogram bag of Somerset's best potatoes over his shoulder, he spotted Thea's Volvo in the car park and made a beeline for it.

'Sorry.' A voice came from behind him as he put the bag down by the boot of the Volvo. 'It's so old, it doesn't have central locking, or a key zapper!'

'It's fine,' Nick replied, turning around to see Thea approaching with the rest of her shopping. 'I'm used to lugging stuff around all day, anyway! And I'm in no rush to get back behind the counter. Annabelle's been nagging non-stop.'

'Oh yeah?' Thea's smile made Nick's breath shorten again. 'About what?'

Realising he'd nearly dropped himself in it, Nick back-pedalled furiously. 'Oh, nothing, really, just stuff to do with the business. She's very particular about the way she likes things done, and I don't think I quite kept everything to her standards while she and Jamie were away.'

'Oh God, I hope it wasn't anything I did – or didn't do.' Thea looked worried, and Nick mentally kicked himself. 'You didn't get into trouble on my account, did you?'

'No, no, nothing like that,' Nick said hurriedly. 'I, er, I mean, I kind of said I'd do something, and I didn't, and now she's on my case about it...'

'So what was it, then?' Thea asked. Nick was sure he wasn't imagining a trace of amusement in her voice, which made him even more self-conscious. 'Anything I can help with?'

'Well...' He started to shuffle on the spot and forced his feet to stay still. 'Actually, there is something, but feel free to say no, and I don't want to be weird about it, and really it's all right if you don't want to, and—'

'Nick.' Thea's voice cut gently through his nervous chatter. 'You know you can ask me anything. Just tell me what's on your mind.'

Sensing that it was now or never, that this moment might give him an answer he'd been searching for ever since he'd reconnected with Thea properly, he steeled himself. Whatever she said next, at least he'd be secure in the knowledge that he'd done something.

'Well,' he said carefully, 'I've been meaning to ask you something.'

Thea's brow wrinkled endearingly. 'Yeah? What is it?'

Nick took a deep breath. 'I've been invited to the Midwinter's Eve Ball tomorrow night at Cherry Tree Court, and I was, er, wondering if maybe you'd like to go with me? The invitation's for me and a plus one, and I know it's rather short notice, but I've been trying to pluck up the courage to text you about it ever since we did the Christmas market together.' He rubbed the back of his head, the nerves starting to get to him again. 'I mean, it's perfectly fine if you've got other plans, and to be honest, I'd understand if you did, it being tomorrow night and everything, but I promised Annabelle I'd at least ask you so that I said I had and—'

'Nick.' Thea's voice interrupted, just as gently as it had before. He raised his gaze from where it had been firmly planted on the ground by his feet, and as he did so, he realised that Thea had put her shopping bag down and was standing right in front of him. So close, in fact, that he could smell the sweet, floral scent of the perfume he'd begun to associate with her when she'd been working alongside him at the shop. It made his senses reel.

'Yeah?'

Thea moved a little closer, until she was properly in his space. With anyone else it would have felt intrusive but somehow having her that close to him felt deliciously right. She raised her eyes to meet his, and as she did so, a smile stole over her lips.

'I'd love to go with you to the Midwinter's Eve Ball,' she murmured.

Her words took a second or two to register, but as they did, Nick felt a huge grin spreading over his face, and a warmth flooded his cheeks.

'Really?'

'Really.'

Thea's face turned upwards and, as their eyes met fleetingly, it was only a split second before their lips lightly touched. The sweet, soft pressure of her mouth on his felt so right, all thoughts and doubts floated away for the few seconds that the kiss lasted. He was reminded of the almost-kiss on her doorstep and how frustrating it had been to be so close and yet so far. He slid his arms around her, and felt a warm surge of excitement when she moved even closer to him. The kiss felt years in the making, and so absolutely right that he never wanted it to end.

'Pick me up at seven?' she said as they eventually stepped back from each other.

'Yeah. I mean, yes, sure, absolutely.'

'See you tomorrow, then.'

'I'm looking forward to it.'

Nick was so flummoxed by how quickly and easily Thea had agreed to be his plus one, and even more so by the fact that they'd ended up kissing that it wasn't until he got back to the shop, he realised he hadn't offered to help her put her shopping in the car.

As he approached the counter, Annabelle gave him a sly smile.

'She said yes, then.'

Nick nodded. 'She said yes.'

'Don't screw this up, little brother,' Annabelle added. 'And for God's sake don't be late. That waste of space partner of hers never went anywhere on time, and Thea doesn't need reminding of that.'

'I'll keep that in mind,' Nick said absently. Wandering off to make himself and Annabelle their customary afternoon cuppa, he wondered whether or not he should slip something stronger into his own tea, just to stop his hands from shaking.

29

'So he just came out with it, while carrying a bag of spuds? And then you kissed him?' Charlotte's laughter echoed down the phone, and Thea felt herself blushing.

'Well, to be fair, he'd put the potato sack down by that point, but yeah, just like that.'

Thea had phoned Charlotte when she'd got back, in need of some advice. She'd also checked with Lorelai that she'd be able to babysit at short notice the following evening. Lorelai had said yes, much to Thea's relief. She was actually happy enough to leave Cora in charge of her little brother, since the ball was only a mile down the road, but she'd asked Lorelai to come over just in case. Cora had been a little put out, but since it was Thea's first date in ages, the girl had eventually seen her mother's point of view. And Cora and Lorelai enjoyed each other's company; the teenager shared the same sense of humour as her grandmother and the same taste in films, too. Given that both of them also had a keen interest in Thea's love life, she knew they'd have plenty to talk about.

Thea mooched over to the living room mirror and glanced at her reflection. Her light brown hair, the same shade as Tristan's, was too long, and the bags under her eyes could have rivalled the shopping bags she'd just unpacked. Not to mention the fact she hadn't shaved her legs in months. 'I've got a bit of work to do to make myself presentable for a posh do at Cherry Tree Court,' she said, half to herself, half to Charlotte, who was still on the line. 'And God only knows what I'm going to wear. The last time I went to a black tie do was when Dylan was a toddler, and he's eleven now!'

Charlotte's tinkle of laughter came down the phone. 'Well, you're asking the wrong person for ideas! I live in jeans and T-shirts, and I can't remember the last time I had a proper haircut, either. We can be two scruff bags together amongst the great and good of the Midwinter's Eve Ball.' She paused and then added, 'Do you fancy getting ready together? I mean, I'm not queen of style, but at least we could get a second opinion.'

Thea grinned. She'd got to know Charlotte well over the time she'd been in a relationship with Tristan, and the thought of a bit of moral support before the ball was a very appealing one. 'Sure. Do you want to come over here tomorrow, late afternoon, and we can pool our resources?'

'Sounds good,' Charlotte replied. 'And I'm counting on Cora to be able to sort out our hair and makeup, if she's willing. She always looks so great when she does her own.' Thea heard Charlotte giving an envious sigh. 'Oh, to have had access to YouTube beauty tutorials when I was a teenager. How things might have been different!'

'You turned out all right,' Thea said. She was still flummoxed by her thirteen-year-old daughter's skills with a cosmetic brush, and quite unsure how she felt about Cora leaving the house with quite so much eyeliner on, and as for the false eyelashes... 'But I'm sure she'd be more than happy to help us out, if bribed substantially.'

'I'll bring cash and a big box of Krispy Kreme donuts,' Charlotte said confidently. 'Good job I'm working in the archive today, so I can pop down to Cabot Circus after work and grab some supplies.' Charlotte spent most of her time in the Department of Astronomy and Astrophysics at University of North West Wessex, which was about an hour's drive from the house she shared with Tristan in Taunton.

'She'll love you forever if you get the ones with sprinkles,' Thea laughed. 'And so will Dylan. You'll be in the top auntie spot for the rest of the decade!'

'Duly noted,' Charlotte replied. 'Er, do you want me to pick up anything for you?'

'No, I'm all good.' But even as she said it, her heart sank. Her makeup was at least ten years old, and she still didn't have a clue what to wear. Somewhere, in the back of her wardrobe, was her old standby, a knee-skimming little black dress, but she hadn't taken it off its hanger for so long, she wasn't sure if it would still fit. It was too late to Amazon Prime something, and by the time she got to Taunton or Minehead, the two nearest towns, the shops would be shut. In desperation, she tried to think of where she could nip out to on Saturday morning. Saying goodbye to Charlotte, she ended the call and started googling for shops nearby that wouldn't break the bank. Her finances were still precarious, and going to be even more so in January, so she couldn't afford to splash the cash on something she wasn't likely to wear again.

Then, she had a brainwave. It was a long shot, but sometimes, long shots paid off. And if she got there before it closed, she'd still have time to nip elsewhere.

'Cora, Dylan, I'm just popping out,' she called up the stairs. 'I'll be back in about half an hour. Call if you need me.'

'OK,' two voices, probably roused from watching things on their phones, called back. Grabbing her bag and car keys, Thea headed out again, hoping that where she had in mind might just save her bacon.

30

The Christmas party gods must have been smiling as Thea pulled up outside the shop, into a parking space that had just been vacated. She was well used to finding solutions under pressure: fifteen years in the primary school classroom had taught her that, and she was hopeful that she'd be able to find one now. Locking the car, she hurried towards the front door, where the staff of the Purrfect Paws Rescue charity shop looked as though they were beginning to wind down for the day.

'It's an emergency!' Thea panted as she pushed open the door to see Mollie Wakefield straightening shelves and putting things away tidily after another day's trading.

'What can I do for you?' Mollie asked. 'I've got those Pokémon cards for Dylan, if you still want them.'

'Thanks, Moll, but I think it's probably best if he comes in himself tomorrow and takes a look at them – I never know which ones he has and hasn't got these days!' She smiled at Mollie, before adding, 'I'm actually here for myself. I need a posh frock for tomorrow night, pronto.'

Mollie smiled. 'Let me guess... the Midwinter's Eve Ball up at Cherry Tree Court?'

'Yup.' Thea began to browse the racks of dresses that lined the right-hand side of the wall. 'I, er, had a last-minute invitation, and by last minute I mean literally an hour ago, and I haven't got anything to wear.'

'Well, I'm sure we can find you something.' Mollie started to bustle around, glancing back at Thea now and again, as if gauging what would suit and fit her. After a minute or two, she came back with an armful of possibilities. Thea, who was feeling overwhelmed by the rows of densely packed dresses, felt grateful. Mollie prided herself on being the personal shopper of the charity shop world, and she had a great eye for it.

'Why don't you start with these?' Mollie said, handing Thea the hangers. 'And don't rush – there's plenty more out the back that haven't made it to the shop floor yet!'

'Thanks so much, Mollie,' Thea replied, hurrying to the small changing room in the corner of the shop. She trusted the woman's judgement, ever since Mollie had found her the perfect dress for her job interview at the primary school a couple of years ago. That was what had triggered her desire to move back to Lower Brambleton, and the pleasing circularity of this logic made her smile. Perhaps Mollie's keen eye would lead to something new this time, too?

Slipping off her clothes, Thea stepped into the first of the dresses that Mollie had found for her. Sadly, the red chiffon number was the wrong length for her, its waist sitting too high up to be flattering, so she put it carefully back onto the hanger and onto the 'rejected' hook. Several others followed, one a close contender with its black velvet, fitted shape and sultry silhouette, but the zip wouldn't go the final inch, so regrettably it had to join the others.

Finally, there was one option left. Feeling her heart sink that, perhaps this time Mollie couldn't work a miracle, Thea slipped the dress over her head and pulled it down carefully. The midnight blue velvet slithered down to just above her ankles, encasing her body voluptuously with just the right amount of stretch. Its Bardot neckline skimmed her collarbones and, as she reached behind her to pull up the zip, she caught sight of her reflection in the mirror. Even in the harsh light of the changing room, she had to admit the dress looked great.

'Any luck, dear?' Mollie called from the other side of the curtain.

Thea smiled. 'I think so. I don't suppose you've got any heels in a size seven I could take a look at?'

'Give me a sec, I'll see what I can do.'

Turning back to the mirror, Thea gave her reflection a smile. Not bad for an eleventh-hour purchase. She wondered what Nick would think of the dress and then shushed that thought. As she stood there, double checking the fit of the dress and making sure it really was the one she wanted, her mind drifted back to the kiss they'd shared. It had drifted in and out of her mind ever since, and every time she remembered it, her lips tingled a little at the memory. When he'd asked her to the ball, she'd wanted to give him a sign that she did like him, but even now, she was second guessing herself.

The kiss, right next to a bag of spuds and a load of shopping, had seemed more natural, like the right thing to do. So she'd done it. And now she couldn't get the sensation and taste of his lips out of her mind. Something inside her had woken up that, apart from an ill-advised two-week casual thing with a colleague in her old job, had lain dormant for a long time. Kissing him felt natural, right, and all sorts of sensations had run through her body when she'd initiated it. As if it was something that she should have done a long time ago.

Thea shook her head. It was likely that she was investing too much in a single action. She'd always had the heart of an incurable romantic, and after Ed had let her down so badly, she'd guarded herself against ever being put in that position again. For years she'd been content to put her children first, pouring all of her love and energy into them, and then, later, her job. But now, after spending time with Nick for the first time in years, and that kiss, she felt as though she was ready to start exploring something new again: something just for herself.

'I've got these, if you want to try them with the dress.' Mollie's voice came from the other side of the curtain again. Thea reached out a hand and grinned as Mollie gave her a pair of glitter-encrusted silver high heeled pumps. 'They came in as a job lot from the Shallowcombe Amateur Dramatic Society,' Mollie added. 'I believe the actress who played the Fairy Godmother in their production of *Cinderella* wore them for the production, but they haven't been worn since.'

'Oh wow!' Thea began to laugh. 'It's been a long time since I've worn a pair of heels this high.' She couldn't resist slipping them on, though. Although a rather outlandish choice with the dress, she figured that, for this event, she'd get away with it.

'There's this, too, if you're in the market for the full look.' Mollie handed her a silk scarf shot through with silver thread. 'Buy the shoes and the dress, and the shawl's on the house.'

'Mollie, you've dressed me in her shoes, but you really are the Fairy Godmother,' Thea said, wrapping the shawl around her shoulders. 'You're a miracle worker.'

'Always happy to help.' Mollie's eyes twinkled. 'It's nice to be able to sprinkle a little Christmas magic around, and, of course, buying from here means you're helping the poor little mites that'll doubtless be abandoned after Christmas to the tender mercies of the animal shelters.' The woman looked serious. 'And we're full to bursting as it is.'

'Cora would love another cat to keep Lupin company.' Thea looked sympathetically at Mollie. 'Maybe in the new year we'll come up and take a look.' She tried not to think about the financial woes she'd be facing in January.

'You're always welcome,' Mollie said. 'Now, why don't you slip out of that lot, and I'll put them in a bag for you.'

'Thanks, Mollie – you're a marvel.'

Thea quickly put her old jeans and jumper back on, and in no time was paying a very reasonable price for the dress and shoes. True to her word, Mollie threw in the shawl for free.

'Have a lovely time tomorrow night,' Mollie said as Thea left. 'I, er, hope your Prince Charming appreciates the effort you've gone to.'

Thea smiled. 'I hope so too.' Feeling markedly more cheerful than she had an hour ago, Thea headed back home to hang up her dress and maybe watch a few YouTube makeup tutorials for herself.

31

Nick couldn't concentrate. This revelation was nothing new to him; he'd often been accused of chronic inattention when he'd been at school, and staring out of the window wanting to be elsewhere, but today the sensation was distinctly obvious. Annabelle had worked in the shop all morning, but was knocking off at lunchtime, leaving him and Roseanna to go through the motions of afternoon trade and then lock up later. It was all routine stuff on a Saturday morning, but Nick had already put some freshly baked sausage rolls in the black waste bin, and only just realised he'd shoved the Chew Moo's Ice Cream in the fridge instead of the freezer in time.

'Something on your mind?' Annabelle asked with a glint in her eye when, muttering, he re-homed the ice cream in the freezer.

'No,' Nick shot back quickly. He'd had enough ribbing from Annabelle last night about Thea saying yes to the ball, and he was starting to go through the roof with nerves about it now. He hadn't told her about Thea kissing him when she'd agreed to go to the ball; he still couldn't quite believe it had happened himself.

If he'd mentioned it to Annabelle, she'd be planning their wedding already.

Annabelle had taken off her apron and was putting it on the hook behind the counter. She turned back around to where Nick was standing nearby, a more sympathetic look on her face.

'She wouldn't have accepted the invite if she didn't want to go with you,' she said gently. 'Just try to enjoy it. You've been waiting long enough to take her on a date.'

'You make me sound like the world's saddest loser,' Nick grumbled. 'It's not as though I've been sitting at home, pining for Thea Ashcombe all these years.'

Annabelle grinned. 'Of course not, but... oh, I don't know. Thea seems really special to you. Thea *is* special. And, without wanting to get too mushy or sentimental, you're special to me, too. The thought that you two might have a future together makes me so happy.' She reached out and hugged Nick, who was pleasantly surprised by the gesture.

'Steady on, Annie, you're going to make me cry!' he joked, to hide how touched he was. Gently disentangling himself from her embrace, he started to rearrange the Christmas gift tags and other festive items that they'd introduced to the counter as impulse purchases at the end of November.

'Well, just make sure you're properly dressed, and you get there on time,' Annabelle continued.

'Yes, yes, I know.' Nick put the tags down again. 'You've already told me she hates lateness. And it's not like I've never been out on a date before. I *am* a man of the world, you know!'

'Really?' Annabelle arched an eyebrow in his direction. 'And when was the last time you left the county?'

'I crossed the border into Wiltshire in the summer!' Nick protested. 'We had an away match against the Malmsbury Marauders cricket team. Thrashed them on their home turf, too.'

'Just don't mess this up, little brother.' Annabelle glanced at the clock. 'I'd better go. I promised Jamie I'd get home and help him move some stuff out of the spare room this afternoon. He's, er, planning on repainting it in the new year.'

Nick paused in his rearrangement of the goods on the counter. 'Really?' he said carefully. 'Any particular reason?'

'Not yet,' Annabelle replied. She gave a brief smile. 'But soon, hopefully.'

Nick smiled back, his nerves about his date with Thea fading into insignificance when set against the bigger challenges his sister was facing. 'I hope so, too.'

Annabelle said goodbye, but before she did, she couldn't resist a last reminder. 'You have got all the bits for your dinner suit, I suppose? Remember, this is a black tie gig and you need to go full Daniel Craig on Thea if you really want to impress her.'

'Yes, of course.' Nick rolled his eyes. 'As far as I can recall, everything's in the suit carrier from the last time I had to get it all out, and my dress shirt's in the wardrobe.'

'Well, I'll see you later then, Prince Charming!' Giving him a merry wave over her shoulder, Annabelle left.

Nick sat out the rest of the afternoon in the shop, filling the time as best he could by getting a jump on next week's jobs. It was at the point when he found himself checking the dates on the milk in the fridge for the third time, and still not taking them in, that he realised he should just call it a day. As the hands of the clock above the front entrance crept their way towards 5 p.m., he turned to Roseanna.

'Go on, you can get off now.'

Roseanna, who at eighteen was old enough to lock up herself, and did the Sunday morning shift on her own, looked pleased. 'Thanks, Nick. I'll make sure I'm in earlier tomorrow to make up the quarter of an hour if you like.'

'No need, honestly. It's bound to be quiet tomorrow morning anyway, with all of us nursing our hangovers after the ball.'

'Have a great time,' Roseanna replied. 'See you next weekend.'

Glancing at the clock, he saw it was two minutes to five. He'd better lock up and get going. Thankfully, Roseanna had taken care of the outside stock, and he just needed to close out the till and set the alarm for the evening. As he did so, he mentally ran through what he needed for tonight. Yes, he thought, it was all going to be fine. Everything was under control. Switching off all but the low-intensity security lights in the shop, he locked up and headed home.

32

'Shit, shit, shit!' Nick's aged ginger tom cat, Marmalade, narrowed his eyes at his master as Nick chucked the vinyl suit carrier, now denuded of its contents, down on his bed. 'Where the bloody hell is it?'

While Nick had been clock watching all afternoon at the shop, willing the working day to go more quickly, he'd now have given his back teeth for an extra hour. But all the time in the world wouldn't have changed the annoying fact that his black bow tie was most definitely not in the carrier with the rest of his dinner suit. The only thing that was, in fact, was a jokey red false bowtie decorated with comedy willies that he vaguely remembered gaining at the last Young Farmers' Ball he'd attended some ten years ago.

With a growing sense of futility, he rummaged through the pockets of his dinner jacket again, but to no avail; the black tie he'd paired with this suit for years was nowhere to be found. In desperation, he even checked the pockets of his trousers, before pulling them on and hastily reaching for his white dress shirt. Buttoning it up swiftly, he reached for his phone.

'Dad? Hi. No, everything's fine. Look, could you do me a favour?' He explained his dilemma, and when Robert Saint had stopped pissing himself with laughter about the tie his son had been left with, he gave a better, but no more helpful answer.

'Sorry, Nick – your mother got rid of my old dinner suit a few years ago after I nearly herniated myself trying to get the trousers on. She donated it to the charity shop along with the shoes.'

'OK.' Nick's heart sank. 'Well, thanks anyway. See you soon.' He threw the phone down on the bed. Nick, to his shame, had a tendency to let small details derail him. He knew he could just show up without a bow tie, that it wouldn't be the end of the world, but all he could think about was that it just wouldn't seem *right*. He contemplated the tie with the willies again. Wearing that, he conceded, would be even worse.

'Jamie? Mate? It's Nick,..'

Jamie, it transpired, only had the one tie, and he was going to be wearing it. Why hadn't he checked the suit before the night of the ball?

There was only one person who, at short notice, might be able to help him. 'Cross your paws for me, Marmalade,' he addressed the cat, who yawned disinterestedly and closed his eyes again.

* * *

'You're a lifesaver!' Nick exclaimed as Tristan handed him an immaculately pressed black silk bow tie. 'I owe you one.'

'Couldn't have you rocking up at my sister's door not looking the part, could I?' Tristan, with a twinkle in his eye, replied. 'Can you remember how to tie it?'

Nick grinned. 'I think so. It's been a while, though.'

'Well, I'd better get off to Thea's.' Tristan, who was looking a knockout himself in a beautifully cut black dinner suit with a rather eye-catching emerald green silk lining, so dark it almost looked black in the evening light, headed towards the front door.

'Thea's?' Nick asked.

'Oh, yeah,' Tristan replied absently, pulling out his car keys from the pocket of his black cashmere evening coat. 'Thea and Charlotte have spent the afternoon getting ready, and Cora's been giving them makeup tutorials, from what I can gather. I said I'd pick her up at seven, and it's almost that now.'

Nick laughed, despite his nerves. 'Sounds like Annie and her mates back in the day. I bet Cora loved being the one in charge.'

Tristan looked sceptical. 'Charlotte's not much of a one for makeup, so I'm a bit worried that Cora's talked her into something crazy.' He shook his head. 'My niece can be very persuasive when she's on a mission!'

'Well, we'll find out soon enough.' Nick grinned at him. 'I'll, er, see you later on. Can you let Thea know I'm on my way?'

'No sense in both of us driving over,' Tristan replied. 'Why don't you come with me?'

Nick could feel himself starting to blush and he dropped his gaze. Tristan cottoned on immediately.

'Oh. Right. OK... forget I said anything!' He gave a slightly awkward grin. 'You and Thea can, er, make your own way there.'

'Thanks, mate,' Nick replied. 'It's just that I kind of want to do things properly, you know, pick her up myself, take her there, bring her home...'

'Say no more,' Tristan said, getting hastily into his car. 'I don't want to know any more, anyway!'

'No, it's not like that!' Nick's face was flaming now. 'Oh God... I've not even picked Thea up yet and I'm fucking this up...'

Tristan paused in the act of closing the car door, and Nick wanted to sink into the floor.

'Nick,' Tristan said gently, 'Thea likes you. She always has. She's been fond of you since school. It might have been a few years since you were properly close, but I'd bet that hasn't changed. You're not fucking anything up.'

'Fond of me? You make me sound like the family Labrador!' Nick shook his head, but he felt touched by Tristan's words. Tristan was notoriously protective of his twin sister. Nick was mindful of that, and hopeful of Tristan's approval now that he'd finally asked Thea out.

'Just be yourself, mate, and try not to stress out about tonight. She said she'd go with you to the party. Enjoy it.'

'I'll try.' Nick swallowed the sudden lump in his throat. 'It means a lot to me that you're giving me your blessing, you know.'

'Just don't make me regret it.' Tristan's face was gravely serious before he broke into a wide smile. 'She might be four minutes older than me but that doesn't mean I can't take on angry big brother duties if a guy messes her around.'

'Duly noted,' Nick said wryly. 'I'll, er see you at Cherry Tree Court, then.'

'See you later.'

Nick watched Tristan pulling carefully out of the driveway and then turned his attention to the bow tie in his hands. His only immediate concern now, apart from getting to Thea's on time, was trying to remember how to tie the damned thing.

33

It had been ten minutes since Charlotte and Tristan had left for the ball, and Thea couldn't stop watching the clock. She also couldn't decide if she desperately needed the loo again, or if it was just nerves.

'This is stupid,' she muttered, leaning against the back of the sofa in her cosy living room. 'It's Nick Saint for goodness' sake; you've known him since you were five.' But they weren't the little kids sitting on the carpet in Mrs Rossiter's Red Reception class any more. The first day of school, he'd tugged the pink ribbon out of her hair and made her cry. After that, she'd ignored him pretty much until Christmas. Gradually, they'd become friends, and, barring the did-it-happen-or-didn't-it moment during the house party when they were sixteen, friends had been what they'd remained.

Maybe that was the problem, though. Maybe she'd kept Nick in the friend zone for so long that she had absolutely no clue what to do now she was beginning to encourage him out of it. *You've done a bit more than that,* she thought. That kiss in the car park, light and fleeting as it was, had sent a very definite signal to him that she wanted to change the boundaries of their relationship. The problem was, she really wasn't sure how much more. But kissing him had been lovely, and she absolutely knew she wanted to try that again.

Thea glanced at the clock again and decided she really did need that wee. But before she could dash to the cloakroom under her stairs for the fifth time in half an hour, the doorbell chimed.

'I'll get it!' Cora yelled, thumping down the stairs and flinging open the front door before Thea could teeter there in the silver stiletto heels. 'Oh, hi Gran...'

Thea let out a breath, and once again told herself to relax. *It's Nick. Nick likes you. He wouldn't have invited you tonight if he didn't.*

'Hello darling!' Lorelai's cheery voice cut through into her reverie. The old lady, still spritely although she was heading towards her eighties, strode into the living room, Cora chatting nineteen to the dozen at her side about how she'd given Thea and Charlotte 'the best makeovers in the world'.

Lorelai turned her attention to Thea, who was standing stiffly by the window, trying not to look as though she was going through the roof with nerves.

'Darling, you look fabulous!' Lorelai exclaimed, hurrying over to plant a careful kiss on Thea's freshly made-up cheek. She glanced back at Cora. 'You've done a great job on your mother,' she confirmed. 'I barely recognised her.'

Thea smiled at Lorelai's indulgence of her great-granddaughter, but a small part of her hoped it wasn't just that. She smoothed the blue velvet over her hips again and scrunched her toes up in the silver stilettos. Her feet were already starting to ache, and she hadn't even left the house. Her blondish brown hair was swept up in a messy bun, and Cora had taken great delight in pulling strands down and using Thea's ancient curling tongs, which hadn't been out of the drawer for years, to give her some wavy tendrils to soften the rather dramatic makeup.

'Thanks, Gran,' Thea replied. 'I hope it's not too over the top.'

'The Midwinter's Eve Ball is the poshest do of the year, as you well know,' Lorelai replied, 'and, from what I can recall from the last time I went, there's no such thing as over the top when you get a bunch of country dwellers together for an evening.' She smiled again at Thea. 'That's to say that you look wonderful, and I really do wish you'd make the effort with yourself more often.'

Thea laughed. 'I'm not sure what my class would make of me if I rocked up in silver stilettos and blue velvet on a Tuesday morning.'

'You know what I mean.' Lorelai's smile assumed a slight sadness.

'What is it, Gran?'

'Oh nothing.' Lorelai paused. 'I can see so much of your mother and father in you. I suppose it hits harder at Christmas, even now.'

Thea reached out and gave her gran a hug. 'I know. I miss them too.'

'But enough of all that,' Lorelai continued, a brisker tone in her voice. 'Tonight is all about making new memories, not dwelling on old ones.' She turned to Cora. 'And you and I, and your brother of course, can argue over which film we want to watch while Mum's out having a nice time.'

'Oh, I've already sorted us a playlist on FilmFlix,' Cora replied breezily. 'Dylan'll just have to suck it up if he doesn't like it.'

Lorelai laughed, and Thea felt herself relax a fraction. She could always count on her gran and her daughter to raise her spirits. She glanced at the clock again, smothering a spark of irritation; Tristan had mentioned Nick was on his way when he'd picked up Charlotte earlier. Why wasn't he here yet?

As if summoned by her emotions, the doorbell rang again.

'I'll get it!' Cora grinned, jumping off the sofa.

'No, you won't.' Thea threw a warning glance at her daughter, who'd been ridiculously excited about her mother *actually going on a proper date*. 'I don't want to frighten Nick off before we even get to the ball.'

Cora slunk back to the sofa, where Lorelai was already scrolling through the playlist. Thea gave her a conciliatory smile. 'You've been so helpful, darling. Now you can just relax with a huge bowl of popcorn and watch all those movies I wouldn't normally let you.'

Beaming, Cora blew Thea a kiss before settling back with Lorelai to choose what to watch.

You've got this, Thea told herself as she walked to the front door. The frosted glass panels of the door meant that she couldn't see Nick, and Nick couldn't see her. She was grateful for a few extra seconds to compose herself, and remind herself that this was Nick Saint, whom she'd known forever, and that she'd been excited and delighted when he'd asked her out. Taking a deep breath, she turned the chrome lock on the door and pulled it open.

Standing on the doorstep, looking like he'd pass an audition for James Bond with flying colours, bow tie draped over his neck and immaculately cut dinner jacket sweeping the top of trousers that looked as though they'd been tailored just for him, was Nick. But as her heart sped up and her face grew warmer, she realised that she'd never seen him looking so gorgeous.

34

'Wow!' Nick's look of undisguised pleasure at her appearance did wonders for Thea's still somewhat fragile self-confidence. 'You look incredible.'

Thea knew she was beaming, and she decided to just embrace it. 'Thank you,' she said, once she felt capable of drawing breath again. 'You look pretty good yourself.'

An expression of pleasure passed over Nick's face, but Thea could sense there was something on his mind. 'What's up?' she asked.

'Only this.' Nick gestured to the ends of the bow tie, which dangled at his collar. 'You wouldn't believe the hassle I went to, to get it, and now I've forgotten how to do the damned thing up.'

Thea laughed. 'Is that all? I can help with that.' She reached out a hand and pulled him into her brightly lit hallway, which had a large mirror to the left-hand side, reflecting them both in all of their dressed-up glory.

Thea felt a definite stirring of lust as she paused in front of him, trying to remember how to tie a 'proper' bow tie. She moved closer, taking the ends of it in her hands, and then, as if some kind of muscle memory had kicked in, she brought them together until she was satisfied that she'd tied the perfect bow. Breathing in the heady scent of Nick's aftershave, an aroma that felt thrillingly unfamiliar, she straightened the bow, ensuring that the ends were tucked safely away.

'There you go,' she said softly. 'Perfect.' Thea raised her eyes from Nick's collar and realised how close his mouth was to hers. Laughing nervously to break the tension, she spun him around to face the mirror. 'Look. Not bad, if I do say so myself.'

Nick grinned at their reflections. 'Looks great. We scrub up quite well, don't we?'

'We do.' Thea agreed. She was jolted, seeing them both in the mirror, just how right they looked together, as if they were an actual, established couple. There was an ease with Nick that she'd never really paid attention to before, but as she caught his eye in the mirror and gave him a smile, it felt as though they were at the beginning of something that should have started a long time ago.

'All set?' Lorelai had appeared in the hallway and had a delighted expression on her face.

'I think so,' Thea turned briefly away from Nick and hurried to kiss her grandmother goodbye. 'See you later.' She grabbed her long black coat from the hook in the hall and then turned back to Nick. 'Ready to go?'

'Yup.' Thea saw Nick glance behind Lorelai, to where Cora was lurking, having obviously wanted to get a glimpse of them both together in their evening finery.

'Don't let your gran watch any scary movies,' he joked.

'Cheeky beggar,' Lorelai replied, but her eyes were twinkling. 'Don't keep my granddaughter out too late!'

'Gran, I'm not fifteen any more!' Thea knew she was starting to blush and suddenly felt the urge to get out of the house as swiftly as possible. 'I've got my keys, so you can lock up.'

'All right,' Lorelai replied. 'And don't worry' – she glanced back at Nick – 'it's Christmas romance movies all the way tonight, isn't it, Cora? Not a murderer or scary villain in sight.'

'Glad to hear it!' Nick's laugh was less nervous now, and Thea again thought how natural this all felt. There was something to be said for dating someone you and your family had known forever.

As they headed out of the front door, Thea felt the warmth of Nick's hand in the small of her back, even through her coat. In the distinctly vertiginous heels, she was glad of the gesture. He led her to his Land Rover, which looked as though it had been cleaned for the occasion and opened the passenger door for her.

'Are you ready for this?' he asked when they were both settled inside.

'I think so,' Thea replied. 'It's been a while since I've been out on a date, let alone a night out as posh as this!'

Nick laughed, and the sound made Thea's pulse race a little faster. 'Me too. It's nice to get the dinner suit out of mothballs.'

'Well, I'm honoured you've done it for me.' Thea smiled across at him.

A pause fell between them. Nick was just reaching for the ignition when he stopped and turned back towards her. 'I'd do anything for you, Thea. I hope you know that.' The nervous laugh was back again. 'I'm sorry. That sounds a bit intense, but I want you to know that I'm here for you, as a friend, or, if things work out that way, something more.' He was holding her gaze, his blue eyes reflecting the intensity of his words.

'I appreciate that, Nick,' she said softly. 'All this...' She gestured down at herself. 'All this is very new for me. I'm kind of taking this one step at a time. But I'm glad it's you I'm taking the steps with.' She leaned towards him, and before she could second guess herself, she kissed him, very gently, on the mouth. Her lips parted slightly, and the kiss became deeper, and when Nick raised a hand to her cheek, she shivered at the contact. As they broke apart again, she let out a long breath.

'Wow,' she said. 'That was quite something.'

Nick stroked her cheek with his thumb, and she shivered at the contact. 'It was. And that felt like a very lovely step to take.'

'I agree.' Thea's hand, which had come to rest on Nick's shoulder, moved slightly so that her fingertips were just resting on the side of his neck, and she felt his pulse hammering under her touch, again suggesting he was as excited by the kiss as she was.

After a few more seconds, Nick moved back from her, clearing his throat. 'If we're going to get to the ball on time, we should probably get going.'

Thea nodded and settled back into the seat. She wondered, having literally just said she wanted to take things slowly, if she'd just put her foot on the accelerator of their relationship with a kiss like that. But it had felt right. As Nick drove the short distance to Cherry Tree Court, she tried to stop thinking so hard. Tonight was meant to be fun, and that kiss had *definitely* been fun.

35

The exterior of Cherry Tree Court loomed up at them as Nick drove up the wide, sweeping approach. On either side of the long driveway, as they got within twenty metres of the house, flaming garden torches lined the boundaries of the frost-bejewelled lawn, and the house itself was a hive of activity. Cars were parked all around the broad, circular sweep of the immediate area in front of the house, and Nick raised a hand of acknowledgement to the steward in a yellow hi-vis jacket who directed him to a space.

'I remember standing out here doing that job when I was a teenager,' Nick said, grinning briefly at Thea before he carefully reversed into the parking space. 'Froze my backside off for two hours and then snuck into the kitchen and guzzled about a gallon of the mulled wine.' He laughed. 'Can't quite remember much after that, but I do remember waking up on Jamie's bedroom floor with the worst hangover I'd ever had.'

Thea giggled. 'Annabelle told me about that – she was so pissed off because she and Jamie had a date that Sunday afternoon and neither of you were in any state to string a sentence together.'

'True.' Nick turned off the engine. 'And I suppose you've never had the hangover from hell and had to cancel something?' His tone was teasing.

'Oh, quite a few times before I had the kids,' Thea replied. 'But being a parent tends to put paid to all of that, for a few years at least.'

'Well, I hope tonight you feel you can have a few glasses if you want to, since I'm more than happy to be the designated driver.' Thea's heart sped up as Nick's gaze, now a little more serious, met hers. 'I'll make sure you get home all right.'

'I know you will,' Thea said softly. After the kiss in the car, the atmosphere felt as though it was crackling between them, and Thea's thoughts were already heading towards the end of the evening, and the inviting darkness of a secluded corner of Cherry Tree Court...

'Ready then?' The click of Nick opening the car door brought Thea back to reality. She clambered out of the passenger side before he had the chance to come around and open the door for her and took his arm when he appeared by her side.

'As I'll ever be. But I'm holding you responsible for keeping me upright in these heels!'

'Challenge accepted.' Nick's eyes shone in the light emanating from the interior of Cherry Tree Court. 'But only if you stay off the mulled wine. Given the long traditions of the Midwinter's Eve Ball, it wouldn't surprise me if it was still made to the same recipe that floored me all those years ago!'

'Ah, but you always were a lightweight!' Thea teased. 'I remember that party at Ben Marsden's gaff where you had one can of Fosters and were convinced you could dance the Macarena on top of his mum's glass coffee table. It's a wonder you didn't fall straight through.'

'Oh God,' Nick groaned. 'I'd forgotten about that.' He paused and gently brought Thea around to face him. 'Look,' he said, 'the fact that we've got a lot of shared history feels a bit like a blessing and a curse. I love that we grew up together, and that we've got so many of the same friends, but also, it feels a bit... weird, too.'

'Weird how?' Thea was perplexed. 'Us being friends was supposed to make things easier, not harder!'

'Well.' Nick looked squarely at her and Thea's heart gave a little skip. 'It's kind of like we've known each other for so long, and there are so many memories and moments from the past, that I suppose I'm worried there'll be nothing for us to discover about each other because we already know it all.' He shook his head. 'Is that just really daft?'

Thea smiled and raised her hand to Nick's face. Gently, she brought her lips to his, and kissed him, the warmth of his mouth in delicious contrast to the evening frost which was setting in all around them.

'Does this feel boring?' she said as they drew breath between kisses. 'Or like we already know how to do it?' Increasing the pressure of her lips on his, she felt a low-down tingle of excitement as he responded to her, wrapping an arm around her and drawing her nearer. 'Because we can stop if you're about to fall asleep!'

Nick groaned into the kiss, and Thea could tell from the way his body had hardened against her that bored was the last emotion he felt. They held the moment for a few seconds longer, until, breathing more heavily, Thea carefully disentangled herself from Nick's arms.

'Well,' she said, raising a trembling hand to a stray lock of hair that had broken loose from the bun maker Cora had used to tie most of her brownish blonde locks up, 'I hope that's gone some way to proving my point, and putting your mind at rest.'

'Something tells me you're not a great fan of being proved

wrong,' Nick teased as he buttoned up his dinner jacket. 'But if that's the way you'd like to do it, then that's fine with me!'

Thea slipped an arm through Nick's again, trying to make sure she didn't trip on the gravelled driveway. 'Duly noted. And if you, er, need another, "reminder" at any point this evening, just let me know. I'm more than happy to refresh your memory!'

They hurried to the front door, which was manned by another steward in a hi-vis vest. Nick quickly produced his invitation from the inside pocket of his dinner jacket, and in a short time they were walking through the elegant, walnut-panelled entrance hall, heading towards the dining room that looked out onto the extensive grounds at the back of the house.

'It's been quite a while since I've been here.' Thea glanced up at the huge chandelier that adorned the sweeping inner hallway, lighting the path up the carved wooden staircase that wound its way graciously up to the first floor. Portraits, some bought from the Treloar family of Roseford Hall, who had a historic connection to the place, and some that had been sourced by the company who now managed the building, lined the walls of the landing, nodding to the history of the place but in pleasing contrast to the more modern fitted carpets and décor that co-existed within the house. The two styles were a reminder that Cherry Tree Court was a thriving venue as well as having a long, auspicious local history.

'Well,' Nick said as they reached the doors to the dining room. 'I hope you're ready for some festive small talk and the joys of hospitality mass catering!'

'Oh, you sell it so well!' Thea replied, laughing. 'I almost wonder why I bothered getting so dressed up.'

'I'm glad you did.' Nick looked her straight in the eye. 'If I forget to say it later, thank you for coming with me tonight. I'm so glad to have you by my side.'

Thea felt an inner glow of pleasure, and she moved a little closer to Nick before they made their way into the dining room. 'Thank you for inviting me,' she said. 'And I promise, no more references to the past tonight. Let's make some new memories that are just for us.'

Seeing Nick's smiling face made Thea's inner glow even brighter, and she couldn't wait to spend the evening getting to know him better.

36

As soon as Thea walked through the door of the dining room, she began to realise exactly how long it had been since she'd been to a function like this. All around her were men and women in formal attire, yakking away nineteen to the dozen and looking completely at home. This was, after all, a chance to network in the cold winter months, which, in a remote area such as Lower Brambleton, was not to be missed. Although, in the twenty-first century, business owners and those on the list of attendees were far more upwardly mobile than their eighteenth or nineteenth century forebears, that comparison wasn't too far off the mark. The impression that the bush telegraph was chattering under the guise of a party was one that wasn't lost on Thea.

What surprised her, though, as people began to notice herself and Nick, was just how recognisable he was to most of the room. The Saint family had farmed in Lower Brambleton for at least four generations, and although the farm was now a large market garden, the shop was a successful replacement for a business that had been in danger of being lost during the recession of the 1980s, and under Nick's father's stewardship, and latterly Nick and Annabelle's, the business was thriving. This meant that Nick had plenty of name recognition, and there were lots of smiles, greetings and brief snippets of conversation as they moved towards the bar, where glasses of Bucks Fizz and other drinks were available.

'Wow, you're giving off minor celebrity vibes!' Thea murmured as they finally got to the bar. 'So much for the unassuming farm boy act.'

'Ha-ha.' Nick picked up a flute of Bucks Fizz and handed it to Thea, before asking the bartender for a pint of Coke. 'Wait until *Christmas at the Farm Shop* goes out in a few days' time – you'll be signing autographs yourself!'

'Not a chance! I made sure I kept to the background, remember?' Thea took a sip of the Bucks Fizz, which was actually rather strong. Cherry Tree Court obviously didn't stint on the hospitality for this bash. The alcohol warmed her and took the edge off the nerves that were beginning to rise again, now they'd entered the party.

'Nick! Looking fly, mate,' Jamie exclaimed as he arrived at the bar. 'Glad you got that tie sorted out. This isn't the kind of gig where they'd let you in with the one you found in your pocket.'

'Tristan came through with a spare just in time,' Nick replied, taking his Coke from the bartender.

'Lucky for you,' Jamie said, a twinkle in his eye. 'Looking good, too, Thea. Hope he's treating you well tonight.'

'So far, so good.' Thea smiled at Jamie, and then, as Annabelle joined them, she gave her a hug.

'Dad's around here, somewhere,' Annabelle said. 'Don't suppose you've seen him?'

'Not yet,' Nick said. 'I'm surprised he's showed up, though. He told me he didn't have a dinner suit any more.'

'Oh, he didn't until this afternoon,' Annabelle said. 'Mum

took him to Moss Bros in Taunton and made him buy another one that actually fitted. But, unfortunately for you, only the one bowtie.'

Thea, who hadn't heard the full story of the bowtie, crooked an intrigued eyebrow, but Nick didn't elaborate.

Just then, she caught sight of Tristan and Charlotte, who were also heading towards the bar. Her twin brother had a look of impatience on his face, and Thea wondered what had happened. She hoped he and Charlotte hadn't had a row. They were two such incredibly different people, but somehow, they made things work between them. The occasional disagreement wasn't unexpected, though.

'All right, Tris?' she asked as they drew closer.

'Yeah.' Tristan gave her a brief smile. 'Just a bit fed up with being cornered by locals who want to talk about the next stage of the Observatory Field development. If I have one more person bellyaching about the plans for the new village hall, or the unreliability of the bin collections up there...'

'Well, now you come to mention it!' Thea teased. She was relieved that it was work and not his relationship that had provoked the irritation.

Tristan shook his head. 'I know I'm seen as the link to the developer, but I was hoping I'd get tonight off, at least!'

'Just get a drink down you and don't worry about it,' Charlotte said soothingly. Thea smiled at her; Charlotte knew almost as well as Thea how to get her brother back in a good mood, and she was grateful that he'd found her.

Grinning, Tristan took a glass of champagne, unadulterated by orange juice. He raised it to his lips but paused before having a sip. 'Are you sure you're OK driving?'

'Absolutely,' Charlotte replied. 'Kick back and enjoy it. You've earned it this year!'

As the group of friends chatted, Thea took the chance to keep observing the gathering of the great and good of Lower Brambleton and its environs. Underneath the sparkling Christmas lights, everyone looked glamorous and festive in their formal dresses and black dinner suits. She was glad she'd found such a great dress in Purrfect Paws. Relaxing slightly as the Bucks Fizz worked its magic, she moved a little closer to Nick, who was in animated conversation with Tristan and Jamie about the shop's plans for the new year. She felt a warm flush of pleasure as he slid an arm around her, and that she was becoming a closer part of the group, in a slightly different way to before.

Nick's look of appreciation made Thea start to think all kinds of things she really shouldn't be thinking so soon into their very new relationship. *Take it slowly,* she warned herself. But those kisses so far had felt anything but slow.

Dinner came and went in a haze of indifferent catering and chatter, and a bit more wine. Thea realised, with a start, that she was enjoying herself a lot more than she'd been expecting at a gig like this. She glanced at Nick, who had taken to holding her hand under the table and thought that much of that enjoyment was to do with being here with him. As the tables were cleared and the disco started, people started to move for drinks, and to stand and watch those brave enough to put themselves on the dance floor. Thea was touched when Nick bought her another drink, and they stood just off to the side of the floor, watching the braver members of the party strutting their stuff.

'Nick, hi!' Another familiar, but much less welcome voice cut into their cosy bubble. 'You made it!'

Only one person she'd met recently spoke almost exclusively in exclamations, and the speaker's tone grated on Thea just as much as it had when she'd been forced to work with her during the filming of *Christmas at the Farm Shop.* That person also had a seemingly innate ability to single out one person and freeze out everyone else, and in the stunningly fitted red velvet body con dress with an almost too-much Arctic white fur trim at the bust line, she looked as sexily festive as Mariah Carey. The dress was a little over the top for a countryside do, but there was no escaping just how well she wore it. If Thea had been feeling pleased with her own appearance a few seconds earlier, those sentiments had changed to a nagging sense of inferiority when standing beside this embodiment of perkily festive cheer.

Bracing herself, and trying to swallow down her irritation, Thea took another sip of her drink.

37

'Hello, Tally,' Nick said. 'I, er, didn't know you were back in the county.'

'Oh, just staying with a couple of friends for the weekend, you know how it is.' Tally's twinkling blue eyes were fixed on Nick and Thea, but, rather than looking jealous, she actually looked quite thrilled. Confused, Thea tried to fix her smile to her face and not show how rattled she was that Tally had rocked up, looking fabulous, to this gig.

'So you two *are* an item, after all!' Tally continued, spotting Nick's arm around Thea's waist immediately. 'You know, I had my suspicions while we were filming.' She suddenly looked a little contrite. 'In which case, I owe you both an apology.' She turned to Thea. 'I'm sorry for grabbing your gorgeous fella under the mistletoe that night at the market. It was out of order, and I should have known better. Forgive me?'

'Shouldn't it be me you're apologising to?' Nick interjected. 'It was me you grabbed, after all.'

'Oh, shush you.' Tally glanced at him. 'If you stand under the kissing shrub looking delectable, what's a girl to do?'

'I don't think that explanation would wash if the roles were reversed, Tally,' Thea said firmly. 'Nick's easy-going to a fault, but he's right. You do owe him an apology.' She wasn't about to correct Tally's misapprehension about her and Nick's relationship; it gave her a certain satisfaction that Tally knew for sure Nick was off limits for her now, especially given their previous hookup.

Tally's expression registered discomfort, but then she smiled in resignation. 'You're right,' she said quietly. 'Just because we had a brief history, it didn't give me the right to impose on either of you.' She looked back at Nick. 'I'm sorry, Nick.'

'No harm done,' Nick said, and then smiled at them both. 'I, er, hope that doesn't mean we're off the filming list for any future episodes of *Britain's Loveliest Farm Shops*.'

'Not a chance!' Tally laughed. 'Channel 5's pre-viewing panel saw the rushes yesterday and they love it, so I expect we'll be in touch next year to do a follow up. Still sure I can't convince you to take up a presenting gig?'

'Nope.' Nick was grinning now. 'I don't mind the odd spot in front of the camera, but I've got enough to do with running the place.'

'Never say never, though, right?' Thea teased. 'I mean, the camera does love you.'

Tally turned to Thea. 'You're *so* right! Perhaps you can persuade our boy to my way of thinking?'

Thea looked straight at her before she replied, 'Oh, Nick's very much his own person, Tally, as I'm sure you know.'

Tally got the message. 'Well,' she said brightly, 'it's been lovely to see you. Enjoy the rest of the evening.'

As she headed off to rejoin her own party of friends, Nick turned concerned eyes on Thea. 'I had no idea Tally was going to be here, I swear. She never let on that she was coming back to the village.'

'It's all right.' Thea smiled. 'I believe you. Now, get me onto the dance floor and show me what you're made of!'

Nick didn't need telling twice. As they walked hand in hand to the floor, Thea slid into his arms just as an old favourite from twenty years ago echoed around the room.

'This takes me back,' Thea murmured. 'I'm never sure if I imagined it, but do you remember that night at Gina Hodge's house party, twenty and a couple of Christmases ago?'

Thea felt the smile on Nick's face against her own as they moved slowly to the music. 'I have a vague recollection,' he murmured into her hair. 'What exactly do *you* remember about it?'

'Well,' Thea breathed. 'I remember the cherry vodka, rather too much of it, in fact, and being at the top of the stairs with some guy.' She paused, then added teasingly, 'He wasn't a bad kisser, actually.'

'Funny,' Nick replied, 'I remember the same thing, although the girl needed a bit more practise! To be fair, she was rather pissed, though.'

'Oh, so you took advantage of a drunken lass.' Thea affected mock outrage. 'Whatever would your mum and dad say?'

Nick pulled slightly away from her. 'As I recall, that drunken lass wanted to take more advantage of me, but gentleman that I was, I took her to the spare room, put a mixing bowl next to the bed and kept an eye on her until she woke up.'

'Really?' It took a lot to surprise Thea, but her memories of that night, especially after over twenty years, were even hazier. 'I don't remember seeing you when I eventually came around.'

'I snuck out when you got up to go to the loo.' Nick looked sheepish. 'I didn't know how much you remembered about our kiss at the top of the stairs, and I didn't want you to feel embarrassed about it if you regretted it.'

Thea felt oddly moved by his complete consideration for her. 'That was very sweet of you.'

'I didn't want to risk losing you as a friend,' Nick continued. 'But there's a part of me now, all these years later, that really wishes I'd taken that risk. I wish I'd told you how I *really* felt about you back then.'

Thea's eyes filled with tears. 'Honestly? I don't know if I was ready. We might have broken each other's hearts if we'd both admitted to each other how good that kiss was.' She shook her head as they continued to move gently to the music. 'All these years I've convinced myself I'd imagined it... why haven't we ever talked about it?'

Nick smiled sadly. 'What good would it have done? You were with someone else, and I... well, as I said, where would it have got us?'

Thea stepped closer to Nick. She felt safe in his arms, and she couldn't help noticing that they seemed to fit perfectly together when they danced. The heels helped, of course, but everything just felt so right, and as if they were the only couple hearing the music.

'Can I kiss you again?' she asked softly.

Nick nodded. 'I would love you to.'

As Thea's lips met Nick's, she suddenly felt as though the years had rolled back and they were at the top of those stairs once more, in the semi-darkness, protected from the rest of the world in their little bubble together. He tasted so good, even without the aid of cherry flavoured vodka, and she wanted that slow, leisurely kiss to go on forever.

'You're still a brilliant kisser,' she murmured as they parted slightly for breath.

'And you're a lot better at it when you're not plastered!' Nick quipped gently.

He might have been teasing her, but she could tell by the way his body was responding to her that the kiss was turning him on as much as it was her. A warm heat pooled in her belly as they continued the kiss for a few more seconds, before they broke apart again, remembering that they were still on a crowded dance floor.

'Well, ladies and gentlemen,' the compère announced as the song faded away, 'if there are any rogues and chancers among you, or if you feel lucky tonight, you might want to chance your arm at the roulette table in the bar. Or if blackjack is your thing, perhaps the cards will win you a fortune, or at least the next round of drinks. What do you say, ladies and gents? Will tonight be the night Lady Luck comes to visit?'

Nick laughed. 'What do you say, Thea? Shall we blow it all on black?'

But Thea was still, and her hands, so relaxed when they'd been dancing, had tensed where they rested on Nick's shoulders. She pulled back from him, and her heart was racing so quickly she thought she was going to black out.

'Can you give me a minute?' she heard herself stammering. She'd not had a lot to drink, but she suddenly felt lightheaded and so short of breath she started to take in huge gulps of air.

'Thea? What's wrong? Did I do something to upset you?'

Thea gave him a quick smile. 'No, I'm fine, really.' She felt her heart starting to speed up. 'Look, can we find somewhere quiet for a couple of minutes? I really need to get out of here for a bit.'

'Sure,' Nick said gently. He put an arm around her, and they walked out of the dining room. The staircase to the upper floors looked quiet, and they both headed upwards, in search of a convenient place to sit for a while.

38

The party was in full swing downstairs with most people taking advantage of the roulette wheel and the other gambling entertainments that had been laid on after dinner. As she and Nick walked along the landing, Thea realised that she was still shaking.

'What's wrong?' Nick asked. His tone was gentle, and Thea felt her eyes welling with tears.

'It's so stupid...' Impatiently, she scrubbed at her eyes, forgetting that Cora had done quite a detailed job with her eyeshadow. 'Bugger,' she muttered as she caught sight of the dove grey powder on her knuckles.

Nick glanced across the landing, and then, seeing there was no one else there, he pushed open the door to the nearest room and led Thea inside.

'Why haven't they locked up?' Thea, despite her upset, gave a nervous laugh.

'Dunno, but let's not worry too much.' Nick closed the door quietly behind them. He didn't switch on the light, as the moon was doing a pretty good job of casting a silver torch across the main part of the carpeted area of the room, which had a four-poster bed to one side and a chaise longue underneath the window. Nick led her to the chaise, and Thea sat down beside him.

'Talk to me, Thea.' Nick spoke softly. 'One minute you were right there with me, the next you seemed like a deer in the headlights. What's going on? Did I do something wrong?'

'Oh, Nick,' Thea sighed. 'Can you just, for one minute, stop holding yourself responsible for absolutely everything?'

Nick looked taken aback, but he rallied. 'OK,' he said carefully. 'But if it's not me, then why don't you tell me what is bothering you?' He reached out and took one of her hands in his. 'I want to help, Thea. Honestly. You can trust me.'

That was the crux of it, Thea thought. Somehow, instinctively, she *did* trust Nick. She wanted so badly to let him in, to confide in him exactly why she had been so freaked out, but she felt so ashamed of it all. Ashamed that she'd been taken in so easily by Ed's lies, that she'd put up with it for so long, that she'd almost allowed herself and her two children to become homeless because of it, and that, even now, she berated herself for allowing things to go on for so long.

'I want to,' she said quietly. 'I really want to be able to level with you, Nick, but it's so hard to say all of it out loud.' She choked back a sob. 'I didn't realise until just now how much it all still affects me. But the last thing I wanted was to spoil our evening like this.'

'You haven't spoiled anything.' Nick moved closer to her, and she felt the warmth of his arms around her. 'I'm here for you, Thea. I want to be here for you, if you'll let me. And if you don't want to tell me everything, or anything, right now, that's fine too. Just know that I'll be here when you want to talk to me.'

'Thank you,' Thea replied. She paused. 'And before you ask...

this isn't about Mum and Dad.' She gave a hiccough that was almost a bark of ironic laughter. 'I mean, I know that you know all about that, and we've all been through it hundreds of times over the years. I can't blame them for this.'

Nick tightened his hold on her, and Thea felt intensely reassured. 'Understood.'

Thea braced herself. Even though she, Nick, Tristan, Annabelle and Jamie had been friends for so long, none of them knew the true extent of her troubles with Ed, and the real reasons for their subsequent split. She'd put on a brave face for the outside world and glossed over the serious issues they'd faced as a couple, and most of the time she felt as though she truly had moved on from the damage he'd done to her trust. Perhaps it was because she'd begun to make herself vulnerable now, embarking on this new relationship with Nick, that she'd succumbed to a trigger she hadn't felt in years.

'Ed had a gambling problem,' she said quietly. 'I didn't know until really late on. When it started, he'd assured me it was nothing more than a bit of fun. Some blokes like the pub, some play five-a-side football once a week, Ed liked casinos. He'd go out once a month with mates from work to a place in Bristol, have a few drinks and a flutter and come back again.' She began to twist the silver bangle she was wearing around on her wrist. 'At first, he'd shrug off any losses – but then, over time I noticed his mood became dependent on whether or not he'd had a lucky night. Sometimes he'd come back euphoric, and other times the gloom would last for the rest of the weekend. I learned not to ask too much after he bit my head off once too often.'

'I'm so sorry, Thea.' Nick's quietly shocked tone illustrated that he really hadn't had a clue about any of it. 'That must have been a real strain for you.'

Thea nodded. 'It was, but it got a lot worse when he started using his phone. Poker, online slots, sports betting... it was suddenly all there, any time he needed a fix. What had been a once-a-month social thing became an addiction. By the time I realised what was going on, we were up to our eyeballs in debt, and we needed to sell the house to cover it.'

'That's when you moved into your gran's annexe,' Nick said. 'I remember you coming back to Lower Brambleton, when the kids were really small. I wanted to reach out to you, but I wasn't quite sure how. No one really knew what had happened between you and Ed.'

Thea shrugged. 'I wanted to keep it that way. Tristan knows, of course, but I asked him to keep quiet – and Gran knows most of it. I had to tell her, when we needed a place to live. The kids were so tiny, and I had nowhere else to go.' She blinked back more tears. 'It's stupid, but I'm so ashamed that I let myself get taken in by what he did. How could I have been so stupid? I turned a blind eye to it, and buried my head in the sand because I didn't want to face the truth. It was only when the court orders and County Court Judgements started arriving in the post that I let myself believe how bad things were. We had no choice but to sell our house, and the money I'd inherited from Mum and Dad had all gone into buying the place. Ed, at least, had the decency to leave once he knew the game was up, but once the debts were all paid off it didn't leave much left for me and the kids. That's why we ended up in Gran's annexe until I could get myself straight again.'

'And the bastard hasn't ever had the guts to make good?' Thea could hear the anger in Nick's voice.

'We've had no contact with him since he left,' Thea sighed. 'Until recently, when Cora got a message from a boy who claims to be her half-brother.'

'What?' Nick's hand stiffened under her own. 'When?'

'Just after her birthday. So it looks as though I might have to make contact with Ed again, for the sake of the kids.'

'You don't have to do anything, Thea,' Nick said gently. 'Just because some boy has been in touch with Cora, it doesn't mean you have to respond.'

Thea shook her head. 'It's not as simple as that.' She felt a slight feeling of unease that Nick couldn't grasp the complexity of the situation. 'I can't just ignore this. There are children involved – not just Cora and Dylan, but at least one other child of Ed's. I have to be the adult in the situation, to protect my kids.'

'Of course you do,' Nick replied. 'And I can't pretend to understand what that feels like. But you've come so far since those awful days, I would hate to see you dragged back into a situation you didn't want to be in.'

Thea turned towards Nick. 'I promise that's not going to happen.' She reached out a hand to touch his cheek. 'I'm sorry,' she added. 'I'm ruining your evening, aren't I? You can go back to the party if you like. I don't mind.'

'I'm not going anywhere,' Nick murmured into her hair. 'I'm staying with you, and when you're ready, we can get out of here.'

'But it's still so early.'

Nick shifted on the chaise longue so that Thea could see the moonlight reflected in the serious expression of his eyes. 'I'm staying with you,' he repeated.

Thea felt a rush of gratitude mixed with something much stronger as she took a deep breath to steady herself. Nick had listened to her and had been there for her as she'd admitted something she hadn't talked about in years. The tumult of emotions she felt as she looked at him was confusing, but some instinct drove her to silence the voices now. Before she could second guess herself, she leaned forward and kissed Nick hard on the mouth. He stiffened in surprise, before she felt him responding to her, and as they continued to kiss, Thea felt the strange, but reassuring combination of passion and security. She wondered, not for the first time, why they hadn't got round to this years ago. Things would have been so different if she'd got together with Nick and not Ed...

As they broke apart again, Thea's heart was thumping in her chest.

'Shall we get out of here?' Nick asked, a husky note in his tone.

'Absolutely.' Thea stood up and pulled Nick to his feet. 'But, if it's all right with you, I don't want to go home just yet.'

Nick smiled at her in the moonlight. 'It's a good job I tidied the house before I left then, isn't it? Shall we have a coffee at my place?'

'I'd like that.' Thea smiled back. 'I'd like that very much indeed.'

Slipping down the stairs, not bothering to say goodbye to anyone else, they headed for home.

39

The atmosphere between them seemed to crackle as Nick drove the short distance from Cherry Tree Court back to his small cottage on the far side of the boundary of Saints Farm. Nick had lived there ever since he'd got back from agricultural college. It was a former farm worker's cottage and had lain empty for many years before Nick decided to take it on and renovate it. His mother and father had agreed to give it to him, so long as he footed the bill for the repairs, and it had been a labour of love for Nick, over the years.

Thea sat quietly in the passenger seat, and Nick glanced across at her from time to time, trying to gauge how she was feeling. It had come to him, as they sat and talked, that despite the fact they'd lived in the same place for a long time, and grown up together, there was still so much they didn't know about each other. The revelations she'd made about what had happened with Ed had shocked him, but it had also ignited a fierce protectiveness within him towards her and her children. He was concerned about what she'd told him about Ed's other son making contact with

Cora, and he wanted to be there for Thea and the kids, to support them during what might prove to be a difficult time. Whatever he'd felt about Thea before, it seemed to have intensified now that she'd trusted him enough to confide in him. That, combined with the fierce physical attraction that had built through the earlier part of the evening, and he was more certain than ever that he'd done the right thing in spending more time with her.

'Well, here we are,' he said, cutting the engine and turning to Thea. 'Are you ready for that coffee?'

Thea's smile assuaged some of the nerves he was feeling. She'd been a whole lot calmer when they'd walked out to the Land Rover, and seemed to have recovered her equilibrium. 'Sounds good,' she said as she swiftly opened the door.

A silence fell between them as he led Thea through to the small kitchen at the back of the cottage. He brewed some coffee in the cafetière and then they walked back to his tiny sitting room at the front of the cottage.

'I don't think I've ever been to your house before!' Thea gave a nervous laugh. 'I mean, not since you've actually *lived* here...' She seemed relieved to be away from Cherry Tree Court and able to talk about lighter things.

Nick grinned as a shared memory surfaced from the back of his mind. 'Oh yeah! I remember when we were eighteen, we all came here for a party after our last exams. God, the place was a mess, wasn't it? But after about five pints of cider, I don't think we really cared.'

'Just as well,' Thea replied, taking a sip of her coffee. 'I think if we hadn't been so drunk, the stone floors would have been really uncomfortable.'

'I don't remember getting much sleep that night,' Nick said. 'I think I stayed awake with Tristan for most of it, setting the world to rights, as only arrogant eighteen-year-olds with no actual real worries could.'

'I don't remember you ever being arrogant,' Thea countered gently. 'Quite the reverse, in fact.' Nick watched as she shuffled closer to him on the red velvet, button-backed sofa where they'd both settled. 'You never seemed sure about anything.'

'Thanks,' Nick said dryly. 'That's a real boost to my ego.'

'You really don't see what I see, do you?' Thea's voice cut into his thoughts, jolting him back to the moment.

'What's that, then?' Nick gave a nervous laugh. He watched, spellbound as Thea carefully put her coffee cup down on the table beside them. Then, he felt a shiver of anticipation as she removed the cup from his hands, too. That shiver intensified as she placed a gentle hand on his thigh.

'I see a warm, sexy, funny, gorgeous man whom I wish I'd got to know better a long, long time ago.'

Nick's heart sped up as the blood rushed somewhere lower in response to Thea's warm fingertips. He ached to close the gap between them again, to feel her lips against his, but the annoying voice in the back of his mind was refusing to go away. She'd been visibly upset not half an hour ago, and he needed to know that she wasn't just riding a wave of adrenaline or trying to chase away the darkness that had made her want to escape from the function room.

'Thea...' he murmured, when she tilted her face towards his. 'Are you sure this is what you really want?'

He saw her pause, pull back, a look of confusion on her face. 'Of course,' she said quickly. 'Don't you?'

Nick sighed. 'You know I do. But you were so upset earlier. I don't want to end up being a sticking plaster one night stand that you'll regret in the morning.'

The speed that Thea withdrew her hand from his thigh made his body scream in protest. Nick tried to ignore it.

'Is that why you think I'm here?' Thea's voice was laced with frustration. 'That I'd really just hook up with you and then walk away?' She'd stood up now and was looking down at him with a look of hurt on her face. 'Do you really think that little of me?'

'Of course not!' Nick jumped off the sofa and quickly reached out a hand. He had the feeling she was going to bolt again, and he desperately didn't want her to leave, not now, not this way. 'I'm sorry. I just don't want you to rush into something you might regret.'

'Oh, Nick.' Thea's eyes were shining with tears again. 'Is that your way of letting me down gently?'

Nick shook his head in frustration. 'No. Christ, no.' He took a tentative step closer to her, breathing in the remnants of the floral perfume she was wearing, and his senses were once again on high alert. 'I *really* don't want you to go, believe me, but I want you to really not want to go, too.' He knew he was stumbling over his words again, and he cursed his inability to get to the point. Thea was still, and her eyes were wide as she looked at him, and he got the feeling that she was weighing up what he'd said, trying to work out what she should be doing.

'I want to stay,' she said softly, bringing the hand he wasn't holding up to his face. He shivered at her touch, and that electricity that had been crackling between them since they'd been spending time together felt almost tangible. Letting out a shaky breath, he brought her hand around to his mouth and kissed her fingertips.

'Then stay,' he said, a husky note in his voice. As he said it, the doubts that had been nagging at his brain quietened down, and before he could second guess himself, he moved towards Thea and kissed her. 'Stay with me. For a little while, at least.'

He felt Thea smiling into the next kiss they shared. 'All right,' she murmured against his lips. 'But I will have to go home tonight. Gran's staying in my spare room, but she's bound to notice if I don't turn up until breakfast time!'

'Understood.' Nick smiled back at her before deepening the kiss. He had the strangest sensation of feeling both relaxed and as if all his senses were at their height. Now that they were both on the same page, his body was aching to touch and be touched, and he couldn't think of anything else but taking Thea straight up the narrow staircase of the cottage and making love to her, for as long as time allowed.

'Come on,' he said softly. 'I think it's about time we made good on all of those kisses, don't you?'

Thea nodded, and he felt himself harden further as she licked her lips. He'd kissed off all of her lipstick, and she looked dishevelled and incredibly gorgeous. He wanted nothing more, now, than to spend the night with this woman, and he felt very confident, as she followed him upstairs, that she felt exactly the same way.

40

For the first time in years, Thea didn't feel any doubt about the decision she was making as she followed Nick up the steep stairs of the cottage and into his bedroom. This had been on the horizon since the first kiss they'd shared in the car park of Saints' Farm. The sensation of Nick's body pressed against hers had awakened a desire in her that had lain dormant for a very long time.

But this wasn't just lust, Thea realised. This was something deeper, something more intense, that was happening because they knew each other so well, and also, despite it. Their long familiarity meant that as Nick lifted the latch on the wooden door that led to his bedroom, Thea felt only the briefest sense of apprehension. This was Nick Saint, her friend, and about to be her lover. This was Nick Saint, a boy she'd known at school but also a man she felt a burning, passionate attraction to. This was Nick Saint; someone she knew she could fall in love with.

'Everything all right?' Nick asked as he let go of her hand and hurriedly drew the curtains in the bedroom.

Thea nodded, and then realised he couldn't see her in the

almost pitch-black darkness of his room. 'Yes,' she murmured. 'Everything's perfect.'

The room gently lit up as Nick flipped the switch on a small, plug-in night light on the wall between where they stood and the ensuite bathroom door.

'Mum and Dad insisted I put in a motion sensor if I was going to be living here alone.' Nick grinned apologetically. 'But I figure it's got more ambience than the bedside light!'

Thea laughed. 'You're such a nerd.' Then, to soften the words, she kissed him again. 'I'm glad it's there. I, er, haven't let anyone see me naked in years, so soft light is fine by me!'

Nick's jaw dropped before Thea saw him collect his thoughts swiftly. 'So, you're OK with all this, then?'

'I wouldn't have followed you up those deadly stairs if I wasn't,' Thea replied. She'd left her silver shoes in the hallway, and on stockinged feet she padded towards him, pushing up against him and pulling his white dress shirt out of his trousers before running her hands up his back. His skin felt warm, and soft, and as she moved upwards, she could feel the muscles of his back and shoulders, firm and taut under her touch. There was something to be said for a man who had such a physical job. She felt a warm surge of desire as Nick arched towards her so that she was in no doubt that he was already aroused by her touch.

'That feels so good,' he murmured as their lips met again and she explored his mouth with hers. The coffee they'd sipped was surging through her system, and she shivered as he raised a hand to her neck, stroking and caressing, before leaning down to kiss her collarbone as his hands slipped downwards over the soft velvet of the back of her dress.

'May I?' he asked as his right hand travelled up her spine and found the top of the zip.

'Be my guest,' she said, and drew a breath in as he slid it

down, gently pushing the dress from her shoulders until it slithered down her waist and pooled at her feet.

Nick's sharp gasp of pleasure did things low down in Thea's abdomen that had her anticipating his next move even before they'd made it to the bed. His eyes were wide as they met hers and travelled down her body, and his hands pressed her closer to him, grinding himself against her until there was no doubt just how much he loved seeing her semi-clothed in front of him.

'You are just as stunning as I imagined,' he said between kisses that travelled from her neck to her mouth and then began to move downward in tandem with his hands, which were stroking her nipples over the black lace of her strapless bra. 'Even more gorgeous, in fact.'

'You've been imagining me like this?' Thea teased, trying to hide how bowled over she was at his lust and his honesty.

'Oh, you wouldn't believe what I've been imagining.' Nick gave her a smile that was unlike any other he'd given her before. It was as if, now they'd consented to each other, he'd been freed of some of the things that had been holding him back. 'Ever since you kissed me that first time, I've wanted to touch you so badly. And feel you touching me...'

'Like this?' Thea whispered, reaching down and caressing Nick's hardness through his dress trousers. 'Tell me how you've imagined it, Nick...'

Nick groaned and kissed her harder, pressing himself into her hand as she increased the firmness of her touch.

'Like that,' he said hoarsely. 'Your hands, your mouth, Christ, Thea, your whole body, just like that...'

She pushed up against him, sliding one of her bare thighs between his legs and feeling him rocking against her, desperate to increase the friction she was teasingly providing. The sounds he was making as she moved with him were such a turn on that she felt an ache between her own legs, and a desperate desire to feel him inside her. Reluctant to break contact, Thea walked forwards until Nick could feel the foot of the bed behind his knees. She pushed him back until he was sitting on it, and then knelt down herself, hands quickly unfastening his dress trousers. He shucked them down, and she allowed herself a long look of appreciation at the sight of his cock straining against the white jersey boxer shorts he'd been wearing underneath. She felt another surge of lust as she imagined what it would feel like to have him inside her.

Thea dropped to her knees and pushed Nick's thighs further apart, glancing upwards as he looked down at her in surprise.

'It's all right,' she said. 'I'm very, very good at this.' She kissed her way up his thigh, and then gently teased him through the fabric of his boxer shorts, the scent and sight of him creating throbs and waves of desire that had her wanting to go over her own precipice, even without the intimate touches.

It was the fact that he trusted her, without question, that was almost as arousing as their physical chemistry. He leaned back slightly, and she slipped a hand into his boxer shorts, encountering warm, aroused flesh and eliciting another groan from Nick. Licking her lips, she began to explore him, until his hips were moving to her rhythm, and she knew she had to slow the pace down.

'Come up here,' Nick said, taking her hand and pulling her up onto the bed. 'I want to touch you.'

Thea smiled down at him, one hand still in contact with the warm flesh between his legs. 'I want to feel you come,' she said, and Nick arched his back again in pleasure.

'Not. Just. Yet,' he ground out, obviously torn between her expert touches and his desire to prolong the sensations. 'Let me feel you, too.'

It took them a few seconds to discard their underwear, and Thea felt that aching throb of desire as she wrapped a leg around Nick's waist, pressing against him until she was the one who needed the rhythm and friction. She looked at him and he gently reached a hand downwards, slipping a fingertip into her warmth and stroking where she needed him the most. The tingling she'd already been feeling intensified, and she pressed against his hand, desperate for her own release. Nick's strokes, gentle, relentless, were guiding her to the edge, and as the waves of pleasure intensified, she pushed up against his hand, feeling his fingers deep within her and needing to feel something substantial. Riding the wave of a first orgasm, she threw her head back, feeling the increased sensation as Nick kissed her neck and continued to give her pleasure.

But that wasn't quite enough. Thea sat up and raised a questioning eyebrow. Nick, despite his evident pleasure and own arousal, reached into the bedside cabinet and grabbed what they needed. Sitting astride his thighs, Thea looked down at him as he readied himself and felt another deep surge of desire and anticipation. When everything was in place, she looked him in the eye. 'Are you still OK?' she breathed.

'Absolutely,' he replied. 'Are you?'

Thea smiled broadly. 'Never better.' She shifted slightly, and then, as their bodies joined, she felt a warmth and pressure that seemed to reach her core. Rocking against him, feeling his hand caressing her once again as he matched his rhythm to hers, she ground down onto him, until the fluttering, pulsing sensation of another orgasm pushed her over the edge. As she broke around him, Nick's thrusts became harder and faster until with a groan, he came too.

Sweating and breathing heavily, they held each other tightly. 'Wow,' Nick said. 'I mean... wow.'

Thea grinned. 'Double wow.'

Nick shifted slightly and Thea felt the loss as he pulled out of her and quickly disposed of the condom. Thea was still sitting on his lap, and she snuggled into his warmth, wondering what happened next.

'Are you OK?' Nick asked gently, stroking her hair back from her face. The bun had been thoroughly dishevelled, and the bun maker was now lying on the floor.

'Yeah,' she said, smiling broadly. 'I'm feeling pretty good, actually. How are you?'

Nick's grin matched her own. 'Fucking amazing,' he said, and then blushed. 'Sorry about the swearing, but it really, really was.'

'You've just made me come twice, had me riding your lap and you're embarrassed about swearing?' Thea was laughing now. 'I will never understand you, Nick Saint!'

'But you do want to try?' Nick teased back.

'Oh, abso-fucking-lutely!' Thea replied. She climbed carefully off Nick's lap and settled back against his pillows. 'But for goodness' sake, don't let me fall asleep or I'll be in so much trouble when I get home.'

'I promise.' Nick settled down beside her. 'We've got the rest of the coffee to keep us awake, anyhow, if you want me to go and get you a fresh cup.'

'That would be amazing,' Thea replied. She gave him a look that she hoped was mischievous. 'On one condition.'

'What's that?'

'You get it for me naked!'

Nick shook his head. 'If you tell anyone I said yes...'

Thea lay back against the pillows and watched Nick's rear view with appreciation as he left the room.

41

Nick shook his head, still unable to quite believe what had just happened. Thea Ashcombe was upstairs in his bed, requesting coffee after the best sex he'd ever had. And it had only been their first time. He didn't want to jinx things, but he was already imagining many more interludes like that. He caught sight of his reflection in the kitchen window (thank goodness his cottage didn't have any neighbours nearby, he thought), and couldn't resist giving the soft-focus version of himself a thumbs up. Then, feeling embarrassed by his own daftness, he swiftly poured two cups of coffee, grabbed a packet of biscuits from the cupboard and took the whole lot upstairs on a tray.

Pushing open the bedroom door once more, he paused when he realised Thea had switched on the bedside light. She was sitting up in bed, staring at him in all of his very naked glory, a look of appreciation on her face. He couldn't help wondering if it was for him or the tray of coffee and biscuits he was holding, as she grinned at him.

'Great idea to bring the cookies – I'm starving after that!' She reached for a biscuit and bit enthusiastically into it, scattering crumbs on the top of the duvet. 'Bugger. Sorry. Where are my manners?'

Nick grinned at her. 'If you were staying the night, you'd be sleeping on that side!'

Thea swatted at him playfully and then shuffled over while he got back into bed with her. They both sipped their coffee, and Nick was surprised at just how natural it felt to be sitting up in bed next to her. The passion of the past hour or so had given way to an easy intimacy, and he felt relaxed and, dare he say it, happier than he'd felt in ages. *Careful,* he chided himself. One evening of fabulous sex didn't make a long-term relationship. He didn't want to scare Thea away by getting too heavy, too soon.

'What's on your mind?' Thea asked, obviously noticing he'd gone quiet. 'Regret ravishing me on your immaculate white bedding?'

Nick laughed. 'Not at all. In fact, I think it's the best decision I've made in ages.'

Thea joined him in the laughter, but he couldn't help noticing a look of uncertainty crossing her face before she did.

'Is everything all right?' he asked her. 'Are you having second thoughts?'

Shaking her head, Thea put her coffee cup down on the tray on the bedside table and then turned back towards him. 'No,' she said quietly. 'And that's what's worrying me.'

Nick's heart gave a little lurch. 'What do you mean?'

'This feels too good to be true,' Thea replied. 'It feels as though the other shoe's going to drop.' She gave him a quick, slightly shaky smile. 'I'm sorry. That probably doesn't make any sense.'

Putting his own cup down, Nick reached out to Thea, who settled into his arms. She felt warm and right, resting against his chest, and he tightened his embrace, stroking her long, brownish blonde hair and trying to give her the reassurance with his body that he wanted to with words.

'I never thought this would happen between us,' he said, kissing the top of her head as she relaxed against him. 'When we were younger, I always hoped it would, but when life took us in different directions, and we both moved on, it just seemed like some silly adolescent fantasy.' He shifted slightly so he could look her in the eye. 'I always fancied you, you know.'

'Oh, shush!' Thea laughed. 'We were kids back then. This is different.'

'What, you mean you didn't fancy me back?' Nick tried to assume an expression of mock outrage but couldn't stop the grin that was spreading over his face.

'You were my brother's mate,' Thea replied. 'That would have been gross!' She squeezed his arm. 'Although, of course, there was that one time on the stairs... but perhaps it's better that neither of us mentioned it again. We might not be sitting here if we'd got it all out of our system when we were kids!' Thea grinned and leaned forward to kiss him. Nick felt his body responding as she deepened the kiss. The coffee had worked its magic, and they were both alert and awake once more, and, from the sensations he was beginning to feel, raring to go.

'Do you have time for a replay?' Nick said as he found himself lying underneath Thea, who was straddling his waist.

'Oh, I think so,' Thea said mischievously. 'I told Gran not to wait up...'

Nick didn't need any further encouragement, and as they made love for the second time, he found himself imagining what the future might look like for them, and this time he didn't chide himself for getting ahead.

42

Thea felt herself drifting off to sleep and realised that she really needed to get home before she crashed out.

'Nick,' she whispered, giving him a little nudge. 'Are you awake?'

Nick gave a muffled groan before he turned over to look at her. 'Yeah,' he said. 'Or I will be in a sec...'

'I'm sorry,' Thea smiled. 'But Gran'll have a fit if I stay out all night, and the kids'll worry, too.'

'Understood.' Nick kissed her again and then swung his legs out of bed and reached for his boxer shorts. The central heating had gone off while they'd been in bed, and the room felt colder. Bracing herself, she reached for her own underwear and slipped her dress back on. It felt like a bubble was bursting, that this lovely little world she and Nick had created over the past couple of hours was disintegrating as reality took hold again. Glancing at the clock, she was shocked to see that it was nearly one in the morning.

Nick had swiftly buttoned up his dress shirt, but hadn't bothered tucking it back in. He'd thrown on a red jersey, and, rummaging through his wardrobe, he pulled out a brown knitted jumper, which he handed to Thea. 'It's going to be chilly out there,' he said.

Thea was touched. 'Thank you.'

They both hesitated at the foot of the bed, and Thea got the impression that Nick was as reluctant to take her home as she was to go.

'This was amazing,' Nick said as he ran his hands up her arms, gently moving towards her for another kiss, which she happily received. '*You* are amazing.'

'Spoken with all the objectivity of a post-orgasmic man!' Thea laughed, to hide how touched she was. 'You're pretty amazing, too.'

Nick groaned into the next kiss. 'Why didn't we do this years ago?'

'Right person, wrong time?' Thea suggested. 'And at least we get to do it all now.'

Thea nodded, and then reluctantly disentangled herself from Nick's warm embrace. 'Well, then,' she said. 'Let's make sure it happens again soon.'

Nick's smirk had her swiping his arm in retaliation. 'That's, er, not entirely what I meant.'

'But a nice thing to think about.' Nick grinned. 'And something to keep me warm when I get back to this big, lonely bed all by myself later...'

Now it was Thea's turn to groan. 'OK, OK... I don't really want to leave, either, but I have responsibilities.'

'I know.' Nick smiled at her, and Thea's own grin got wider as he playfully kissed the tip of her nose. 'Would it be too much, too soon if I said that I hope one day you won't have to rush away somewhere else.'

'Maybe,' Thea said hastily. She still needed time to get her head around all that had happened between them. 'Give me time, Nick. It's not quite as simple for me as it is for you.'

Nick's brow furrowed. 'I get it. And I don't want to put pressure on you, I promise.' He drew her closer to him, and she luxuriated in the warmth of his body. 'Now, let's get you home before your gran sends out a search party.'

They drove back to Orion Close in companionable silence. For Thea, reality was starting to hit now they'd left Nick's cottage. She wasn't good with late nights, and she didn't look forward to the grogginess that only a few hours' sleep would leave her feeling. It struck her, as they drove, just how different their circumstances really were. Nick was free of wider responsibilities – he had his share of the family business, and she knew how hard he worked, but he had his own house, and a steady income. He'd lived a charmed single life, from what she could see.

She, on the other hand, had responsibilities coming out of her ears: two children, both nearly teenagers; an ageing grandmother; a rising mortgage rate and only a part-time teaching job to cover it; a not-entirely-cordial relationship (let's face it, *no* relationship at all), with the father of her children and a pathological fear that everything was going to get taken from her. Not to mention the most recent, unsettling development between Cora and this son of Ed's. Could she and Nick really be thinking about a future together, or would her life be too much of a culture shock for Nick to contemplate?

Thea tried to shut down that line of thinking. She was often guilty of running fifteen steps ahead in her desire to keep control of things, and she ended up having to backtrack when things changed. She and Nick had spent one pleasurable evening in bed together; that didn't mean she was ready to commit to him, or, indeed, he to her.

The trouble was, she could keep telling herself that, but every time she looked at Nick, she couldn't help wondering what it would be like to be in a relationship with him, to do the simple, everyday things that couples did. They'd fallen into bed, enjoyed each other, but the lead up to that had been full of laughs, shared smiles and a developing affection that she hoped had the potential to last the course.

But hoping something and knowing it for sure were two different things. Sure, Nick had hung out with her and the children a few times, and they'd all got on well, and she knew that her gran liked him too. That, however, didn't mean Nick would be comfortable just fitting into her rather more complicated life. The trouble was, every time Nick looked at her, she could see the love and affection in his eyes. She had the feeling that if she was falling for him, he was falling for her even harder. What she didn't know was whether or not he'd really thought through what being in her life meant. Lust and attraction, and deepening friendship, were something, but were they enough?

'Well, here we are.' Nick's voice broke into her thoughts as he pulled onto the driveway of her small house on Orion Close. They got swiftly out of the Land Rover and Nick walked Thea to her front door.

'I had a great time tonight,' he said softly.

'Me too.' Thea paused, glanced quickly at the window of her front room, realised the curtains were shut and it was in darkness, and then leaned up to kiss Nick goodnight.

'Can I see you again soon?' Nick asked as they broke apart.

'I'd like that.' Thea smiled up at him. He looked sexily dishevelled in the soft moonlight, and the red jersey contrasted well with his smart dress trousers and the tails of his untucked shirt. 'I'll, er, text you?'

'I'll be waiting.' Nick paused. 'Look, Thea... I don't want to rush you, but I do want you to know. I like you. A lot. More than like you, if I'm honest. And I know that's a lot to land on you after one "proper" evening together, but... well, I, er, wanted you to know that.'

He looked so adorably uncertain, standing there, that he'd said the right thing, that Thea couldn't help kissing him again. 'I like you too. A lot. But let's take this slowly, OK?' She glanced up at the front windows of the first floor of her house, and Nick immediately understood.

'Slowly is fine.' Nick smiled. 'I know you've got a lot to think about. But I want to be a part of your life, Thea, and, if you want me to be, part of Cora and Dylan's lives, too.'

'Thank you,' Thea replied. She knew Nick was sincere, but she also knew he hadn't really had a great deal of experience with children. So, slowly was fine.

'See you soon,' Nick murmured, leaning in for one last kiss. 'Sweet dreams.'

'You too.' Thea watched him as he got back into the car, then, rummaging in her bag for her keys, let herself into the house as quietly as she could. All was silent as she sneaked up the stairs, feeling, to all intents and purposes like the teenager she'd once been. As she reached the landing, she checked in on Cora and Dylan, both sound asleep, and noticed the door to the spare room was closed, suggesting Lorelai was too. Smiling into the darkness, she mulled over the events of tonight. Things were changing for her in so many ways, and she couldn't help feeling optimistic.

43

The next morning, Thea, unused to such a late night, ambled down from her room to find breakfast in full flow in the kitchen. Lorelai, true to form, had risen early, had a pot of tea on the go and had made sure the children had eaten a decent breakfast. Dylan, noshing his way through an enormous bowl of porridge, glanced up at his mother before fixing his attention back on the TV series he was watching on his Kindle. Cora, slightly less of a morning person, was staring at her phone and making slower progress with her bowl.

'Morning!' Lorelai chirped, handing Thea a cuppa. 'How was last night.'

'Great, thanks.' Thea couldn't quite meet her grandmother's gaze, although she had nothing to be ashamed about. After all of her protestations about seeing how things went with Nick, last night, in the cold light of day, felt like a bit of a leap. She couldn't quite believe they'd fallen into bed on literally their first 'proper' date, but then, she supposed, they had thirty years of friendship to set the groundwork. And what a revelation last night had been!

Thea hadn't enjoyed sex like that in years; in fact, if she was being honest, ever.

'So, any gossip from the social event of the season?' Lorelai asked as she placed a generous bowl of porridge, topped with cream and raspberries, in front of Thea.

Thea stared at it in confusion. She didn't recall buying any of the ingredients in front of her that had gone into the delectable breakfast.

'Oh, I brought this all over with me,' Lorelai replied when Thea gave her a quizzical look. 'I remember how you used to love a bowl of this after a night out, and the kids always request it when they come over to stay.'

Thea smiled at her grandmother. 'Thanks, Gran, it's just what the doctor ordered.' She took a spoonful and instantly felt better. 'I can't think of anything too scandalous – except that Robert Saint was persuaded to buy a new dinner jacket, having sworn he'd never get into one again!'

'Maggie got her way, then!' Lorelai laughed. 'It's good to know they're both up on their feet again – hopefully that'll take some of the pressure off Annabelle and Nick in the new year.'

Thea nodded. The mention of Nick made her face feel hot, and she hoped her grandmother wasn't going to press her for more details. She wanted to keep things to herself for now, to hug the memory of their wonderful night close for as long as she could.

'So, what are your plans for today?' Lorelai asked, breaking into her reverie.

'Not sure yet,' Thea glanced out of the window. 'It's a lovely, sunny day – perhaps we'll go for a quick walk, blow away the cobwebs.'

Stereo groans from her two children greeted this suggestion, which made Thea even more determined to get them off screens and into the fresh air. She hurried upstairs for a shower, making it clear that she expected them to be dressed and ready to go in twenty minutes. Checking her phone before she went into the small ensuite shower room that adjoined her bedroom, she smiled to see that Nick had sent her a message:

> Hope you got some sleep in the end... wish it could have been with me, though! x

Replying, she suggested they make another date after the Christmas rush. She wanted to suggest something sooner, but it was three days until the big day now, and she still had a lot to organise, and she owed it to her children to be present for them now that the holidays had started for them all. She and Nick had lots of time to spend together; Christmas needed to be spent with the other people in their lives. All the same, she felt a sudden pang; she missed him.

As she got back out of the shower again, she couldn't resist re-checking her phone to see if Nick had responded. He had, and her smile turned to a grin. He'd sent her a shot of himself, towel strategically placed low on his waist, torso still wet from the shower, a suggestive half smile on his face. The message simply read:

> Next time...

If saucy texts were about as close as she was going to get to him for the next three days, then she'd look forward to receiving more of them. Dithering about what to send back, since she herself was pink and dishevelled from her own shower, she made do with:

> Nice view to keep me warm on these long, lonely nights.

Perhaps she'd send him something more 'visual' later on. Saturday night had unleashed Nick's naughty side, it seemed. She'd have to make sure she kept her phone away from the kids, if this was going to be the way their communications were going.

A little later on, as Thea, Cora, Dylan and Lorelai wandered through the woodland between Thea's house and Nightshade Cottage, Thea reflected that, even with the unsettling situation with Ed and his other son not yet resolved, things were looking up. Annabelle had taken her aside between courses last night and offered her a few more hours at the farm shop, as well, which she definitely said she'd consider. Although the money wouldn't match her teaching salary, every little would help. For the first time since she could remember, Thea felt optimistic about the future, and as she strolled along with her family on a bright, wintry Sunday morning's walk, even the weather seemed to be celebrating.

44

For Nick, the next couple of days flew by in a flurry of activity, as the farm shop got ready to close for Christmas. He'd spent a leisurely Sunday at home, mulling over the previous evening and trying to keep the grin from his face whenever he thought back to how much fun it had been. Even Thea's reaction to the roulette tables hadn't derailed either of them for long, and he felt privileged that she'd shared the reason for her upset with him. They were building on many years of trust, and taking their relationship to the next level had felt like the natural next step. He knew, now, to give her the space she needed to celebrate Christmas with her family; she'd made it clear that this was what she wanted, and he felt optimistic that they'd be going into the new year having established something very new, but very precious.

To that end, he'd promised he'd keep his distance, that he would enjoy Christmas with his own family, and he and Thea would get together after the festive furore was over. That didn't stop him thinking about just jumping in the Land Rover and heading over to Orion Close at least thirty times a day for the next day or so, but he managed to restrain himself. The last thing he wanted to do was scare her off.

Annabelle, of course, had been driving him bonkers with her knowing looks when they'd been on shift in the shop together, but he'd resolutely refused to give her any ammunition. There'd be plenty of time to talk to the family when he was surer of the ground he and Thea were breaking. But he couldn't resist mentioning to Annabelle that yes, she'd been right, and yes, he hoped, finally, that things were going to work out between them. Annabelle, seemingly content with that, had made do with Cheshire cat grins in his direction ever since.

At close of business on Christmas Eve, Nick was alone in the shop. Annabelle had left earlier in the day, since she was cooking Christmas dinner for the family and needed to get started on the mammoth task of catering for them all. She'd hugged him goodbye as she'd left, and he'd promised to get round early on Christmas morning to give her a hand and mediate between the relatives. Their mother's sister, Gladys, was coming down to stay with their parents, and was a stickler for things being done just so on Christmas Day, so Nick wanted to provide some extra support.

As he switched out the lights and locked up, he remembered a comment Thea had made about Dylan being into Pokémon cards. He was pretty sure that the collection he'd had when he was a kid might still be in the attic at his parents' place and wondered if he'd have time to root them out before he saw Thea and the kids again. He hadn't got anything planned, for once, on Christmas Eve, so he thought he'd pop round and see if he could find them.

At Holly Ridge Cottage, his parents' house, his mother was pleased to see him. While she made him a cuppa, he ascended the rickety ladder into their roof space and was soon immersed in the archived memorabilia he found. Although his parents had downsized some years ago, a lot of the stuff that he and Annabelle had been given as children had, unaccountably, ended up at their smaller place, and he'd been meaning to reclaim his portion of it for quite a while. Searching through the boxes of possessions he'd not seen for decades, his walk down memory lane was in danger of distracting him from what he'd come over to find. Delving into one of several plastic storage boxes marked 'Nick', he smiled when he came across a wallet of old photographs from the mid-noughties. He spent a couple of minutes flipping through them, noting with amusement the clothing and hairstyles of himself and his friends, and wondering why they'd ever thought the styles that looked so great on the popstars of the time would ever suit them. His heart sped up when he saw a picture of Tristan, Thea, Annabelle, Jamie and himself, snapped during some party or other, looking young, carefree and completely at ease in each other's company. He remembered, with a jolt, that this must have been the infamous night at Gina Hodge's place, but it had obviously been taken before they'd all got plastered on stuff they were too young to drink. His arm was around Thea, and he wished he could go back and tell his younger self to be brave and tell Thea how he'd felt back then.

Shaking his head, he put the photo in his back pocket and returned the others to the archive box. He vowed to himself that his new year's resolution would be to get all of his stuff out of his parents' attic once and for all, but for now it would have to wait. As he looked in the next box, he found what he was searching for, the boxed set of Pokémon cards, and just before he put the lid back on, he noticed a small jewellery case tucked away in one corner of the storage box. Carefully pulling it out, he smiled as he flipped it open. A gift from a relative many years back, he remembered wondering when on earth he'd ever have reason to wear it. But now, it seemed like the perfect last-minute gift for Thea. He didn't want to give her anything extravagant, but it didn't seem right not to mark the season, somehow. Carefully descending the ladder once more, he headed downstairs to have the cup of tea with his parents.

'You and Thea looked pretty cosy on Saturday evening,' his father said as they sipped their tea in the small, neat living room of the cottage. 'Anything we should know, at last?' Rob wasn't blessed with his wife and daughter's diplomatic skills, and Nick had braced himself for an interrogation.

'Early days, Dad,' he said quickly. 'But we have been spending a bit of time together.'

'Funny... didn't see you much after dinner. You youngsters lack the stamina to stay out all night!' Rob snorted. 'Not like your mother and me. We didn't get home until half past two!'

'And you were like a bear with a sore head all day Sunday,' Maggie chided. 'Leave Nick alone. It's about time he got his act together with Thea. Don't jinx things with your questions.'

Nick threw his mum a grateful look. 'Is there anything I need to take to Annie's for Christmas Day?' he asked, keen to deflect the focus from his love life.

'Not that I can think of,' Maggie replied. 'I'm sure she's got it all under control, but you could always check with her.' She gave a stage whisper. 'A pair of ear plugs to filter out the worst of Aunt Gladys's rhetoric might be advisable.'

Nick grinned. He knew his mother loved her sister, but they did not share the same outlook on life. 'I'll bear that in mind,' he said. Kissing his mum and dad goodbye, he headed back out of the door with what he'd salvaged from the loft. As he drove the short distance back to his own cottage, he found he couldn't pull his mind away from Thea. He wondered how cross she'd be if he dropped by. Looking at his watch, he shook his head. She'd be really busy now, getting stuff ready for the next day. All the same, as he drew up outside his house, he felt an almost irresistible urge to play Santa Claus and drop the cards and the small gift he'd discovered in the box over to her tonight. Perhaps, if he only stayed for five minutes, it would be OK. If she didn't answer the door, he'd leave them on the step.

He managed to last four whole hours before he gave into the temptation.

45

'Ssh!' Thea hissed as she pulled Nick through the front door and closed it quietly. 'The kids are finally asleep, and I really don't want to wake them up again.' It had been a hectic Christmas Eve, and Thea had been looking forward to flumping on the sofa and relaxing for a couple of hours before heading off to bed herself. Tomorrow was going to be a busy day of family, fun and, if Lorelai was on her usual form, far too much food, so a couple of hours to herself was a must. However, Nick was on her doorstep now, and her body and mind were telling her she wanted something entirely different.

'Your wish is my command,' Nick murmured. 'I won't make a sound, I promise.'

'What are you doing here?' she asked. 'Shouldn't you be bracing yourself for the Saint family Christmas shindig?'

'I'm not expected at Mistletoe Barn until mid-morning tomorrow,' Nick replied. 'And since Charlotte, Tristan, Annie and Jamie are all tied up with their own last-minute preparations, I found myself lonely and at a loose end on the night before Christmas.'

He turned hangdog eyes on her that looked so self-consciously gloomy, Thea couldn't help but laugh.

'Well, I'm sorry to hear I'm your last resort!'

'You were my first, actually, but I didn't want to interrupt your family celebrations.'

'The kids would have been pleased to see you,' Thea replied. 'You can do no wrong in their eyes since you rustled up the tree for them.'

'Glad they liked it,' Nick said. His face suddenly grew serious. 'There was something else, as well.' He reached into the pocket of his thick winter jacket and pulled out a small, gift-wrapped box. 'Don't panic,' he said. 'It's not *that*. I'm not quite so impulsive as to propose three days after we've slept together.'

Thea snorted back a laugh, still mindful of the kids upstairs. 'Sometimes I forget we've been friends forever.'

'Me too.' Nick's eyes met hers, and she felt the warm, welcome pressure of his lips as he somehow managed to keep the present in one hand and move her closer to him with the other. His mouth began to explore hers, and her knees grew weak. It had only been a few days since their night together, but she was suddenly aching for more. Deepening the kiss, she pressed closer to him, slipping her arms inside his jacket so she could feel him against her. Thea could feel Nick's body stirring, too, and she wished she could just whisk him upstairs and make love to him with the same freedom they'd had on the night of the Midwinter's Eve Ball.

Gasping slightly, she eventually pulled away again. 'You are *far* too good at that,' she murmured. 'You're a dirty kisser, Nick Saint.'

Nick raised an eyebrow. 'I'll take that as a compliment.' His tone might have been confident, but the flush on his face gave away the effect the kiss had had on him, too. 'I can't believe I'm going to have to leave here with this ridiculous hard-on!'

Thea smirked. 'If my children weren't upstairs, I'd deal with that, but they're both light sleepers, and it's far too risky.'

Nick pulled her close again and groaned. 'My ears hear you, but the rest of me is determined to ignore the warning...'

Thea giggled, then, shocked at the sound, she kissed him again. 'So I can feel.' She reached a hand downwards and felt Nick pressing back against her. It was so tempting to keep playing, right here in the hallway. Nick gently pushed her back against the wall, and they continued to kiss for a little longer, until both of them were flushed and breathing heavily.

'I want you so much, Thea,' Nick breathed into her neck, sending tingle after tingle over her skin.

'I want you too,' Thea replied, her voice low and slightly shaky. 'You are the best Christmas present I could ever have.'

'And I'm desperate to be unwrapped.' Nick's voice was little more than a groan. 'Promise me you won't leave me hanging for too long...'

'Oh, God.' Thea felt as though every inch of her was on alert, and desperate to touch and be touched. 'How the hell are we going to get through Christmas Day?'

Nick laughed. 'I'll be thinking of you every minute.'

Slowly, tantalisingly, they disentangled themselves.

'I'd better go,' Nick said. 'If I don't leave now, you'll have to explain why you've got a breakfast guest on Christmas morning to the kids.'

Thea pulled back from him. 'I wish you didn't have to go, but it's better we take this one step at a time. The kids have never seen me with anyone else other than their dad. I want to give them the chance to get used to the idea that there might be someone new in our lives. Maybe dinner together sometime after Christmas would be a good start.'

'I absolutely understand,' Nick said. 'I'd love to.'

Thea grinned. 'Shall we say teatime on the twenty-eighth, then? Unless you've got other plans?'

Nick smiled. 'It's a date.'

Thea's head spun as they kissed again. 'Lovely...'

Nick shook his head. 'I still can't quite believe that things are happening between us.'

'Neither can I,' Thea agreed. 'But I like it. I like it a lot. And I like you more than a lot.'

'Glad to hear it.' Nick smiled down at her. 'Now. Take this present and put it under the tree. I hope you like it, too.'

Thea's face fell. 'I didn't buy you anything...'

Nick's warm hand on her cheek reassured her before he spoke. 'I don't want anything else other than you,' he said. 'I know that sounds sappy, but it's true. You're the best Christmas present anyone could ever have.'

Thea's eyes filled with tears. No one had ever talked to her like Nick did. He'd always been a good talker, but now, seemingly smitten, he'd developed an eloquence that made her heart soar and ache at the same time.

'Have a lovely Christmas,' she said as she walked him back to the door.

'You too.' Nick smiled at her. 'Call me when you're ready to see me again. I can't wait to pick this up where we've left off.'

Thea smiled back. 'Neither can I.'

As he walked down the short path to the kerb where his Land Rover was parked, Thea followed him with her eyes. How was it that someone she'd known her whole life could mean something so new, and so different to her now? She had the very real feeling that, if she wasn't careful, she was going to fall head over heels for Nick. The thought should have scared her, but instead she felt as though something had finally fallen into place in her heart. For the first time in a long time, she, too, was smitten.

46

Nick woke up on Christmas Day with a slight hangover, having had a generous tot of whisky as a night cap when he'd returned from Thea's, but a feeling of excitement he hadn't felt in years. And it had nothing to do with the season. Rolling over in bed, he reached for his phone, and his heart gave a little flutter of pleasure when he saw that Thea had already texted him to wish him a merry Christmas. He shouldn't be surprised; even though her children weren't toddlers any more, he imagined they'd still be up early on the day itself. He allowed himself the luxury of imagining Thea, Cora and Dylan opening their presents, enjoying a festive breakfast and sharing the day together. He was surprised at how much he wanted to be a part of that scene, and wondered, with a pang of curiosity, how Thea's former partner, Ed, could have walked out on his family the way he did. Thea's account of the end of her relationship with Ed had explained a lot, but to Nick the whole thing seemed unfathomable. What could possibly be more important than the family you'd helped to create?

He shook his head slightly. Annabelle was always accusing

him of naiveté; he figured that this was just another example of where he 'just didn't understand the ways of the wider world'. She was wrong, of course: he did understand. He just believed that people could, and should, be better for those they loved. The best versions of themselves.

Smirking at himself for his own stupid idealism, he texted 'Merry Christmas' and a few too many kisses back to Thea before getting out of bed. Soon after that, he decided to walk over to Mistletoe Barn, where Annabelle was already sorting out the preparations for Christmas lunch.

'Hey sis,' he said as he ambled through the back door into the kitchen. He'd brought a couple of bottles of champagne with him and clunked them down onto the kitchen counter. 'Merry Christmas.'

'You too.' Annabelle paused briefly from basting the roast potatoes and gave him a hug and a kiss on the cheek. 'Help yourself to a drink. There's a bottle open in the fridge if you want champagne.'

'Can I get you one?' Nick asked.

'Just a top up.' Annabelle gestured to her glass and went back to the potatoes. 'I don't want to be drunk and in charge of boiling pans!'

'Anything I can do to help?'

Annabelle rolled her eyes. 'Get in there and referee between Mum and Aunty Gladys? Dad's trying to keep the peace, but you know how they are when they've had a couple of glasses of champers. There's a reason they only see each other at Christmas!'

'Will do.' Nick grinned at his sister. Ever since she'd taken over the Christmas dinner preparations from their mother a couple of years back, Annabelle ran Christmas Day like a well-oiled machine, leaving the rest of the family to just get well oiled. He sometimes felt guilty that the responsibility had landed with her, but since she and Jamie now lived in the farmhouse, it seemed to go with the territory.

Entering the large but cosy living room, he glanced quickly at his phone screen, hopeful of a message from Thea, before slipping it into his back pocket. Thea had sent him a cute, animated gif of a rabbit blowing kisses under the mistletoe, and he resolved to slope off later and find an equally cute one to send back to her. In the meantime, he had the family to referee.

'Hello, Aunty Glad,' he said as he approached the group of family by the fire. 'Nice to see you.' He kissed her cheek, and then turned to his mother, who was sipping a flute of champagne by the large stone fireplace that dominated the living room. Jamie was stacking logs into the wicker basket and glanced up, giving him a smile as he settled himself on the sofa next to his aunt.

'Hello, Nicholas,' Aunty Gladys responded. 'Still single, I see?'

Nick nodded. 'Afraid so, Aunty Glad.' He wasn't going to be drawn on his relationship quite so early in proceedings.

They made the usual small talk, and Gladys filled him in on the activities of his cousins who were both living with their families in Australia and celebrating Christmas around the barbecue.

'Have you never thought of visiting them out there for Christmas?' Nick asked. He tried not to smirk as he caught his mother's eye.

'Too hot for me at that time of year.' Gladys shuddered theatrically. 'But I'm planning on going out for a few weeks next summer – it'll be cooler then.'

'Makes sense,' Nick said. He sat back on the sofa and let conversation drift around him, wondering, yet again, how Thea's Christmas was going. He wouldn't want to be anywhere else but with his family on Christmas Day, but there was a part of him that wanted to have Thea and her children by his side to share it.

'Of course, people split up too quickly, these days,' Aunty

Gladys was saying, on her third glass of champagne. 'In our day, marriage was for the long haul, thick and thin, in sickness and in health, for richer for poorer. Now it's easier to walk away, people just don't commit to each other.'

After his recent experiences with Thea, Nick wanted to disagree, but he kept quiet. Aunty Gladys was entitled to her opinions, and nuance had never been part of her vocabulary.

'Oh, I don't know, Aunty Glad,' Annabelle, who'd come in from the kitchen, said. 'People are under so much pressure these days. It's not always easy to keep things going. Especially when there are children involved.'

'All the more reason to stay together,' Gladys replied, accepting another top up from Annabelle, who was offering around the bottle. 'Too many single-parent families these days, all on benefits and scrounging off society.'

Nick caught Annabelle's eye and shook his head. They'd learned not to argue with Gladys, especially not on Christmas Day. Some topics – Brexit, politics and family dynamics – were always off limits once a year. But Nick couldn't help feeling irritated by Gladys' point-blank statements: she'd obviously been mainlining the right-wing news channels again.

'Well, everyone, dinner's almost ready, if you want to go to the dining room,' Annabelle said.

The table, set for six, looked stunning. A white tablecloth was topped by a green and red festive runner, which in turn was adorned with holly and mistletoe wreaths, and red and green candles, already lit. The family crystal, inherited from Annabelle and Nick's grandparents, glinted in the candlelight, and the dinner service Jamie and Annabelle had been given as a wedding present had already been set out.

'Jamie, the table looks fabulous!' Maggie said, giving her son-in-law a smile of appreciation.

'It's the least I could do, what with Annie being our resident Nigella Lawson all day!' Jamie joked. 'But thank you, all the same.' He hurried back out to the kitchen to help Annabelle bring in in the tureens of food, and Nick made himself useful doing the same.

'I'm going to need a lot more of this if I'm going to get through lunch without braining Gladys with the red wine decanter!' Annabelle muttered to Nick as she piled roast potatoes into one of the serving dishes.

'Don't let her get to you,' Nick grinned. 'I mean, what would Christmas dinner be without our annual serving of swivel-eyed lunacy courtesy of Aunty Glad!'

'I know.' Annabelle smiled briefly at Nick. 'I suppose it's just the way she speaks about single parents that gets to me. Some of us are struggling to even become parents, and it kind of hits a nerve.'

'No news, then?' Nick asked carefully. He'd been hoping, like the rest of the Saint family, that Annabelle and Jamie's holiday would have enabled a Christmas miracle, but it seemed that it wasn't to be.

Annabelle shook her head. 'Not as yet, no.' She seemed torn between sadness and laughter and seemed to opt for the latter as she took a generous glug straight from the champagne bottle. 'Ah well, at least it means, now that dinner's almost on the table, I can get pissed without guilt!'

Nick threw an arm briefly around his sister's shoulders and then grabbed a couple of the tureens. 'Well, let's get on with it, then,' he said. 'A united front against Gladys will do the trick, I'm sure.'

Annabelle grinned. 'Whatever you do, don't mention you're dating Thea, or she'll have a blue fit when she finds out you're seeing *one of those bloody single mothers*!'

'I have no intention of mentioning it.' Nick grinned back. 'I don't want to be given the third degree by the right-wing mafia around the Christmas table!'

'Fair enough.' Annabelle paused, before adding, 'Did you manage to see Thea again before Christmas Day hit?'

Nick's smile gave him away.

'So you did, then?' Annabelle laughed.

'Let's just say I'm very much looking forward to the new year.'

'Glad to hear it, little brother. Now let's get this food to the table before Mum throttles Gladys with the holly wreath!'

'I'll be there in a sec,' Nick said. He checked his phone again. He was hoping for another message from Thea, but he also knew she'd be busy with her own family Christmas, so he wasn't going to be too surprised if he didn't hear from her until later. He wondered if she'd opened his present yet. Hopefully, he'd been right in his choice to give it to her. Smiling when he saw she'd sent him a photo of herself and the unwrapped gift, he paused before joining his family in the dining room. He texted a quick, 'It looks great on you. Wish you were here with me,' to her, along with a goofy gif of Bugs Bunny blowing kisses.

47

Thea leaned back on Lorelai's sofa and groaned. 'That was amazing, Gran. I honestly don't know how you do it.'

'Years of practise, dear,' Lorelai replied. Tristan and Charlotte were finishing up the washing up in the utility room, ably aided by Cora and Dylan, who were loading the dishwasher and squabbling about whose turn it was to bring the last plates through.

'Well, I hope you don't intend to hang up your apron any time soon,' Thea joked. 'I'll need all of the recipes and tips if you do decide that one of us needs to take over next year.'

'I'll keep you posted, but I'm probably good for a year or two yet.' Lorelai smiled indulgently. Taking advantage of the fact that the rest of the family was occupied doing the clearing, she added, 'Have you given any more thought to what you're going to do about Ben, and his father?'

Thea hesitated. She needed to talk things through with someone, but she didn't want to burden her grandmother with it all, especially not on Christmas Day. 'Not really,' she admitted. 'But I suppose I can't hide from it forever.' She sighed. 'At least Dylan seems reasonably OK with the development – Cora and I sat down with him and told him about Ben, and all he said was, "Does he play football?" I suppose that's a good start!'

'Could have been worse,' Lorelai agreed. 'And it might be better to be the one who takes control of the situation, rather than allowing Ed to dictate things, as he surely will once he's got wind of Ben contacting Cora.'

'You know, I honestly don't know if he does know or not,' Thea's brow wrinkled. 'I mean, I've kind of been assuming that he must know, but what if he's still in the dark? That could add a whole new layer of complications.' Just thinking about what might and might not be happening was enough to give Thea a headache. 'But that's for another day,' she added. 'Not Christmas.'

'I'm here if you need me,' Lorelai said gently. 'You know that.'

'I know.' Thea smiled at her grandmother. Then, turning to the bag of board games she'd brought over with her, she grinned. 'So will it be Monopoly, Cluedo or Twister this year?'

Lorelai gave a laugh. 'I think my days of playing Twister are well and truly over, but I'm sure you've got a few left in you!'

'Maybe if I hadn't had so much wine with dinner,' Thea replied. She loved days like this, just hanging out with her grandmother, waiting for the rest of the family to join them. She was well aware of the passing of time, these days, and how, now Lorelai was approaching eighty years old, they had more of those days behind them than in front of them, so she was determined to make the most of the time they had.

That got her thinking, reluctantly, of the situation with Ben and Ed. Surely, she owed it to her own children to allow them to make contact with their half-brother? She needed to take control of things and resolved, after the Christmas holiday was over, to do just that.

'Right' – Charlotte entered the living room – 'now all that's out of the way, who's for Twister?'

Tristan, following behind her, rolled his eyes good naturally. 'I don't intend on exerting myself any more than to reach for my glass of wine this afternoon, so count me out.'

'Spoilsport,' Charlotte chided him. 'Come on... I know how flexible you are!'

'TMI, future sister-in-law!' Thea laughed. 'Didn't you get the memo about not discussing that sort of thing in front of the other twin?'

Charlotte grinned. 'Don't get me started on you, or I'll demand all sorts of gory details about why you disappeared so suddenly from the Midwinter's Eve Ball!'

It was Thea's turn to roll her eyes. 'That can wait for another day.' Thankfully, the children came into the room just as she said it, so Charlotte didn't probe any further.

A riotous game of Twister ensued, with Dylan victorious, after a close-run contest with Tristan. As Tristan collapsed across the mat trying to make an impossible reach to a red spot, Dylan jumped on top of him before doing a victory lap of the living room.

Thea, on the fuel of another glass of champagne, couldn't stop giggling. There was nothing better than being with the family on Christmas Day.

'Rematch!' Dylan shouted.

Tristan groaned. 'Not right now.' He heaved himself up off the floor and flopped onto the sofa beside Charlotte. 'Your go, I think.'

Charlotte shook her head. 'Co-ordination is definitely not my strong point!' She glanced at Thea. 'How about you, Thea?'

Thea shook her head. 'Nope. All I'm good for is the monarch's speech and a snooze right now.'

The afternoon carried on much the same way until, finally, feeling laughed-out and replete, Thea rounded up Cora and Dylan and made her way back to Orion Close. Tristan and Charlotte were spending the night in Lorelai's spare room and would probably be up for a hangover-curing woodland walk at some point on Boxing Day. Thea looked forward to it. She never took having family around for granted; it was the most valuable privilege she had. Even allowing for the sentimentality that an extra glass of wine enflamed, she felt as though she'd really filled up her emotional wells this Christmas. She laughed at the self-reflection; she'd talked about the same thing with her class before they broke up for the Christmas holiday, encouraging them to try to think as much about the gifts of spending time with loved ones as they did about the gifts under the Christmas tree. Perhaps it was just a festive, hazy glow she was feeling, but she felt as though she'd got a lot of things into perspective lately. She fingered the lapel of her winter coat, where she'd pinned the pretty, silver and pearl pin badge in the shape of mistletoe and berries that had been inside the box Nick had given her the night before. His handwritten note, which she'd tucked back into the box, had simply read:

So you can use this to kiss me whenever you want... not that you need an excuse!

With that in mind, Thea fumbled in her pocket for the house keys. Just as she was about to open the front door, determined only for a cup of tea and an early night, her phone pinged. Pulling it out of her pocket, she saw that she had a Facebook message request. Somehow, before she even opened the app, she had an inkling as to whom it might be from. Her heart started to race as she waited for the message to load. Timing had never been his strong point, but even she had to question what made him think that eight o'clock on Christmas Day was the right time to make contact. The message was short, to the point and didn't give much away, but she knew it was going to be the gateway to a much longer conversation. It wasn't a conversation she wanted to have, but it seemed, now, it was inevitable.

48

After a night spent in less than peaceful slumber, Thea decided she wasn't going to let Ed continue to play on her mind. He'd had too much power over her and their relationship when she'd been living with him, and she wasn't going to allow him to do the same after so much time apart. If he wanted the children to meet, then it was going to be on her terms, not his. She looked at the message he'd sent again:

> Thea, Sorry to contact you out of the blue. I understand Cora and my son Ben have been in touch. We should discuss how to proceed.
> Please message me when you have a moment to discuss next steps, and we can arrange a conversation. Ed.

Thea wasn't sure whether to be annoyed or relieved at the curt tone of his words. The message said all it needed to say, and no more. But there was so much she wanted to know – the details that would make this meeting easier. Was Ed still in a relationship with Ben's mother? If so, where were they living? How long had they been together? She felt a sting of something she couldn't quite identify: not jealousy, but a sense of injustice that he seemed to have moved on, to have made a new life for himself after summarily wrecking the life they'd had when he'd walked out on her and the children. Anger was there, too; if his other son hadn't contacted Cora, would he have bothered to get in touch with her? Was his message just a reaction to an unfortunate situation enabled by the children's use of social media?

But all of this was getting her nowhere. She sighed. She'd spent far too long already composing replies, which ranged from courtesy to rage. She just needed to respond and then forget about it until they'd come up with a strategy. Grabbing her phone, she texted back as neutrally as she could, suggesting a phone call when it was a good time. Then, determined not to let Ed and their past get her down while she had another lovely day with the children to enjoy, she deliberately left her phone upstairs, and went down to make breakfast.

Later on, as she'd predicted, Tristan and Charlotte arrived on the doorstep, having chosen to walk off the excesses of the previous day. Persuaded off the sofa by Comet, who was raring for a longer walk, the children headed off into the woodland, leaving the adults to natter and stretch their legs.

'It was such a nice day yesterday,' Thea said. She'd grabbed her phone again, but as yet hadn't had a reply from Ed. Nick had sent her a couple of texts, though, and she'd replied to him. She was hoping she might see him over the next day or two.

'It really was. Here's to many more to come.' Tristan, who had the ability more than anyone to sense when there was something on Thea's mind, looked at her intently. 'Everything all right?'

Thea paused. She needed to talk to someone, and since Charlotte was ahead with the children and Comet, it seemed as good a time as any to confide in her brother. As she filled him in, Tristan's expression turned from shock to outrage.

'That absolute twat!' he fumed. 'How dare he waltz back into your life, on Christmas Day of all days, and start making demands about the kids. Who the fuck does he think he is?'

Thea shrugged. 'He's the kids' father, if nothing else.'

'Not that you'd know it, after all this time.' Tristan stopped walking and put a hand on Thea's arm. 'How are you handling it?' His tone was a little gentler as his anger subsided.

'I'm OK, I guess,' Thea kicked at an embedded stone on the path with the toe of her walking boot. 'It's all been a bit of a shock, but Ed and I owe it to the kids to do things in a civilised way, even if he has been out of my children's lives for so long.' She took a breath. 'I'm going to suggest I meet him, without any of the kids, and then we can work out what happens next.'

'Are you sure you want to do that?' Tristan asked. 'It's been over eleven years since you split up. And if this new child of his is only ten, he didn't really hang around, did he? Doesn't that piss you off, even a little bit?'

'Of course it does!' Thea booted the stone, having dislodged it from the ground. 'But what's the point in holding onto all that? It is what it is, and we've both moved on with our lives. All I need to be sure of is that he's not in the same place with the gambling addiction that he was when he left. I won't put my children at risk.'

'You're a whole lot calmer about this than I thought you'd be, sis,' Tristan replied. 'I mean, I wasn't living with the guy, and I still want to feed him to the loan sharks – feet first!'

Thea laughed. 'That's my brother – protective until the end.' She hugged Tristan. 'I know it's difficult to understand, but I've managed to build a life of my own, to move on. Ed can't hurt me any more. If there's a way that Cora and Dylan can get to know him, and this half-brother of theirs, without our old emotions and our past getting in the way then I have to try to make it work.'

'Just don't go promising anything that'll backfire on you, sis.' Tristan hugged her back. 'I don't want you getting hurt again.'

'I won't.' Thea paused. She felt a little emotional as she asked the question she'd been wanting to broach since they'd started talking about the Ed situation. 'When I do agree to meet him... will you come with me, Tris? I think I need my brother by my side if I'm going to get through this.'

Thea saw Tristan swallow hard before he replied gruffly, 'Of course I will. Name the time and place and I'll be there.' He paused before adding more playfully, 'And I'm not joking about the bloody sharks!'

That afternoon, feeling a whole lot better about what she was going to do, Thea took a deep breath and arranged a meeting with Ed.

49

Two days later, with the kids safely ensconced on the sofa at home, arguing over who got to play which character on Dylan's newly acquired *Sword Fighter 3* game, Thea headed out of the house and down to the Star and Telescope pub in the centre of Lower Brambleton. Ed had been more than happy to travel to meet her, so she figured she might as well gain the upper hand and meet on familiar territory. As she pulled up in the car park, she wondered which of the cars was his. When he'd left her, he'd only the clothes on his back.

Tristan, glowering in the passenger seat beside her, turned and looked her in the eye. 'Are you sure about this? You don't have to do it, you know.'

Thea smiled at her brother. 'You and I both know that's not true. It's better all round if the kids get to know each other and the adults behave in a civilised way.'

'You don't owe him *civilised*,' Tristan muttered. 'You don't owe him anything.'

Thea was grateful for his protective streak, but she also knew she was right. 'I'm glad you're here to keep an eye on things,' she said. She reached out and touched his arm. 'I'm sure Ed won't want any trouble, either. It's been a long time.'

'I'll be at the bar if you need me,' Tristan said. 'All you have to do is say the word, and I'll be right there next to you.'

'I know. And I appreciate it.' Thea and Tristan headed into the bar of the Star and Telescope, which was reassuringly busy on this 'Betwixtmas' day. Lots of locals, it seemed, had taken the time off between Christmas and New Year, and while Thea felt nervous about being spotted conversing with Ed, she was grateful for the public place. Taking a deep breath, she headed through to the lounge area of the pub, keeping her eyes peeled for him. If this meeting went well, then she'd consider allowing the children to come along next time.

Over in the far corner, near the large fireplace that dominated the space, a man was sitting alone at a table. He was looking down at his phone, and so as she paused at the entrance to the lounge, Thea had the advantage. She noticed that his hair was grey, and that he was heavier set than he had been when they'd been together. He was dressed tidily in a polo shirt and dark jeans, with a jacket slung over the back of the chair. She couldn't help wondering if he was playing the online slot machines while he waited. Heading across the lounge towards him, he looked up as she approached the table.

'Hi,' he said, and she could tell from his tone how nervous he was. 'Thank you for coming.'

Thea nodded. 'Hello, Ed.' She took a seat as he gestured to the one across from him. The silence felt loaded, uncomfortable. Thea waited while he closed an app on his phone and put it flat down on the table.

'I was just texting Ciara, my wife, to let her know I'd got here

OK. She was, er, a little worried about all this, as you can imagine.'

'You got married?' Thea could hear the incredulity in her own voice. 'When?'

Ed looked sheepish. 'Shortly after Ben was born. Ciara comes from quite a religious family. They, er, weren't too happy about our situation, so it seemed the right thing to do.'

'Ah yes, Ben. The reason we're having to do this.' Thea's tone was sharper than she'd intended, and Ed's shock registered on his face. 'I'm sorry,' she said. 'This has all come as a bit of a shock. I've not really had time to process it all since Cora told me she'd been in touch with your son.'

Ed laughed nervously. 'Well, it's not exactly been a walk in the park for me, either.'

'Which part? Leaving me and the children homeless, getting married and having kids again or not bothering to let me know any of this before your son got in touch with our daughter?'

'Thea...' Ed began. 'This isn't really the time or the place for a wider discussion, is it?'

Thea's irritation began to rise. 'Oh, isn't it? Well, all right then, what *would* you like to discuss? The last contact I had with you, a month after you left, you were broke and sofa surfing, and then, nothing. Not a phone call, not a birthday card to your children... and now this? What am I supposed to think?'

'There's a lot of ground to cover, I get that,' Ed replied. 'And we'll get there, I promise. But there are some things you need to know. And the most important thing is that I'm sorry. I know now that I was in the grip of something bigger than me, and that you and the kids became collateral damage. It took me a long time to come to terms with that, and even longer to get the help I needed. But I've done the work, Thea, and if Ben hadn't jumped the gun and contacted Cora, I was going to reach out myself soon. Ciara gave me an ultimatum when Ben was a toddler: go into rehab or she wouldn't let me be a part of her and Ben's life. I didn't want to make the same mistake with them as I did with you, so I did it. And I've been in recovery for eight years now. I haven't placed a bet in all of that time, and I never want to.'

All this talk of *reaching out* and *doing the work* made Thea want to vomit with rage, but she swallowed hard and tried to force her emotions back down to a manageable level. Ed had always been able to push her buttons, and, much as she hated to admit it, he was right, there were more important things at stake now than what their own past relationship had been.

'So what now?' she asked. 'Have you given any thought to that?'

Ed nodded. 'Well, since Cora and Ben have made contact, I think it would be a reasonable next step to allow them to meet, if you think that's a sensible idea. Ciara wants to be present, too, if you're happy to have her there. She feels... insecure about the, uh, unresolved nature of our relationship.'

'It's unresolved because you cut off contact with your own kids!' Thea snapped. 'You haven't been there for them at all since you walked out. And now you want to come back into their lives? Give me one good reason why I should agree to any of this?'

Ed looked pained. 'Because, you know as well as I do that it's better we manage this as adults. If we don't let the kids get to know each other now, while we still have some control over it, they'll do it anyway when they're older. At least this way we've both got some say in the matter.'

It wasn't lost on Thea that this was exactly the line of argument that Lorelai had pursued when she'd talked this through with her grandmother before Christmas. She just hated that Ed was right, as Lorelai had been. She let out a long sigh. 'All right,' she said. 'But we do this slowly. And I'm warning you, Ed, if you're just going to disappear again, then we can forget this right now. It took me a long time to get back on my feet when you left, and the kids can't cope with you swanning back into their lives if you're just going to leave again.'

For the first time, Ed looked genuinely remorseful. 'I can't forgive myself for what I did to you and the kids, Thea,' he began, 'but I can tell you now that I was in the grip of an addiction so strong that it overwhelmed everything else. I couldn't help myself back then, and I was no use to you, or Cora and Dylan. If I hadn't got away, when I hit rock bottom I'd have dragged you down with me, and I'd never have forgiven myself for that.' He looked down at his hands. 'I know it was the coward's way out, just to run, but believe me when I say I've pulled myself up through hell, and it's only now that I feel as though I won't just be a burden of shame around your neck. I treated you appallingly, and I will always carry that with me. But I want to be a part of my children's lives, and if Ben hadn't reached out to Cora when he did, I'd have done the same thing anyway.'

It wasn't often that Thea was stunned into silence, but it seemed that, if nothing else, Ed could still have that effect on her. She swallowed hard. 'I appreciate what you've said,' she began. 'I suppose having a shared history counts for something.' The irony wasn't lost on her that she'd been saying much the same to Nick, in a different context. 'In a way, it's good to see the shorthand between us still works.'

Ed looked relieved. 'I'm not expecting miracles, but I am serious. I think we can make this work. I have a lot to make up for, and I really want to prove that to you.' He reached out and touched one of her hands where it rested on the table.

Thea pulled away. 'Don't. I'm prepared for the kids to meet, and I'm even prepared to be polite to you in their company, but don't push your luck, Ed.'

'I'm sorry,' he said humbly. His gaze was distracted by something over Thea's left shoulder. 'Tristan's still not my biggest fan, I see.'

Thea glanced behind her and saw her brother nursing a pint at the bar and staring daggers in Ed's direction. 'He doesn't think I should have come,' she said. 'He had to pick up the pieces, along with Gran, when you left.'

'Can't say I blame him, then.' Ed gave a rueful smile. He paused, and then added, 'Let me know when it's convenient for the kids to meet. I'm based in Wiltshire, just outside Salisbury, these days, so it won't take long for me to get over to you. That's where I met Ciara, in fact.'

'Things must have happened pretty quickly between you two, if Ben's ten years old,' Thea observed. 'You gave it a whole three months before finding someone else?'

'It wasn't my intention,' Ed replied. 'I was lucky that she stood by me, but there was never any question she wouldn't have the baby. It was the wake up call I needed.' He looked genuinely remorseful. 'I'm so sorry, Thea. This must be a lot to take on board all at once.'

It was. Not least that Ed could be living relatively close by and still not have made contact, but she swallowed the emotion. There would be plenty of time later to mull it all over. For now, it was essential that the lines were kept clear: it was the best thing for all of the children involved.

'Do you, er, have any more children?' she asked as silence fell between them again.

'A little girl – Maisie,' Ed replied. His face softened as he mentioned the name. 'She's the spitting image of Cora at that age. She's another reason why it felt important to make contact with you and the kids.' He paused, and then added. 'My plan had been to write a letter and send it to your gran's place.'

'What makes you think she'd have passed it on to me?' Thea asked. 'She's not exactly fond of you, either.'

'I can understand that.' Ed shook his head. 'It was a gamble...' He gave a nervous laugh. 'Sorry, poor choice of words. I'm glad, in a way, that Ben took the initiative. It's made things a bit easier.'

'You think this is easy?' Thea shook her head.

'Not exactly, but it's done now.' Ed gave her a small smile. 'I'd like to make the best of it, if you're willing to do the same.'

Despite the emotional rollercoaster of the past few days, Thea could feel her anger starting to abate. Ed had obviously picked up the pieces of his life, and despite the lack of actual contact over the years, he seemed sincere now. It still felt unreal; when he'd left, penniless and in the grip of a gambling addiction that had bankrupted them, she had never wanted to see him again. But time was a reasonable healer, and now, it seemed, it was time to face the next phase of their relationship.

'Let's get through to the new year first,' Thea said, surprising herself with how calm she now felt. 'I'm sure we can work something out and get us all to meet. Cora's great with young children, and I'm sure she'll be thrilled to meet Maisie.' She gave a brief smile. 'And if Ben's into football, he and Dylan will be fine.'

'He's a Bristol Rovers supporter, so I'm not sure if that counts!' Ed quipped. 'But hopefully they can bond over a couple of goalposts.'

Thea stood up again, once they'd swapped mobile numbers. 'I'll be in touch.'

Ed rose, too, and, taking another look in Tristan's direction, he said, 'I hoped your family would look after you after what I put you through. And I'm so sorry I haven't been there for you and the kids.' He paused and looked suddenly nervous. 'I'd like to make it up to you all. The business I started a few years ago has been very successful. It's about time I accounted for everything, financially as well as emotionally.'

Thea put up a hand. 'We've done fine without you,' she said firmly. 'We don't need your money now.' Even if she'd been destitute again, she wasn't ready to take Ed's money. Not after all this time. The financial worries still ate away at her, but she'd find her own solution.

'I understand.' Ed met her unflinching gaze. 'But there may come a time when that changes. I'd like to talk about how I can help, eventually. Please, Thea, promise me you'll think about it.'

Thea nodded. 'If you want to help, then give the money to the kids you walked out on. Open a savings account for each of them. I'm sure they'd appreciate that, when the time comes that they need the money.'

'Sensible as ever.' Ed smiled at her. 'Some things never change.'

Thea tried not to smile back at him. She needed some time alone now to mull things over.

'Speak soon,' Ed said as he headed back towards the door. Thea watched as he nodded at Tristan, who gave a curt incline of his head back. Then, she let out a long, shaky breath.

Tristan was by her side in a trice. 'Are you all right?'

Thea slid an arm around her brother's waist and leaned against him. 'I'm fine. I think it's going to be OK.'

'I meant what I said, Thea; if he dicks you around, he'll have me to answer to.'

Thea gave a laugh at the protective vehemence of her twin brother's tone. 'I think he's on the level. He seems to want what's best for the kids – all of them.'

'I hope you're right,' Tristan said, as they broke their hug. 'For your sake, as well as theirs.'

As Tristan drove Thea back to her house, she felt grateful, not for the first time, that Tristan had her back. Her brother had always been there for her, and she felt stronger for it. She smiled as her phone vibrated with a WhatsApp, and her smile turned to a grin when she realised it was from Nick. Her head was still spinning from the maelstrom of the past few days, but Nick felt like another anchor in the storm. She was looking forward to seeing him, to update him on recent events.

50

Nick smiled broadly as he checked his phone. He and Thea had firmed up their plans for tonight and she'd asked him to come over after work for a bite to eat and a chat. He knew the kids would be around, so he'd have to curb his more passionate impulses, but he also felt hopeful that this might mean she was ready to introduce him to Cora and Dylan as someone other than just a good friend. He suspected they'd worked it out already, after the Midwinter's Eve Ball, but it would be good to put things on a more 'official' footing with them. He set to completing his final jobs of the afternoon, so he could make a quick getaway when the shop closed.

As he was tidying the shelves and doing a last date check on the fridges, the shop's bell tinkled and in walked Tristan.

'Happy New Year, mate,' Nick called, 'if it's not too early to say that!'

Tristan wrinkled his nose. 'Might be, a bit. Where are we, 28 December?'

They exchanged pleasantries for a minute, before Tristan made a firm subject change. 'Just a heads up, Nick, Thea's a bit wobbly right now. If you're seeing her over the next few days, be aware of that.'

'What's happened?'

'Thea met up with that bastard ex of hers today at the pub. She's agreed he and his new kids can meet Cora and Dylan, and they're supposed to be working out some logistics so they can do it soon.'

'Christ...' Nick's head spun. 'I thought he was well out of the picture?'

'Not out of it enough,' Tristan muttered. 'According to Thea, he's in recovery, in a relationship and has a couple of new kids. Thea, for some godforsaken reason, thinks that means the kids should meet each other.' He paused. 'Cora's been in touch through social media with Ed's other son.' He ran a hand through his hair. 'She reckons if they don't manage things between them, then the kids'll do it anyway, eventually.'

Nick's heart thumped. He tried not to feel hurt that he was finding this out from Tristan and reasoned with himself that it had all happened so swiftly, and that was probably why Thea hadn't filled him in on all of the developments herself. He forced a smile at Tristan. 'Your sister's got her head screwed on, Tris, I'm sure she'll do the right thing.'

'I hope so.' Tristan looked so worried, Nick forgot his own concerns.

'I've known you both for a long time, Tris, and you've weathered worse. She'll get through this, and we're both here to help her, aren't we?'

Tristan smiled then. 'You're right. And she'll have my guts for garters if she thinks I've been talking to you about it all, so can you not let her know I've told you? She'll tell you in her own time, I'm sure.'

'My lips are sealed.' Nick smiled at his friend. He walked

Tristan to the door and flipped the closed sign. They were still closing a little earlier in the relaxed days between Christmas and New Year, and Nick was relieved. It would give him time to get home and changed before heading out to Thea's place.

As Tristan went out of the door, he turned back to Nick. 'I'm so glad you and Thea are finally getting it together,' he said. 'It's taken you both long enough. Don't let this thing with Ed put you off. Thea's been over him for a long time, and she's handling things the way she should. He won't come between you two, and if he tries, he'll have me to deal with!'

'I appreciate that.' Nick smiled. 'Take care, Tris.'

Driving home to his cottage, he mulled over what Tristan had told him. He wasn't worried, not really, but he didn't want to say the wrong thing to Thea, either. What they had was so new, and so special, that he didn't want to jeopardise things before they'd really got started. He'd let her take the lead and tell him what she wanted him to know, and hopefully she'd allow him to help her face this difficult situation. He knew how headstrong she was, though, and that he'd have to be careful how much he offered to help her. She'd been so used to dealing with things independently since Ed had gone that she might think he was trying to take control, otherwise. He shook his head in frustration. It felt as though there was suddenly a layer of complication to their relationship that hadn't been there before Christmas. He'd always known it wasn't going to be easy, starting a relationship with Thea and her children, but, he told himself firmly, none of it was going to jeopardise things. They'd take each day at a time and build something new. And today's brick in that new structure was dinner with Thea and the children. That was something to feel optimistic about.

51

Thea took a deep breath and focussed on letting it go as slowly as she could. She wasn't going to let Ed get back into her head again, not after all this time. Their reconnection had been necessary, and logical, but that didn't mean she had to like it. She'd do what she needed to do for the children, but nothing more. She hadn't told Cora and Dylan about their meeting, in case it had all gone pear shaped. Thea couldn't bear them getting their hopes up if it was all going to end in tears again, but she knew she couldn't keep it a secret from them much longer, especially not with Cora and Ben in regular contact via Snapchat. She'd sat them both down when Cora had told her about the initial communication with Ben, so they were both in the loop, but she hadn't wanted to raise their hopes or stress them out about everyone actually meeting. That was a bridge she needed to cross now.

In a way, it felt reassuring that she could view it so dispassionately. She'd been angry, initially, when she and Ed had spoken, but now, with the benefit of an hour or so's breathing space, and Tristan's presence beside her before and after the meeting, she felt better about the whole thing. There was just one thing she needed to do, though, to fully clear the emotional space before Nick came round for dinner with her and the children, and that was to talk things through with them. They had a right to know what had been discussed, and she needed to know how they felt about allowing him back into their lives. They weren't babies any more, and they had the choice about how they wanted to proceed. It wasn't just a decision for the adults.

'Cora, Dylan, can you come down here a minute?' Thea arranged the three mugs of hot chocolate on a tray and added a selection from the box of biscuits that Lorelai had given her when she'd popped in a couple of days back. She hoped this would go some way to making the discussion a little more palatable.

The thump of two sets of feet on the stairs signalled the kids' arrival into the living room, and Thea took a deep breath. Although Cora was still messaging Ben, Thea wasn't sure if Ed would have had the chance to speak to him since their chat. She hoped not. This was something she wanted to broach first.

As the kids flumped on the sofa, Thea settled herself in the armchair and, with murmurs of appreciation, Cora and Dylan sipped their hot chocolate.

'Mmm, this is lush, Mum.' Cora grinned, and the smile became wider when she glanced at her brother, who had a frothy moustache of squirty cream. She reached for a chocolate digestive from the tray and before Thea could blink, it had vanished into her mouth.

'So.' Thea's stomach gave a little flip. 'I went to meet with your dad this morning.'

Cora's hand, holding a second chocolate biscuit, paused halfway to her mouth. 'Why didn't you tell us?'

'I didn't want to get your hopes up. It's been a long time since he and I have been in the same room together, and I wanted to make sure we could both cope with it before I brought you two along.'

'And are you both still alive?' Cora gave a brief grin.

Thea grinned back. 'Just about.' Then, she became serious again. 'I know it's a lot to take in, even with the contact you've had with Ben, but it was important that your dad and I ironed out a few things before getting you both involved.' She briefly told them about Ben's sister, Maisie, too, so that they were completely in the picture. Cora wasn't surprised – Ben had already told her about Maisie – but Dylan just nodded. Thea looked at her son, who was staring intently into his mug of hot chocolate. 'What are you thinking, Dyl?'

Dylan raised his eyes, and Thea's heart began to ache. 'It's all right,' she said gently. 'You don't have to say anything if you don't want to.' She reached out the hand that wasn't holding her own mug and gave his messy mop of brown hair a stroke. 'As I said... it's a lot to take in. And I know you haven't had as long as Cora has to get used to the idea of meeting Ben. And your dad, of course.'

'It's not that,' Dylan said quietly. 'It's just... do you think Dad loves his new kids more than he loves us? Is that why he stayed away so long?'

Thea's eyes filled with tears at the pain behind that question. She shook her head. 'No, darling, of course not. Your dad loves you. We both do. And we want to make sure that you're both happy for him to come back into your lives.' She hated having to defend Ed, but she needed to make sure Dylan didn't feel that it was something about himself or Cora that had caused the distance between the family. They'd had conversations like this before, when Dylan had been old enough to realise that his father wasn't around, but the fact that there were new children in the mix had obviously re-ignited some of his anxiety.

'But why has he waited so long?' Dylan asked. 'I can't, like, even remember anything about him. It feels weird.' He furrowed his brow. 'And what if he doesn't like us now? What if we don't like him?'

Thea, who'd spent enough time over the years trying to get past the fact that *she* didn't like Ed very much any more (and that was putting it mildly), gave Cora and Dylan what she hoped was a confident smile. 'Then I promise you don't have to see him. I'm not going to force you to do anything you don't want to do. This is a lot to ask of you both, and just because your half-brother, Ben's found you, that doesn't mean you can't choose what to do. This has to be something you want, and Dad and I aren't going to push you either way. We might not see eye to eye on a lot of things, but we both love you very much. It might not be right for you at the moment, but perhaps sometime in the future you might feel differently. If you don't want to go any further with it now, I promise you we'll both understand.'

Cora, who'd been keeping quiet up until now, suddenly interjected. 'But won't that be, like, really rude if I suddenly stop talking to Ben?' Her brow furrowed in that all-too-familiar stressed-out teenager way. It was an expression that Thea had learned to identify, and she called it 'social media anxiety'. She hated seeing it in her daughter, but at times it felt inevitable.

'You don't owe anyone anything,' Thea replied. 'Remember that. My job is to keep you two safe and happy, and if that means putting things on hold with Dad and his new children, then that's OK. If you decide you do want to meet them, then that's fine, too.' She reached out and pulled them both close to her. 'You are the most important people in my life, and I'll support you, whatever you want to do.'

They cuddled for a moment, and Thea bit her lip. She didn't want to say anything else to them: Cora and Dylan had to make their own choices about what happened next. She thought she'd done a decent job of trying to stay neutral about it all, under the circumstances, but she realised, to her surprise, that it hadn't really been that difficult. Making contact with Ed earlier that day hadn't been pleasant, but it could have been far worse, and for the first time since the bomb had dropped about Ed, Ben, Ciara and Maisie, she felt strong enough to be able to face it.

'So.' Cora disentangled herself and looked mischievously up at Thea. 'Now that's all done, can we talk about Nick coming round for dinner? I mean, are you two *a thing* now or what?'

Thea shook her head. She was still getting used to the speed at which her daughter could change emotional lanes, and not even feel the bumps in the road. 'I'll let you know. But he seems to like you two, so I thought it was about time we sat down together for some grub.' She smiled at them both. 'If that's still all right with you two?'

Cora and Dylan both nodded, and Thea felt relieved. They'd had a lot to deal with lately, but at least Nick's presence in their lives seemed to be something they were happy with. She realised, with a pleasurable jolt, that she was more than happy with it, too.

52

A little later on, Thea glanced in the mirror in the hallway before opening the door to a smiling Nick.

'Hi,' he murmured as he walked through. She relaxed as he slid his arms around her for a tentative kiss. 'I've missed you.'

'It's only been a few days!' Thea laughed, but she was flattered and warmed by his obvious affection. She allowed herself to kiss him back before they made their way to the living room. Cora was flumped on the sofa, texting or scrolling, and Dylan was sorting through a huge stack of Pokémon cards ready for swapping with his mates when he got back to school. Nick smiled at them both and then sat down in the armchair nearest to Dylan. He glanced at the pile of cards on the arm of the chair.

'Some of those look familiar!' he said. 'Glad to see my old collection's getting some use.'

Dylan glanced up from the pile and grinned. 'They're pretty old,' he conceded, 'but you had a lot of rare ones so that's cool. Thanks for sorting them out.'

'No problem.' Nick grinned back.

'Hi Nick.' Cora looked up from her phone, but was soon drawn back into whatever she was watching.

'Got to love the conversational skills of Generation Alpha!' Thea quipped, which earned her an eyeroll from her daughter. Then, she turned back to Nick. 'Can you give me a hand in the kitchen?'

'Sure.' She and Nick ambled out, ostensibly to put the finishing touches on dinner, but as soon as they were alone, Thea pulled the door closed.

'You might as well know, Ed's been to see me. He wants the children to meet his new family.' Thea slumped back against the kitchen counter.

Nick didn't say anything at first, but he crossed the kitchen and offered her his arms. She settled gratefully into his embrace, feeling the warmth and support as it seemed to flow from him to her. 'I'm here for you, Thea. I've said it a lot, but I mean it.'

Thea looked up at him. 'You don't seem overly surprised by what I've just said.'

Nick hesitated, and for Thea, the penny dropped before he confirmed it. 'Tristan came to see me on the way home this after-noon. He told me what happened.'

Thea sighed. 'Of course he did.'

'He just wanted to make me aware, so I didn't go blundering in and saying something daft, I'm sure.' His gaze was earnest as it met hers.

'Or to brief you about the extra complications in my life,' Thea muttered. She loved her brother, and deep down she knew Tristan had her best interests at heart, but she couldn't help feeling irritated that he'd broached the subject before she'd had the chance to fully discuss it with Nick, herself.

'I don't mind the complications,' Nick said. 'I want to be part of your life, Thea, and if they come with you, then that's fine by me.'

'It's a lot to ask of someone whose life is so ridiculously simple,' Thea insisted. 'You've never had kids, never lived with anyone, never had to look for a job outside the farm... what makes you think you can take all of this on, straight off the bat?'

Nick looked hurt and then irritated. 'Don't treat me like an idiot, Thea. I might not have had all of those things but that doesn't mean I'm stupid.' He stepped away from her. 'I thought, over the past few weeks, I might have been able to convince you that I'm serious, and that I want to be a part of you and your children's future.'

'You have, Nick, you really have, but this is a lot. I'm not sure what impact re-establishing contact with Ed is going to mean in the long term, and if I don't know, then I can't expect you to, either. That's not part of what you signed up for when you started getting to know me better, I'm sure.'

'I signed up for you!' Nick's voice was more vehement now. 'And if that means having to deal with Ed, then so be it. I want to help you and Cora and Dylan to get through this, the best that I can. I only wish I'd been able to be here for you years ago.'

Thea's eyes filled with tears. 'I'm sorry,' she said. 'I'm so used to being on my own, making the decisions for myself and the kids, that I don't know how to handle it when someone offers to help. Gran and Tristan are forever getting the rough edge of me because I just need to do things my way. I'm not sure I'm cut out for sharing that responsibility, after all these years of being alone.'

'What are you saying, Thea?' Nick's voice was calmer now, but Thea could feel the hurt running in an undercurrent through it. 'We've barely got started.'

'I know.' Thea dropped her gaze to the laminate floor of her kitchen. 'I guess... I don't know what I'm saying.' She swallowed hard. How had everything changed so suddenly? Ten minutes ago, she'd welcomed Nick through the front door with a wide smile and a delicious kiss. Now it felt as though there was a huge gulf between them. She raised her eyes again, to find Nick looking speculatively at her. She knew what he was going to ask, even as he said it.

'Tell me, if you hadn't met up with Ed this afternoon, would you still be thinking like this?'

Thea paused before she answered. Eventually, bracing herself, she looked back up at Nick. 'I don't know,' she said quietly. 'Honestly, I just don't know.' She moved towards him and reached out a hand to take one of his. 'What we've done has been wonderful,' she said softly. 'And you're the nicest, loveliest man I know.'

'But...' Nick's voice was quiet, and his expression had a look of resignation.

'Sometimes I can't help wondering if we just started this because it was convenient. Because we were both in the same place at the same time. I can't help wondering if you'll wake up one morning and realise that, or perhaps I will.'

Nick shook his head, and Thea could see the hurt written all over his features. 'You might think that, Thea, but I can tell you, I won't.' Then, he turned, opened the door and walked out of the kitchen. A few seconds later, Thea heard the front door open and close, and the rumble of Nick's Land Rover as he drove away.

53

Thea put on a brave face through dinner, fibbing that Nick had received a call from his parents and had needed to rush off to their place, but she got the feeling that neither child was convinced.

'Can you text him and ask him to check if he's got any more Pokémon cards?' Dylan asked as the children tucked into Thea's casserole with considerably more gusto than she did.

'Yeah, sure,' Thea replied, although Pokémon cards were the last thing she wanted to contact Nick about. As soon as he'd left, she'd started kicking herself, and although she was trying to project a calm exterior for the sake of her son and daughter, inside, she was churning.

Cora jumped up from the table and started to clear away the dishes. 'Come on, Dyl, give us a hand,' she said. She locked eyes with Thea. 'Maybe you could call Nick and, er, remind him about those cards while we do the washing up?'

Thea shook her head. 'He's probably busy.'

'Ohhhhkaaaay...' Cora looked sceptical. 'Well, go and sit down, anyway, and I'll make you a cup of tea.'

'Thanks, love,' Thea replied. She settled down on the sofa, and listened to her children's friendly bickering about who should do what in the kitchen and tried to put the quarrel with Nick out of her mind. She'd been right to point out that it had all been a bit rushed. They'd fallen into bed together after their first official date, for goodness' sake! Who on earth did that? The little voice that told her she'd known Nick for a lifetime was resolutely ignored. She'd been lonely, as had he. They'd enjoyed themselves over Christmas, but now the festive season was nearly over, it was time to get real.

This was her life. This was her house. And in the kitchen, those were her beloved children. She didn't need anyone else, and she didn't want anyone else. She'd coped for years after Ed had left, and she'd got quite good at it. Why should she sacrifice her independence for a pair of loving arms, a friendly ear and absolutely dynamite sex?

But this was Nick. And, much as she hated to admit it, she knew he loved her. And much as she wouldn't admit it to herself, she loved him. Set in her ways she might be, but she couldn't ignore those two facts. Had she just blown him out because she was afraid to take a risk? Had the renewed contact with Ed put her even more on her guard? If so, was that really fair to Nick, who'd been nothing but patient, kind and steadfast, not just recently but for all of the years she'd known him?

'Oh, for fuck's sake!' she exclaimed.

'You OK, Mum?' Cora was standing in the doorway of the living room, looking curiously at her mother.

Thea smiled. 'You know what? I think I just might be. Do you think you'd be all right to keep an eye on your brother if I pop out for a bit? There's something I need to do.'

Cora grinned. 'I think we'll cope.' She handed Thea her cup of tea. 'Do you want this before you go?'

Thea took a sip – Cora always knew how to make a decent cuppa. 'That's just the thing I needed.' She looked at her daughter, and smiled at Dylan as he, too re-entered the living room. She reached out an arm to her daughter, who snuggled up to her briefly, and the other to her son. 'I know it's all been a bit weird, lately, but I promise you, things are going to be fine. We'll make it work, darlings, I promise.'

'And what about you and Nick?' Cora asked, her voice slightly muffled from the cuddle. 'Are you going to make it work with him?'

'That depends,' Thea said carefully. 'Are you sure you two are OK with it, if we do?'

'Only if he finds more Pokémon cards!' Dylan quipped, a cheeky gleam in his eye.

'I'll make sure he knows that.' Thea grinned at her son. She held her son and daughter close, and they were eventually joined by Lupin, who could never resist a warm cuddle. They were the most important people in her life, and they always would be, but perhaps it was time to let someone else into their protective little bubble. She knew it was going to be incredibly difficult to let go of the tight hold she had on everything in her life, to begin to share it anew with someone else, but she also knew if she didn't take that risk and give Nick the chance to be a part of it, too, she ran the risk of being lonely, and wondering what might have been between them. After everything they'd experienced lately, her heart knew she couldn't allow that to happen. Taking another sip of her tea to fortify her, she kissed the tops of her children's heads, and headed out to see if she could make amends.

54

Thea hadn't really registered the snowfall before she left the house: it had just been a few flakes before dinner, but it was turning into something a little more beautiful and dramatic as she shut the front door. It seemed that Mollie Wakefield had been right about the long-range weather forecast. She'd chucked on a hoodie and a pair of trainers, reasoning that it was just a short journey to Nick's place, so she wouldn't need to wrap up. Hopefully, what she had to say to Nick wouldn't take too long. Now she'd made up her mind, she couldn't back out. She didn't want to wait another minute.

'Mum, Dad, wish me luck.' She hadn't 'spoken' to them for a while, she realised, not since Nick had taken on a more significant role in her life, but she felt as though she needed their ghostly reassurance now. She'd idealised her parents' marriage over the years, and when her own relationship with Ed had ended, she'd blamed herself for not being able to sustain something as powerful as her parents had. With age had come experience, and she realised that all relationships faced challenges, but she'd never stopped hoping that one day, she'd find something as strong.

Who'd have thought that the answer had been under her nose the whole time? She thought back to that favourite film of hers, *13 Going on 30*, and suddenly felt as nervous as that gawky teenager, going to tell the boy she loved that yes, she really did love him. She hoped he'd still listen to her, despite the fact that she'd put the brakes on in her kitchen not two hours before.

'Nick Saint, you'd better be home,' she muttered as the snow began to get heavier. Snow in Somerset wasn't common, but when it came it had a tendency to blanket the county. She switched her wiper blades up a notch and shivered. The Volvo's heating system left a lot to be desired, and she regretted the decision to leave her coat and gloves behind.

Visibility was getting poorer, and she was grateful that Nick's cottage was only a couple of miles away. She flipped her headlights to full beam and crawled along the main road, feeling more and more nervous by the second. She wasn't sure if it was the sudden blizzard or what she was going to say to Nick when she got there that made her more on edge. Yelping and dipping her headlights a fraction too late as a 4X4 came barrelling around a sharp bend towards her, she slowed down even further.

Slowing down was probably the wrong move, though. The car, once so reliable, had been getting more and more temperamental as it aged, and with a final arthritic splutter, the engine died.

'Shit!' Thea thumped her steering wheel as the car coasted to a halt. She was, irritatingly, halfway between the centre of Lower Brambleton and the long, winding lane that led to Nick's cottage on the edge of the land Saints' Farm owned. Manoeuvring the car into the verge as closely as she could, she cut the engine. Now what?

'Oh, for fuck's sake!' Thea felt the urge to scream aloud when she realised, in her haste, she'd also left her phone on the living room table. Great. There was only one thing for it. Thrusting open the car door, thankful as she did so that there was no oncoming traffic, she slammed it shut and started the freezing walk to Nick's place. At least, she thought, it would give her time to think about what exactly she was going to say to him when she got there.

55

To say Nick had endured a restless evening was an understatement. He'd sped home, mindful that the weather was closing in, and slammed the door of the cottage, hoping to lock out some of the frustration that the conversation with Thea had caused. Playing their last words over and over again in his memory, he'd realised, with twenty-twenty hindsight, that he had, as per usual, done things completely wrong. How many years had he known Thea? Too many. And he knew that when she was cornered, she got defensive; she dug in and pushed back out with everything she had. He should have just walked away, left her to cool off, but instead, desperate for some kind of resolution, he'd pressed her, and in the end, she'd given him an answer that was the last one he'd wanted. Now, instead of sitting around her dinner table and spending time with her and the children, he was back in the cottage with only Marmalade for company and a long, freezing night ahead.

'You're a bloody idiot,' he muttered. Marmalade looked disinterestedly up at the sound of his owner's voice. 'When will you ever learn?' He reached for his phone and then chucked it back down again on the kitchen table. There was no point: Thea would, hopefully, cool down in her own time and they could talk things through. Looking to take his mind off things, but not feeling very hungry, he popped a couple of slices of bread into the toaster and waited. Marmalade provided a welcome distraction by loudly reminding him about dinner, so Nick duly obliged.

'Probably all for the best, anyway,' Nick said to the cat as he popped the bowl down in front of him. 'I can't see you and that tortoiseshell minx, Lupin, playing happy families together under one roof!' It was a lame joke, and it failed to raise a smile from him or any response from Marmalade.

Munching on his toast a couple of minutes later, he reached for his phone again. Maybe he should try calling Thea. He still liked to make actual phone calls, and he wanted to do more than just text. Should he?

'Oh, fuck it!' He dialled before he could change his mind.

'Hello?'

'Er, hi.' Nick felt confused. 'Who's this?'

'It's Cora. Why are you phoning Mum's phone? I thought she was with you?'

Nick's heart beat a little faster. 'No, Cora, she's not. Why, was this where she said she was coming?'

'Yeah.' Cora's tone grew more concerned. 'The snow's got really bad, now. I was worried when I realised she'd left her phone behind at home. Are you sure she's not there?'

Nick gave a little laugh. 'I think I'd know if she was! I promise you she's not hiding in my wardrobe.'

'Eww, gross!' Cora gave a giggle, but then she grew serious again. 'Can you ask her to call me when she gets there? I mean, she might have, like, stopped off somewhere, but she left here about an hour ago, so...'

Nick nodded, and then remembered Cora couldn't see him. 'I

will.' He realised that Cora probably needed a bit more reassurance. 'Don't worry, lovely,' he added. 'I'm sure she's fine. I'll let you know the minute she gets here.'

'Thanks, Nick.' Cora's voice sounded a little shaky. 'It's just I can't help worrying. My grandparents crashed their car on an icy night, and I can't, like, imagine what it would be like if Mum did the same.'

'I promise, I'll ring you the minute I see her,' Nick said. 'Even better, I'll get her to ring you. Keep her phone next to you and we'll speak again really soon.'

As he ended the call, he shook his head. Dealing with anxious teenagers wasn't something he was used to, and he hoped he'd said the right things to Cora. Her concern for Thea was making him even more worried. What if she had skidded in the snow and was stranded in a ditch somewhere? Her car was so bloody ancient, he wouldn't trust its brakes in good weather, let alone a sudden snowstorm.

'Right, that's it, Marmy!' He glanced at the cat again, who'd finished his dinner and was now padding softly past him ready to settle in his favourite bed on one of the radiators in the living room. 'If she's had a shunt, I'm going out there to help.' Grabbing his coat and, as a second thought, a large, navy blue cashmere scarf, he headed out of the door. What the Volvo might not be able to handle, his Land Rover certainly could. He only hoped Thea would appreciate the help.

56

Never had a walk seemed longer, or colder. Shivering in just the hoodie and jeans she was wearing, with the snow rushing past her that was slicing her face to bits, Thea pressed on. At the very least, even if Nick was still cross with her, she knew he would offer her a lift home.

The snow was impeding her progress, though. Her trainers didn't have a lot of purchase on the newly covered road surface, and she was walking gingerly, trying not to add a sprained ankle or worse to her woes. Hugging her arms tightly around herself, she pushed on. It wasn't much further; perhaps someone would drive by and offer her a lift in a minute. She wasn't surprised that she hadn't seen any other cars since she'd broken down – this wasn't the weather to be out and about, and Lower Brambleton wasn't on a through road to anywhere.

'You'd better be home when I get there,' Thea muttered. It would be sod's law if Nick had gone to the pub to drown his sorrows. She began shivering. What had seemed like a great idea before she left the house now seemed ridiculous. They could have arranged to meet properly, talked things through like adults.

This daft, teenagerish mission was seeming less and less sensible with every step she took.

But maybe that was the point? She shook her head, exasperated with herself. She'd spent so long thinking about everyone else's happiness: her children's, her grandmother's, even Tristan's. Perhaps, for the first time in a long time, she was reconnecting with the teenage girl she used to be and acting on her own impulses and desires. And sixteen-year-old Thea, who'd had a brief kiss with a good-looking farm boy at the top of the stairs at someone's party, was cheering her on, reminding her that yes, she, too, deserved to be happy.

The bright, shining lamps of an oncoming vehicle distracted her attention from her own thoughts, and she shuffled in a little closer to the grass verge. Its fog lights were on, and she was dazzled before it slowed down as it approached her. In surprise, she realised it was flashing its headlights at her. The lights were so bright that she couldn't make out the licence plate, but in a few more seconds she realised the rickety old vehicle looked familiar. Her heart thumped painfully in her chest, in a combination of relief and nervousness, when she caught sight of Nick behind the wheel.

'What on earth are you doing walking on this road on a night like this?' he asked as he opened the driver's door and strode towards her. He, unlike Thea, was wearing sturdy boots against the weather.

'My car broke down about half a mile back,' Thea said, through chattering teeth. 'I thought your place was closer than mine, so I've been walking.'

Nick whipped off his jacket and scarf and wrapped them around Thea's shoulders. 'You bloody idiot. There are no streetlights down here and dark blue is a stupid colour to wear at night in the winter, even without the snow.' She felt the warmth from his body as he pulled her closer to him and wrapped his arms around her.

Thea, grateful for the contact, found her eyes were welling with tears. 'I know.' It suddenly dawned on her how daft this decision really was. 'But...'

'But what?' Nick looked her straight in the eye, and his gaze was so sincere that Thea couldn't help the tears that started to fall. She moved towards him, wrapping her arms around him and feeling how warm, solid and safe he was.

'I've been such a twat,' she murmured. 'But I've been listening to someone I hadn't spoken to for a long time, and she made a lot of sense.'

'Who?' Nick asked. Thea could feel him tightening his arms around her, and she knew they should get out of the snow, but she needed to say something to him before they did.

'My sixteen-year-old self.' She looked up at Nick, who looked back down at her in surprise. 'She told me to stop being so stubborn and just go for it. So that's what I'm trying to do.'

Nick's expression of bemusement made Thea smile. 'It's all right,' she said gently. 'I can explain later. But for now, can we get out of this bloody snow?'

'Definitely!' Nick released her from his arms, and they both scrambled up into the Land Rover.

As she opened her mouth to speak, Nick held up his phone. 'Hang on a minute.' He dialled, and the phone was answered immediately. 'Hi Cora. Yes, she's here. No, she's fine. The car broke down. Yup, hang on.'

Nick passed the phone to Thea. 'You should probably talk to her.'

Thea quirked an eyebrow. She quickly reassured Cora that she was fine, and the car would be, too, before letting her know she'd be home soon. Then, she handed the phone back to Nick.

'Now I really *do* feel like a teenager, with you and Cora being the ones to keep tabs on me!'

Nick's expression grew serious. 'She answered your phone when I tried to ring earlier, said you'd come to see me, but got worried when you weren't with me. I said I'd let her know the moment I found you.'

'I'm so glad you did,' Thea gave a nervous laugh. 'I was freezing my arse off, out there.'

Nick gave an equally nervous chuckle, but then his face grew serious again. 'Look, Thea, before you say anything else, do you mind if I do?'

Thea nodded. 'You rescued me from the road – I think you've earned it!' She looked at him, and she could see he was already finding a way to formulate the words. Patiently, snuggled into his jacket, she waited.

57

The relief Nick felt when he'd seen Thea trudging up the road had rapidly given way to a mixture of exasperation. He was frustrated with himself, for not communicating well enough with her earlier in the evening and cross with Thea, for being so damned stubborn. And the nerves were rising because he had the very distinct impression that if he cocked this next couple of minutes up, that really would be the end of whatever they'd started.

'Thea,' he began. 'I want you to know something. Something I should have told you a long time ago. Something I should have told you after the Midwinter's Eve Ball. Something, if I'm being totally honest, I should have told you more than once since we started seeing each other.' His hands started to tremble, and since he'd given Thea his jacket, he had nowhere to put them, so he willed them to stop.

'What's that, then?' Thea's voice, gentle but with an undercurrent of her own nerves, prompted.

'Whatever happens next, whatever you decide about us, I want you to know that I love you.' He shook his head, willing himself to stay put, even though every instinct he had was urging him to fling open the door of the Land Rover and run away. 'I've loved you for a long time. Getting to know you better this Christmas made me realise that I can't just walk away from what I feel about you. You're important to me, Thea, and I want to be there for you, to be in your life, if that's what you want, too. If it isn't, then I can live with that. But if there's any chance that you feel the same, then I promise you that I will try my best to make you and Cora and Dylan happy.'

Thea was just staring at him, as if she couldn't work out how best to let him down and allow him to keep his dignity. Despite the cold, the flames of embarrassment that he'd managed to damp down while he'd been talking were now licking up his neck, his face, making the sweat on his brow feel like a cascade, and it was no good pretending that his hands weren't shaking, as well as pretty much the rest of him, too. Everything they'd done this December, every smile, every laugh, every kiss, every moment together, seemed to have propelled them to this point, and now he felt as though he couldn't proceed into the new year without knowing exactly where he stood.

'I'm sorry,' he stammered. 'I've no right to put you on the spot like this. Forget I said anything. I'll take you home.' Feeling the hot lava of mortification beginning to run down his spine, he went to turn the ignition key.

'Just shush a minute, will you?' Her hand had covered his and he paused, the engine remaining still. 'Honestly, Nick, you're as big an idiot as I am, sometimes.'

Nick shook his head. 'Have I messed up again?'

Thea's smile, tentative at first, broadened. 'I said shush. It's my turn.'

Shaking his head, he put his hand in his lap. 'That depends,' he said quietly. 'Am I going to want to hear it?'

'Why don't you just wait and see?'

Fight was out of the question. Flight seemed impossible while the snow kept falling, so the only thing left for Nick to do was freeze. Barely managing to breathe, he waited.

58

Thea didn't think she'd seen anyone look as nervous as Nick now did. She realised what a lot it had cost him to tell her how much he loved her, and immediately she knew she'd have to choose her next words very carefully. Nick, once he was in, was all in, and she felt the responsibility of that. She knew what she had to say to him, but it still scared her. If things didn't work out between them, it would break both of their hearts. Perhaps his, even more than hers. Was she ready to finally make that jump?

'No,' she said firmly. 'You don't just get to drop a bombshell like that. You need to hear what I have to say.' She squeezed his forearm gently. 'Nick. Look at me. *Look* at me.'

It seemed an eternity before Nick raised his gaze to meet hers. She was taken aback at the look in his eyes, as if he'd just told her something far worse than that he loved her. She realised now, just how true it was; how he'd struggled with that fact over the past few weeks, with the pain and ecstasy of beginning a relationship with her. She also now knew that she'd have to tread carefully. There was so much to say, but if she got it wrong, things would get far worse.

'I'm sorry, Thea—'

Thea's other hand found its way to Nick's mouth, and she hushed him firmly. 'No. You don't get to say anything now. And you certainly don't get to apologise again. It's my turn to speak, and you'd better bloody well listen.' She was amused as his eyes widened, but she willed her face to remain serious.

'Firstly,' she said, gently removing her hand from Nick's mouth, 'you need to stop apologising for everything. Annabelle always says you spend your life saying sorry for things that are nothing to do with you. Stop taking responsibility for stuff that is literally not your problem.'

'But Thea—'

Thea gently covered his mouth again. 'Shush, or it's staying there until I've finished.'

Nick nodded, a trace of amusement in his eyes.

'All right.' Thea fixed him with her hardest stare, but she had the feeling it wasn't having the desired effect, as his gaze softened, and he moved closer to her. 'As I was saying...'

Seeing him relaxing a little sent Thea's senses into overdrive, and she found that she, now, was the one who was struggling with what to say. The words screamed in her mind, but she couldn't seem to articulate them.

Fuck it, she thought, after a beat or two. There was only one way to make clear what she needed to tell him. Thea closed the remaining gap between them and brought her hand up to Nick's face again.

'No...' she said gently as she saw him draw breath to speak. 'I'm still talking.'

'I didn't say anything...'

Thea's hand stroked his face and came to rest on the back of Nick's neck, feeling the warmth of his skin contrasting with the texture of his collar.

'That's better.' She leaned upwards until her lips met with his. Increasing the pressure, she deepened the kiss, exploring his mouth with her tongue, and pressing into his embrace, as she felt him, tentatively at first and then more confidently, reciprocating the kiss and sliding his arms around her. They remained that way, locked together, until Thea breathed in again, and gently started to disentangle herself.

'As I was saying,' she murmured. 'You're not the only one who feels that way. It's taken me a while to see it, but I'm in love with you, Nick. These past few weeks have opened my eyes to something I should have seen before. You are the kindest, loveliest, sexiest man I've ever met, and while I could live with fewer apologies, I'm prepared to overlook that because being with you is the best thing I've done for a long, long time. This thing with Ed is complicated, but we'll work that out. It's *you* that I want.'

Nick's eyes widened, and Thea smiled at his adorable surprise. 'Don't even pretend that you didn't know that was what I was going to say.'

'No,' Nick replied. 'I'm not pretending.' He shook his head. 'Even now, I still can't quite believe that you love me. God, Thea, you love me!' He looked down at her in wonder. 'And I love you. I love you so fucking much. And I'm sorry, I shouldn't be swearing but I just can't—'

As they broke apart once more, Thea was sure that the smile on her face was mirroring the one she could see on Nick's. 'I know it's a bit late, but Merry Christmas, Saint Nick,' she said. 'Here's to the future.'

Nick started the Land Rover again, and they navigated the winding, snowy road back to Orion Close. It had been a long time coming, but despite the snow falling on the windscreen, Thea had never seen things more clearly.

EPILOGUE

'No, I'm bloody well not going to fill in, just for the sake of the cameras!' Thea's broad smile belied the stridency of her words as she walked away from Nick and Annabelle, who were both behind the shop counter, looking at her with the same beseeching expression. 'And the two of you looking at me that way isn't going to make any difference.'

'Really?' Annabelle grinned at her. 'I mean, do you really want your heavily pregnant nearly-sister-in-law to be on her feet more than necessary for the duration of the Christmas season?'

'That's not fair, Annabelle,' Thea muttered. 'And you told me yourself that the midwife said everything's perfectly fine, and doing some light work would be good for you and the baby.'

'But Tally and the team said you were a real hit with the viewers in last year's Christmas special,' Nick chimed in. 'She seems to think that the viewing figures'll be through the roof if we're in shot together this year.'

'What is this, *The Real Housewives of Burnham-on-Sea?*' Thea laughed. 'I'm not a reality star, and neither are you, Nick Saint.

And the last time Tally tried to convince you otherwise, you turned her down flat.'

'Well, yeah, but that was before I saw how much the camera loves you...' Nick sidled out from behind the counter and slid an arm around Thea's waist. 'It makes you look so sexy, Thea Ashcombe, and you know how gorgeous I think you are already...' He dipped his lips towards hers, an expression of barely disguised lust in his eyes, and if it hadn't been for the sound of Annabelle's grossed-out groaning behind them, Thea probably would have given in and kissed him right back.

'The answer's still no,' Thea murmured, but she knew her resistance was futile: ever since she and Nick had finally got together, she found it hard to refuse him anything. These past twelve months had objectively been the happiest of her life, and although she'd maintained her independence and was still living in her little house on Orion Close, thanks to the couple of days a week she was now working at Saints' Farm, she knew that eventually she and Nick would make a home together, when the time was right.

'Tally's coming up tonight,' Annabelle interjected. 'She wants to run a few things past us all before the cameras start rolling the day after tomorrow. Would you at least be happy to meet with her as a team?'

Thea sighed, but she knew she was going to agree. 'Of course. Let's see what she's got in mind.' She looked back up at Nick. 'Just promise me there won't be any grand gestures on camera. This is meant to be a show about the farm shop, not some trashy fly-on-the-wall docudrama!'

'Don't worry,' Nick grinned. 'I promise not to drop to one knee and pop the question on camera.' He brushed his thumb gently against her lips. 'When that time comes, it'll be between you, me and the engagement ring, I promise.'

Thea's knees, accustomed to going weak whenever he looked at her like that, felt their familiar lurch. 'I'm glad to hear it.'

'So now we've established that, are you up for attending the meeting?'

Thea grinned. 'For you, anything. But I'm not sure if I have it in me to be so polite to Tally.'

'Don't worry,' Annabelle interjected. 'Word on the WhatsApp says she's hooked up with some gorgeous camera operator, so she'll be keeping her hands off Nick while he's around.'

'Glad to hear it,' Thea laughed. 'You know, I think I could get to like her if she's no longer intent on getting Nick into bed!'

'Ugh!' Annabelle replied. 'You might be besotted with my brother, but please don't make reference to him and sex in the same breath. It's weird enough for me that you took this bloody long to get together – I don't need to think about him shagging anyone!'

'Fair enough!' Thea was laughing now. 'That good old shared history is a doozy, sometimes, isn't it, Annie?'

'True, but it comes in handy at others.' Annabelle paused and patted her prominent baby bump before adding, 'I mean, who else am I going to trust to hold the sprog when Jamie and I fancy a night out?'

'With pleasure,' Thea responded. 'I couldn't think of anything nicer.'

Still smiling, she wandered out of the shop. Cora and Dylan were spending the night at Ed's place, and Nick would be along later to take advantage of the child-free house with her. The past year had wrought some pretty spectacular changes for her and her family, but as the cusp of another new year was just upon the horizon, Thea's life felt more complete than it ever had before.

* * *

MORE FROM FAY KEENAN

Fay Keenan's next title is available to order now here:
https://mybook.to/FayKennanBackAd

ACKNOWLEDGEMENTS

This novel, as ever, would not have been possible without the help and support of so many people. Firstly, to my wonderful editors, Victoria Britton and Sarah Ritherdon, who steer the course brilliantly, curb my excesses and push me hard to get the job done – thank you. Also, many thanks to Alice Moore for the wonderful cover, and the copy, proof and marketing teams at Boldwood.

My thanks, also, to all of the friends and family who support me in this endeavour – you know who you are, and I've mentioned you many times before. Writers need networks, and I have the best of them. A special shout out has to go this time to the wonderful Mavis and Margaret, whose encouragement and support I so greatly appreciate – I hope you've enjoyed this one, too!

Finally, thanks to you, reader, for walking this path with me. I hope you've enjoyed reading this one as much as I've loved writing it. See you next time!

ABOUT THE AUTHOR

Fay Keenan is the author of the bestselling Little Somerby and Willowbury series of novels. She has led writing workshops with Bristol University and has been a visiting speaker in schools. She is a full-time teacher and lives in Somerset.

Sign up to Fay Keenan's mailing list for news, competitions and updates on future books.

Visit Fay's website: https://faykeenan.com/

Follow Fay on social media here:

 facebook.com/faykeenanauthor

x.com/faykeenan

instagram.com/faykeenanauthor

bookbub.com/authors/fay-keenan

ALSO BY FAY KEENAN

Willowbury Series

A Place to Call Home

Snowflakes Over Bay Tree Terrace

Just for the Summer

Roseford Series

New Beginnings at Roseford Hall

Winter Kisses at Roseford Café

Finding Love at Roseford Blooms

Winter Wishes at Roseford Reloved

Coming Home to Roseford Villas

Brambleton Series

A Sky Full of Stars

Could It Be Magic?

BECOME A MEMBER OF

THE SHELF CARE CLUB

The home of Boldwood's book club reads.

Find uplifting reads, sunny escapes, cosy romances, family dramas and more!

Sign up to the newsletter
https://bit.ly/theshelfcareclub

Boldwood

Boldwood Books is an award-winning fiction publishing company seeking out the best stories from around the world.

Find out more at www.boldwoodbooks.com

Join our reader community for brilliant books, competitions and offers!

Follow us
@BoldwoodBooks
@TheBoldBookClub

Sign up to our weekly deals newsletter

https://bit.ly/BoldwoodBNewsletter

Printed in Dunstable, United Kingdom

67277335R00179